CONTEMPT

(Grandma BB's shenanigans)

The Jamieson Legacy

BY

PAT SIMMONS

ISBN: 978-1-733831680

Developmental Editor: Chandra Sparks Splond
Proofread by Stuart Budgen
Proofreader: Miriam "Cookie" Mitchell
Beta Readers: Stacey Jefferson, Evangelist Charlotte Townsend
Interior Design: Kimolisa/Fiverr.com
Cover Design: Wayne Parker/designerboard18/fiverr.com

Praises for Pat Simmons Work

5 stars Queen's Surrender is fantastic!

I just finished reading, #10 in the Jamieson Legacy Series. I love this family and their commitment to God and each other. Philip and Queen's story was refreshing despite the conflicts they suffered throughout the novel. They were realistic and their live story was wonderful. I hope that we see more from the Jamiesons. –Reviewed by Robin Holland

5 stars The Confession forgiveness

This is a great example of how we should seek God's forgiveness, forgive ourselves, and ask for forgiveness from others. Even if forgiveness is not granted, we need freedom from our past sins. Through Pat's characters, Sandra and Raimond, along with their children we experience many examples of forgiveness. –Reviewed by Juanetta P. Frazier

5 stars The Acquittal magnificent romance!

The romance of Josephine and Rainey was superbly narrated, it was as if while reading I could visualize every move, love touches, sadness, happiness... everything. What is glorious, the steps of prayer, lights shown, conviction and repentance of each character.— kindle reader

5 stars Guilty of Love you gotta read this read!

Where do I begin?!?! First let me say Mrs. Simmons is an anointed, master writer in her field. Omg! I just love the way you tell a story. Although you write beautifully Christian love stories, you can't help but connect with god on a personal level because she weaves him into the story so well. Not to mention the Jamieson men sound so yummy, you wish you had one in your life :) –kindle customer

The Jamieson Family

Parke and Cheney's family

Parke VIII (Pace)—Parke's son
Kami—adopted daughter
Victoria—Kami's biological sister (same mother)/also Parke and Cheney's adopted daughter
Paden—biological son
Chance—biological son

Malcolm and Hallison's (Hali) family

Malcolm Junior (MJ)
Major
Mallison

Cameron and Gabrielle's family

Twins: Camille and Gabriel

Kevin (Kidd) and Eva's family

Kennedy
Kevin Junior

Aaron (Ace) and Talise's family

Lauren
Diamond Queen

The Robnetts (The Jamiesons' maternal cousins)

Queen, called Queen Bee by the Jamiesons to differentiate between Queen Robnett and Queen Jamieson Dupree. (Queen Robnett's name has been traced back four generations.)
Queen's sisters are Rejoice and Princess
Queen's cousins are sisters Sapphire, Jewel, and Duchess

CONTEMPT

(Grandma BB's shenanigans)

The Jamieson Legacy

Chapter 1
Grandma BB's Death Rehearsal

Beatrice
PRESENT, Ferguson, Missouri, 2023

Beatrice Tilley Beacon, also known as Grandma BB, had never seen two grown men bawl like babies who needed diaper changes and warm bottles.

Perfect!

She grinned.

It took some practice—more than an hour—but Chip and Dale, her muscular and menacing bodyguards, were convincing enough when pretending Grandma BB had died. Once they had mastered that, she sent the Jamiesons a group text to summon them to her house.

This was the planning stage for her actual funeral.

Practice makes perfect, and Grandma BB had thought of every detail for a marvelous homegoing—the musical selections, the officiating minister, and mourners handpicked to speak highly of her.

Now, all that remained was for her to take her last breath. Grandma BB sighed.

Happy times and devastating lows.

She passed down the oral history to her great-granddaughters, who shared no bloodline with her, but were dear to her heart. She instilled into Kami and Victoria Jamieson the confidence to tell it like it is.

For this occasion, Grandma BB dressed in her finest satin burial clothes, ladies' lace dress socks, and her newest pair of two-tone wingtip Stacy Adams shoes.

Her long silver curls fell past her shoulders. The diamond studs in her ears were a wedding gift from her late husband Henry.

Grandma BB wanted authenticity. Of course, this was only a dress rehearsal—literally.

"I might change my mind and switch it up some." She chuckled.

She'd sent out a group text to the Jamiesons and a few others an hour ago. So now, she waited in her master bedroom with a sitting area that was large enough to be divided into two rooms, like the one she and her husband first rented when they married. Henry wanted a life of grandeur for his wife, and the splendor of this house was proof. The house had his-and-hers closets before it was a thing. The second-floor balcony off the bedroom, overlooking her manicured backyard hosted many romantic dinners at sunset. The bitter pill to swallow was that the original oversized nursery that was never used became a library of collectible books and periodicals.

Patting the armrest of her plush velvet chair, she admired her furnishings. After the death of her husband, Grandma BB decorated the room in a Victorian-era style with scalloped lace Priscilla curtains and thick rose-colored satin drapes.

She lived on Darst in historic Old Ferguson, a suburb of St. Louis where the large homes would be called the big house on plantations in the Deep South. Grandma BB's red brick bungalow with three large dormers gave her story-and-a-half home the appearance of a full second floor. An enclosed breezeway between her house and the garage was the perfect spot for people-watching, her specialty.

The Beacons' property, which was among the first Black neighbors to cross the city to the county line, served as the block's model home because of its upkeep and meticulous landscape.

Humph. She grinned proudly.

Her mind continued to drift as she waited for her family to arrive. She loved this. Grandma BB remembered when that hippy neighbor

Cheney Jamieson—who had first been Cheney Reynolds—moved next door. *There goes the neighborhood,* she had thought. A single young woman with a house needing more than a spruce-up and no husband to help. It couldn't be done, Grandma BB had thought, but she was wrong.

Who knew that the lives of perfect strangers would be connected for better or for worse, or that they'd be intertwined forever?

Where were they? Grandma BB grew impatient as she tapped her Stacy Adams shoe on her carpet.

Chip, one of her bodyguards, appeared in her doorway, sniffing, eyes glossed over. "Out of the thirty-plus kinfolks, I thought some of them would show by now."

"I know. Keep practicing. You're supposed to be mourning my demise." Grandma BB huffed, picked up her state-of-the-art monocular telescope from the table, and moved to her favorite spot on the cushioned window seat where she had spent many hours doing neighborhood surveillance.

All quiet. Not even a stray dog, she thought. In the distance, she spied a couple strolling with a pamphlet in their hands. Judging from them pointing at houses, Grandma BB surmised they were on the Old Ferguson West walking tour to see houses built in the mid-to-late-1800s, like the former house of Charles Ferguson whose extra-wide front door was built to accommodate caskets for wakes, or the house of Louis Maull, the founder of the barbecue sauce company. Today, she knew all her neighbors by name, their work schedules, and their criminal activities.

Parke and Cheney's black SUV ground to a halt in front of her curb.

"Yeah!"

The roar from his brother Malcolm's motorcycle's could be heard approaching, but his wife, Hali, and their children beat him to a parking spot across the street. Parke and Cheney's oldest son, Pace, drove up behind his parents with his sisters and younger brothers. That was a surprise. When did college students have time to visit?

Cameron; his wife, Gabrielle; and their twins arrived in their red Porsche SUV.

More and more Jamiesons descended on her neighborhood like they were responding to a house fire.

They rushed to her house as if they were late for one of their church services, and Grandma BB heard voices before the doorbell rang, so she scrambled back to her Queen Anne chair.

Chip turned up his hysterics as Grandma BB instructed him to, as Dale opened her front door and let out a wail.

"What's going on?" she heard Parke ask.

"She's…she's upst—" Dale began.

A pack of footsteps reminding her of a herd of cattle rushed up the stairs to her master bedroom.

Seconds later, her room exploded with her family. There wasn't an ugly one in the bunch. The men were handsome, and their wives were pretty. Seemingly clueless of the occasion, the children raced toward her with smiles, happy to see her, while Parke and his two brothers stood back with their arms folded. Cheney, Hallison, and Gabrielle didn't look happy either. Parke's older children looked confused.

"Took y'all long enough. I could have been dead," Grandma BB scolded.

"That's what we all were thinking with your bodyguard boohooing at the door. Now what is going on here?" Parke asked in his normal no-nonsense manner. "Do we need to call an ambulance because my vitals are probably off the chart?"

The man was always over-the-top serious.

"This is not about you, Par-kay." Par-kay was Grandma BB's nickname for him whenever he annoyed her. "They're simply practicing for my demise."

A chorus of "What?" floated around her packed room as Chip shoved his way in and began to pass out programs.

"What is this?" Malcolm demanded. Without removing his signature dark shades, Parke's second oldest brother looked menacing.

"What does it look like? It's the order of service for my eulogy," Grandma BB stated.

"Who died?" Queen Jamieson Dupree pushed her way through her cousins to make a show-stopping appearance with her husband, Philip, who trailed her, wearing his ministerial collar—perfect for the occasion.

"If there weren't children in the room, I would strangle you for scaring *us* to death." Cheney squinted and waggled a finger at the matriarch.

"Mom!" Kami, Victoria, and Pace said in unison.

"I'm going to die eventually. I'm seventy-something already."

Grandma BB was brought up in an era when a woman never told her age and always hid it well with hair dye. Depending on her aches and pains for the day, she could be seventy-or eighty-something.

Her guests groaned.

"Why don't you add a decade or two?" Cheney shook her head, then scanned the program that Chip began to hand out. "And why are we rehearsing a funeral?"

"This is the schedule of my service and the way I want it. Since I won't be there to supervise it, I want us to go through a practice run."

"Are you serious?" Queen said as Philip pulled out a chair for her. He was another cutie pie. The couple was proof that opposites attract—and clash. Queen and her brothers, Kidd and Ace Jamieson, were Parke's cousins.

"You want me to give the eulogy and fill in the blanks with good stuff? I'm a minister. I don't want to stand before God and lie." Philip gave her a blank expression.

"No worries. I'm sure God will give you inspiration." Grandma BB fanned her hand in the air. "Chip, will you place an order for delivery?"

Tears vanished, Chip grabbed his cell phone off his belt and stepped into the hall to do her bidding.

"Now, as you can see from the lineup, Victoria will be the mistress of the ceremony. The order of service will start off with a marching band. I'm a cornerstone donor to Harris Stowe University. Henry was an alumnus, and I'm an alumna. If Victoria becomes too overcome with emotion, then Kami will step in to keep the program flowing."

"Wait. You never mentioned you attended an HBCU." Cheney seemed hurt that she didn't know every tidbit of Grandma BB's life, including that she'd attended a historically Black college and university.

"I can't reveal all my secrets." Grandma BB winked and nodded for Victoria to begin reading the obituary since the children had settled on her plush carpet and the adults were seated in chairs or on her chaise.

Victoria, Kami's half-sister, wasn't the same guarded teenager as she was when Parke and Cheney adopted her at fourteen. The eighteen-year-old was now a college sophomore who boasted confidence and excelled in intelligence. She was savvy and creative. Her beauty wasn't understated—she glowed. The sisters could pass for twins despite Kami being two years older.

Pace and younger brothers Paden and Chance will have their hands full protecting their sisters who had different fathers. Their misfortune in life led them on different paths to foster homes.

The Jamiesons rescued Victoria from a cycle of abuse and became her protectors.

They were truly a blended family.

Although they'd adopted Victoria, her comfort level was maintained when no men were within close range. Living with Grandma BB in the same neighborhood was the solution.

It took two years for Victoria to accept the Jamieson men's love for her. When she let her guard down, she received the love she'd always craved from a father but still kept her brothers, cousins, and uncles at arm's length to take in small doses.

This was Grandma BB's reason for giving Victoria the honor of memorializing her. They both had suffered in life.

Victoria stood poised. "Born circa 1970, Beatrice Tilley Beacon also known as Grandma BB—"

"Hold up." Parke squinted. "You're not ancient. A forensic dentist could give us a closer birthdate than before 1970. That would make my parents older than you, and they are in their late fifties."

Grandma BB glared at Parke. "You're interrupting my service before it begins. Hush."

"Dad…" Victoria smiled, then continued "Grandma BB leaves to mourn her memory, grandchildren Cheney (Parke) Jamieson, Hali (Malcolm) Jamieson, Gabrielle (Cameron) Jamieson, Queen (Philip) Jamieson Dupree—"

"Wait a minute," Cheney said, following her daughter along on the program, "you listed all the great-grandchildren by name?" Cheney asked.

Jutting her chin, Grandma BB gave her former neighbor a shrug. "And? They're Jamiesons. You're not supposed to interrupt a funeral. You and your husband may be banned from attending. Now, hush."

She cleared her throat. "As you all can see, the Scriptures are blank, so our family minister can select the best ones to set the tempo of my service."

Philip studied the paper and twisted his lips before looking up at Grandma BB. "You want Jonathan Nelson's 'I Believe [So Long Bye Bye]' for the music selection? I mean, it's upbeat, but…"

"What? You don't think it's upbeat enough?" Grandma BB gnawed on her lips. "I want my celebration of death to mimic my celebration of life."

"Oh boy," Philip mumbled and rubbed the back of his neck. "Death is celebrated if you die in the Lord because you will rise with Him when He returns for His believers. Are you confessing your sins so you can profess Christ as your savior?"

Grandma BB folded her arms. He sounded serious, but she had to stop him before he took it too far. "I don't want an altar call at my funeral." It was not on her program.

"As the minister in the family, I feel it's my duty to remind you of Second Corinthians, chapter five and verse ten: *For we must all appear before the judgment seat of Christ; that everyone may receive the things done in his body, whether it be good or bad.*' All of us in this room can celebrate if you died living a life that's pleasing to God."

"Who said I haven't?" Grandma BB eyed her grandchildren and great-grands.

"You've cursed out a neighbor, shot—"

"I did not kill your father. It was meant as a warning only." Grandma BB silenced Cheney.

"Doesn't matter," Cheney said. "I'm not the only one here who knows all your dirty secrets. Your name is legendary."

"Excellent." Grandma BB sat smugly. "Now, will you and your husband stop interrupting your daughter who is leading this service?"

"Sorry, sweetie." Cheney blew air kisses at Victoria, glanced back at the paper, then raised her hand. "Sorry, but *ah*, you got twenty people to give tributes, and they have a maximum of five minutes each? We're going to be there all day. A bit much, don't you think?"

"I've lived a long life." She wanted to acknowledge everyone who would comfort the Jamiesons on her passing. She had debated whether to include a parting view, but it was for the benefit of those who arrived late, which would be against protocol.

Kami stood next to Victoria who nodded for her to take over and Kami did. "Come on, Mom and Dad. Let's get through this."

The arrival of the first baby in the Jamieson family, Kami, made Grandma BB a proud great-grandmother. While Kami was speaking, a dark-skinned pretty young woman tiptoed into the room, scanning faces and searching for someone.

"Excuse me. Are you Grandma BB?" She blinked.

Pace, Kami and Victoria's older brother, stood and stepped toward her. "You're in the right place. This is my great-grandmother Grandma BB."

Humph. The girl didn't know her well enough to call her anything besides Mrs. Beatrice Tilley Beacon. "Who wants to know, and how did you get into my house past my security detail?"

Chip appeared and cleared his throat. "She came at the same time as the chicken wings. I was taste-testing." He chewed and swallowed. "The food's here."

"I'm Deli Fox." She approached, about to shake Grandma BB's hand. Her eyes were just as chocolate as her skin. Her teeth were white as if from dental bleaching.

Was that a stage name for an exotic dancer, stripper, or worse? Grandma BB wasn't shaking anybody's hand until the woman stated her purpose. "And what are you doing here?"

Pace clasped Deli's hand and gently tugged her closer to him. "I texted her when Dad thought something was wrong at Grandma BB's house. She's a nursing student."

The room remained quiet as Pace and Deli's interaction upstaged Grandma BB.

Pace was Parke's firstborn son with another woman who had died. Cheney had adopted him as her own son, and their bond was strong.

"What kind of name is Deli?" Grandma BB put the rehearsal on hold. She had never met any of the children's dates except for Kami's first boyfriend who was a disaster covered in tattoos, which the family had nipped.

"It's short for Delilah."

"Delilah, Delilah," Grandma BB said, as she repeated the name that sounded familiar.

"You mean Delilah like in the Bible? She was lying and scheming to take Samson down," Chance, Parke's youngest son of five children, said in horror.

"*Awww* naw." Grandma BB gripped her chair as if she needed support to stand.

Chip and Dale wiped their fingers and came to assist her. She was about ready to blow some steam.

"In Hebrew and Arabic, Delilah means delicate. I prefer that reference." Deli graced the audience with an innocent smile.

Ummm-hmm. The uppity young thang could hold her own. Grandma BB respected that, but this was her house.

She eyed Pace. A girlfriend, huh? He was a third-year engineering student at Washington University less than twenty minutes away. When did he have time to date?

"Grandma BB," Pace said soothingly, "remember your blood pressure." His mannerisms and politeness were so much like Parke's.

Deli pulled a monitor from her purse. "I can check it." Her smile was a winner.

"She's fine." Queen stood and stepped forward. Her eyes sparkled. She was more protective of her young cousins who called her Auntie than a mother hen.

"You must be special if my nephew asked you to come and you came. If Pace hasn't already warned you, the Jamiesons aren't your ordinary boring family."

"We're out of control," Cheney said. "I'm Pace's mother."

"I'm supposed to be dying or dead, remember? Can we put the introductions on hold?" Huffing, Grandma BB shook her head. She squinted at the guilty parties.

Deli frowned and looked concerned. "If she knows she's dying, shouldn't we call the paramedics?"

"I'll explain later," Pace said and guided her to the seat he'd given up.

"Okay. Let's take it from the top!" Grandma BB clapped.

Chapter 2
Let the Show Begin

Victoria
PRESENT, Ferguson, Missouri, 2023

Clearing her throat, Victoria felt as if this was an audition for a school play. "My name is Victoria Jamieson." A slight smile graced her face. It felt good to belong to a family who loved her. Parents. Siblings. Grandparents. Aunties and uncles. And, of course, a great-god-grandmother. The works. "I'm the younger daughter of Parke VI and Cheney Jamieson's clan."

"Whoot-whoot!" The room exploded with applause, cheers, and whistles. Victoria blushed from the attention.

Grandma BB released a piercing whistle between two fingers, then inhaled to recover the oxygen she'd expelled.

"I've learned that being a Jamieson is more than about a bloodline. It's about the heartbeat." Victoria choked and patted her chest. In the past, she had learned not to trust anyone, especially adults. But her family—this family—the Jamiesons backed up whatever they said. They didn't make idle threats or false promises. She loved them more than she could ever express. "I wear my name like a badge."

Her sister, Kami, would come to the rescue whenever she became emotional. The two didn't even like each other when they'd met in high school, not knowing they were half-siblings. Victoria accepted the blame for that.

Hate and anger consumed her, and Victoria didn't know how to cope with the hurt and betrayal she felt for adults. Yet they found their way to each other despite different experiences in foster care.

Cameron, Parke's youngest brother, and Gabrielle's six-year-old twins ran to Victoria. She squatted to receive their hugs. They were the sweetest children. Their love was ready to give to her.

She composed herself. "Sorry."

"Nothing to be sorry for," the Jamiesons mumbled through the room.

Victoria smiled her thanks and continued. "Before Beatrice Tilley Beacon became our beloved Grandma BB, she lived a full life as a little girl in Little Rock, Arkansas."

And I will give you a full life. For I know the thoughts I think toward you, the Lord whispered, *thoughts of peace, and not of evil, to give you an expected end.*

How many times had the Lord spoken that Scripture to Victoria's spirit? It was a comfort to know she was on Jesus' radar.

"Grandma BB was a little girl like me?" Camille's eyes were wide in disbelief.

"We all were little kids," Chance told his five-year-old cousin. At twelve years old, he seized any opportunity to pull rank.

Before the children could engage in more bickering, Grandma BB lifted her servant's bell. "*Shhh.* This is a solemn moment. Please give reverence to the dead."

"Who's dead?" Camille's twin brother, Gabriel, asked.

"Son..." Cameron gave his children a stern look to stop their questions. "I'll explain later once I know what's going on myself," he mumbled.

Victoria contained a giggle and continued reading from her script. "She was the only child of Nellie and Joseph Tilley. She was born in..."

The adults leaned forward, awaiting the one answer that Grandma BB never revealed—her age. She preferred to be vague since everyone complimented her on her youthful appearance and agility. Victoria knew, but she wasn't giving it away. It was simple math. All they had to do was crunch the numbers from events, and her secret would be uncovered. Grandma BB didn't look her age.

Victoria had shared many secrets with Grandma BB when she lived with her. They both suffered pain and loss. Victoria would miss her the most when she transitioned from life to death. They had cried and laughed together. Most importantly, Grandma BB had taught her how never to be a victim again. A gun wasn't required. "It's who you know," she always said, "to get things you need done."

"Black don't crack." Grandma BB winked in response to everyone's disappointing groans. She crossed one leg over her knee, then swung her newest pair of Stacy Adams shoes, which none of them had seen.

"This is Grandma BB's life reflections," Victoria said as she turned the page. "Joseph Tilley provided for his family as a mechanic. Her mother was a domestic worker for Agatha Rothman…"

Chapter 3
Beatrice Tilley

My mama, Nellie Tilley, said she couldn't keep any babies, then I finally came along. She said I was a beautiful ball of sweetness.

Yep. That's me. I have survived childhood illnesses, Jim Crow restrictions, and strangling my young and only cousin, Lily Rae Swann. The brat was a thorn in both my sides, backside, and head.

Lily Rae was Estelle Swann's—Auntie Stella's—only child, so I had to put up with her as kin.

Mama and Auntie Stella were close, and they reckoned their daughters would be best buddies.

Wrong.

Lily Rae was six years younger, more spoiled than me, a whiner, and annoying. I learned how to cuss babysitting that brat.

Papa was older than Mama, and he had two brothers who died before I was born.

Auntie Stella lived in a pale blue house on Pulaski Street, a block from our pristine white house on Cross Street near Ringo Street. All the homes on this side of Little Rock are called shotgun houses. Papa says it's because a bullet could go from the front door, through the house, and out the back door. I don't know if he was kiddin' me, but I don't want nobody shooting at our house.

The houses were long. They were lined up side by side from corner to corner. A small patch of grass separated the sidewalk from the front porch, then another patch to the alley. Some neighbors' houses are so close I had seen boys climbing to roofs with one foot anchored on each home.

Papa would run those bad boys away if they tried that stunt outside our house.

Some neighbors had two front entrances. Other houses, like ours, had one door and a smaller porch. Mr. Swift, next door, had hedges around that bordered his house at the sidewalk. Papa built a white picket fence for our yard. Mama planted a rose bush on the corner and flowers around the porch.

Mama liked to get compliments when people walked by.

Our home was nice inside too, although the rooms were divided like one side of an ice tray—one square was the living room, the next was my bedroom, a smaller square was the bathroom, followed by Mama and Papa's bedroom until we stood in the kitchen next to the back porch. One long box.

Papa says our house, at twelve feet, is twice his height.

Mama didn't like some folks' houses whose wooden porches leaned to one side like a sliding board because the three brick pillars that anchored them had begun to sink underneath. Our porch was brick and sturdy. Papa had built it.

Two doors down was my best friend Peggy Bellamy's house. We were in the same class.

"They make our neighborhood look bad," Mama always said when we walked past them on our way to Ninth Street where all the Coloreds went to shop, eat, and have fun.

"I want a big house like Mr. John Bush on Ringo Street," I told Mama.

He was a rich Colored man, and Lily Rae's papa worked for him. One day when I grow up, I'm going to marry a handsome man, have five kids, and have a big house too.

"That will be nice." Mama smiled. She did that a lot—smiled until her eyes sparkled, whether she was tired or not.

A few weeks before I was to start my sophomore year, Mama opened my bedroom door early on a Saturday morning.

"Watch Lily Rae while your daddy and I are gone to work."

"You don't work on Saturdays," I whined, prying open an eye. As a mechanic, Papa always worked on Saturdays, but not Mama.

"School is starting, and you'll need things. Mrs. Rothman's neighbor is letting me clean her house today for extra money."

My eyes were fully opened, and I watched the expressions play on Mama's face. She wasn't happy about it either, although she tried to sound upbeat.

I didn't hide my disappointment. Mama, dressed in her long-sleeve white blouse and dark skirt, sat on the side of my bed. She mustered a smile and tweaked my nose.

"Beatrice, I'm doing this so when you turn eighteen, you can go to college, get a real job, and won't have to be a domestic worker to earn a living. Now watch Lily Rae, you hear?"

"Yes, ma'am."

Nellie Tilley was wrong. Mama was too pretty to be cleaning White folks' houses, but that is what Colored women did, clean or launder White folks' clothes.

I would go to Auntie Stella's, but her house wasn't as tidy as Mama's, so she liked to drop off Lily Rae at our house.

Lily Rae liked to play in my bedroom instead of outside. She knew I had a closet full of toys, including dolls with blond hair and blue eyes. Lily Rae liked them because they were fairer skin like her. Not me. Mama said it reminded her of brown sugar. My hair was long enough for a ponytail. Lily Rae's was stuck in its roots because a rubber band couldn't hold it. I'd tie her up first before I let her break any more of my stuff.

Lily Rae seemed to enjoy picking fights, knowing I better not hit her back because Mama says, "She's family. Pay her no mind." I gave her the licks she was asking for, then my mama gave me the licks I didn't ask for when she came home.

By the time school started, Mama and Papa had bought me a lot of stuff like we were rich. I received straight A's right off with little effort and even helped others in my class.

But my mouth seemed to get me in trouble, according to my tenth-grade teacher Miss Holland.

"Beatrice is well-behaved," she told Mama at the parent conference, "but she's developing a habit of challenging me in class. That's disrespectful."

With my hands folded in my lap and my back against the chair, I did my best to copy an angelic expression I had seen on *Bugs Bunny* and *Tom and Jerry* cartoons. I was innocent. It's not my fault that the truth slips out of my mouth. Papa and Mama taught me to always tell the truth, and that's what I did. Folks don't like to hear the truth. I was in trouble last year with the gym teacher because I asked her how she could expect us to be healthy when she was fat. I had to apologize to her too.

"Is that right, Beatrice?" Mama lifted her left brow. Translation: I had embarrassed her, and I was going to get it now. I was getting too old for butt whuppings—five licks from my daddy because he said discipline builds character and Colored people had thick skin—or three from Mama because she didn't like Papa whupping me.

It'll hurt.

I'll cry.

They'll forgive me until the next time I am falsely accused.

I lowered my head in repentance, but I wasn't sorry. The teacher had been wrong about President George Washington having dentures because he had no teeth. I read in a book I had checked out from the library on Ninth Street that George Washington had two sets of false teeth. One was in a museum; the other was buried with him, and he had some teeth. "I'm sorry, Miss Holland." I hoped I sounded convincing.

When I got home, Papa and Mama had no mercy.

"I expect better of you, Beatrice!" Papa roared. "Life is about letting folks think they're right, especially White folks. Play nice so you can graduate, go to college, then get a job to show people how smart you are." He frowned. "Understand."

It wasn't a question. "Yes, sir." Then I got my five licks.

Mama didn't give me a lecture or licks. I got no dessert.

Good behavior at school, even though I was right in my answer, and doing my chores at home without being asked, put me in good graces.

I started to earn money babysitting neighbors' kids along with Lily Rae. Got paid two bucks each kid so I could shop.

Everything was sold on Ninth Street between West Broadway and Chester. Everything!

Folks called Ninth Street the Line because Coloreds had to accept disrespect if they crossed the boundary into the White community.

"Why?" I asked.

Mama and Papa never answered me, so I asked my teacher.

"That's a question you're never to ask," Miss Holland said. "It's just the way things are." She gave me a stern look that forced me to shut down a rebuttal.

I walked away wondering what would happen if I did cross the Line.

"Beatrice, you must learn not to question adults," Mama said one time after she and Papa returned from a movie at the Gem Theatre on Ninth Street. "You let people think they're right."

That didn't sound intelligent, but I held my tongue.

Papa liked to go to the barbershop so he could talk with other Coloreds about their time in World War II like it was fun. Mama and my teachers said war was sad, but people had to be freed like those who enslaved Negroes.

When he returned from the war, Papa worked as a mechanic. Mama said he learned skills at the Negro school.

Ninth Street had a lot of stores and businesses. There was the grocer, Red's Pool Hall, where some of the older boys hung out on the weekends, and the library. It was quiet, and I could read anything, even stuff Mama didn't want me to read. Mr. Taylor's barbershop, where Papa got his hair cut, was next door to Mr. Donald's shoe company where Papa got his church shoes shined.

The walk was long, but Mama and I didn't mind. If we got tired or our bags became too heavy, we'd go to the cab company and pay for a ride home. It was on Ninth Street too.

We paused outside Gem Theater to see what was playing so Mama could tell Papa to take her.

There were three beauticians besides Miss Beulah who pressed Mama's and my hair from their kitchen. Since my birthday in March, Mama had let me wear heels to church on Sundays—because little girls couldn't wear heels. That made me a grownup and Lily Rae jealous. I even learned to sway my hips a little like Mama. Today Miss Beulah was pressing my hair real straight. She didn't burn me much, but when she did, the skin on the tip of my ear sizzled from touching the metal comb. She would dab a bit of Royal Crown on it, and the oil seemed to melt on it.

She tried to distract me, but the damage was done.

"Beatrice, your hair is growing like weeds in a yard," Miss Beulah said.

"We don't have weeds. Papa don't like them," I told her.

"I'm sure he doesn't, child. It was an old wise folks' expression. How old are you now?"

"Sixteen. I'm wearing heels, and Mama lets me wear lipstick sometimes," I boasted proudly.

"Nellie, looks like our little Beatrice is getting some gray strands early."

"What?" I whipped my head around and also got a mark on my cheek with the hot-pressing comb. "But I'm too young to be old." It was a frightful thought.

"Gray comes in early on my mother's side of the family. Don't you like my gray?" Mama patted her curls. "Your papa likes it." Her eyes sparkled.

"But you're old, Mama. You're supposed to have gray hair. Not as much as Miss Beulah who really looks old."

Silence from mama and a scowl from Miss Beulah.

When we left Miss Beulah's, I didn't get the promised strawberry sundae. I didn't get a whupping either, and it would be another month before I could wear heels again. Lily Rae laughed. I pinched her on the arm.

So unfair! I would be old by then.

The more well-off folks like Lily Rae's daddy worked at the Mosaic Templars Building. Mr. Bush sold insurance to Coloreds and made a lot of money, and so did his employees.

My papa wasn't much of a talker like salesman, but he had skills and knew how to use his brain and hands.

One time when Lily Rae tried to act high and mighty, I told her, "Uncle Calvin can't be too smart because he can't fix his own car."

The truth caused hurt feelings and landed me on punishment again. My cousin was such a tattletale.

Mama attended the Negro School for Industrial Arts, too, where she learned her education and home skills like sewing, but for some reason, she cleaned Mrs. Rothman's house instead.

"You should get all the education you can, Beatrice, but if the opportunities to use those skills are limited, you have to make adjustments to earn a living."

Must not be a lot of opportunities, I thought because all my friends' mothers cleaned, cooked, or washed White folks' clothing for a living.

My mama would ride the bus and come home tired, so after I did my homework, I started off cooking simple meals to help Mama, then she taught me about seasonings.

Sundays were the best. No school or work. We dressed up to attend church at Wesley Chapel. For me, I wore nice dresses but still couldn't put on heels. Once Mama said something, she never changed her mind. She was pretty in her black patent leather heels, nice dresses, and big hats. Mama and the other ladies looked nothing like they did when they cleaned White folks' houses.

Papa exchanged his greasy overalls for a suit and tie. He was handsome. There were two churches in the Dunbar neighborhood. The well-to-do Coloreds attended one, and the laborers worshipped at the other one.

The sermon, which I had memorized, was usually a continuation from the previous Sunday. "This world is not our home," Reverend Rufus preached until some mothers jumped up, holding their skirts down, and started dancing up and down the aisles. Others would join in until they passed out on the pews.

After the long sermon, the offering was even longer if they didn't collect enough money, then Reverend Rufus would dismiss us. On the way home, we would see neighbors who didn't attend morning service. Mama would always wave or speak.

Peggy's mama, Mrs. Bellamy, had invited us to Sunday dinner and the left church earlier to warm up our meal. After dinner, Peggy and I sat on the front porch to gossip like our parents did.

"All the boys in our class are ugly or stink," Peggy said. She was six months younger than me and wore cat-eye glasses.

"That's why I don't like any of them." We were both sophomores, and the handsome boys were in our upper classes.

"What you want to be when you grow up, Beatrice?" My friend was taller than me with a round face. The front of her hair was cut into a big fat bang. The rest was tied back into a ponytail. She put more Royal Crown in hers than me so not one strand moved, even when the wind blew.

Not mine. I wore my hair down in a tight curled flip whenever I came from Miss Beulah's. About a week or so later, I had a ponytail but no bangs. I didn't like to cut my hair at all. Not even for trimming.

"I want to be rich and have White people clean my house."

Peggy giggled. "You mean like the Bushes who built those four big houses on Ringo Street? They're like mansions. One's the size of two of our houses. But I ain't seen no White folks around here cleaning anything. Mama says their daddy or grandpa was a slave."

"He must have been real smart to become rich—" Mrs. Bellamy's high-pitched voice blasting through the open front window interrupted them.

We weren't supposed to listen to grownup conversations, but that was the only way we knew the good gossip, so Peggy and I exchanged knowing looks and eavesdropped. "The school council's talking about building a new high school for Coloreds."

"Lord knows ours is falling apart," Mama said.

"You want to go to a new school?" Peggy questioned in a hushed tone.

Dunbar High and Junior College in our neighborhood was all we knew. I shrugged. "Yeah. It would be nice, but we only got one and a half years after this semester."

"I heard the White high school is taking all the funding. A million dollars," Papa chimed in. "I don't think there's going to be enough money to go around."

Peggy and I exchanged sighs. We had heard enough. I stood and walked to the door, knocked, and peeped my head in. "Mama and Mrs. Bellamy, can Peggy and I walk to Evergreen Park?"

It was a small amusement park in the neighborhood.

"Yes. "You girls stay together," Mama said.

"And don't talk to no boys!" Papa said first, then Mr. Bellamy.

"Yes, sir," Peggy answered.

I nodded, knowing that's why we were going to the park.

Chapter 4
The Barbershop

Beatrice
PAST, Little Rock Arkansas, April 1957

The following Saturday, Papa was hot enough to boil a pot of water. Mama was cleaning another house again for extra money.

"Nellie, the only house you need to clean is ours, and we help you," Papa fussed.

This was the only thing I heard them argue about—not the money but Mama cleaning houses.

"I'm sorry, honey, but Mrs. Rothman changed my wages again, and her neighbor pays better. She even asked if Beatrice could babysit her child sometime on the weekend."

My bedroom door was closed, but I could hear every word clearly. If the woman had children like Lily Rae, I could answer for myself: no. But this was grown folks' conversation, and I wasn't allowed to butt in or listen. Plus, I didn't want to go to work with Mama. I wanted her home with us.

"Aw naw. Nellie, you tell that woman that I said no. Slavery is over. Having my Colored daughter watch over a White child doesn't sit right with me." Papa was on a tirade for the next five minutes.

Whether or not Mama would tell the woman what Papa said didn't matter. My services weren't for hire to White folks. I didn't hate them. I just didn't like how they treated Mama.

Papa had calmed down and hugged Mama before she left the house. I smiled. I liked my parents to be happy. The house was quiet for a long time until Papa knocked and opened my door.

"Come on, Beatrice. We've got to do your mama's shopping today," he said it in a pleasant tone but he didn't hide that he was unhappy about it.

We drove to Ninth Street, and Papa escorted me to the grocer. "Do all your mama's shopping. You can get something extra for you."

"Okay, Papa." I hugged him, and he squeezed me tight. "You know I love you and your mama, right?"

I looked into his kind eyes. Mama said I had his eyes. Papa was handsome with his mustache and black hair with bits of gray. I wanted to marry a man just like my papa. "Yes, sir. I know." I grinned wide and went inside Mr. Jasper's grocery store.

Papa waved, then continued his way down the street to Glass Front Barbershop. Mr. Taylor owned it, and Mr. Beacon was one of the barbers who worked there.

After I finished my purchase, I walked to Redman's Department Store. It wasn't as big as the one on the other side of the Line, but Mama said they had nice enough stuff. Instead of going in the direction of the barbershop, I turned and headed toward Main Street toward Pfeifer Brothers Department Store.

Maybe I could buy Mama the smallest bottle of perfume with the money I saved. I stood in front of the entrance in amazement. The building was intimidating up close. I felt like an ant about to be crushed. A handful of Coloreds didn't go through the front door but around the back, so I followed them. We entered through a hall that housed the restrooms—one for Whites and the other for Coloreds.

The inside was like a palace—clean, white, sparkling. I walked up to the perfume counter. The White saleslady gave me a blank expression. No smile was forthcoming, but she wasn't rude. "May I help you?"

"I want to buy my mama some perfume."

She lifted a brow. "Oh?" Did my request amuse her? "Why don't you try some fragrances on your wrist to see which one you would like and can afford?"

"Okay." I probably didn't have enough money, but Peggy and I played pretend a lot. My eyes widened as I inhaled traces of carnations and peaches, but a faint spice tickled my nose.

"Like that?" She snickered. "It's Nina Ricci's L'Air du Temps. It means the air of the time," the sales clerk said, transporting me out of Little Rock to a world far away.

"French?" I quizzed her, and she nodded as I pulled money out of my purse. "How much?"

"Nine dollars for a two-ounce bottle." Her smirk dared me to have enough money.

I had six bucks from babysitting, but I counted my money anyway. "I'm short."

"Of course, you are. Would you like a sample to take home to your mama? Only one." She scooted a basket filled with colorful vials close to me, and I picked a purple tube the size of a toothpick and as wide as a drinking straw. "Thank you."

I left out of the same entrance, then retraced my steps to Ninth Street to the Glass Front Barbershop, passing the pharmacy and Gem Theatre where Papa and Mama liked to go some Saturday nights. Mama would be too tired tonight.

Too bad because I liked seeing Papa's eyes light up when he looked at Mama, and she would blush. That must be love.

The bell chimed when I entered the barbershop. All conversations ceased. There weren't a lot of customers. Four pairs of eyes looked up at me. One man looked older than Papa and was in his barber's chair. Mr. Beacon cleared his throat. "We have a lady present. Be respectful. This is Joe's daughter."

"I won't be long. Take a seat, Beatrice. Men, mind your manners around my baby girl."

Teenager, I wanted to correct Papa. *Hmmmph.* I wasn't a baby anymore because I had started menstruation and could become a mother myself. That's what Mama told me. I wanted to wear heels again, but I kept quiet.

I took my seat, crossed my legs at my ankles, and sat like a lady. I thought about Mama working and wondered if there was a place in the world where Coloreds could get real jobs and make a lot of money to buy expensive perfume and have big houses. I glanced around the shop. Mr. Beacon's son was tucked away in the back nook. He was still and so quiet I hadn't realized he was there.

A book held his attention. It had glossy wrapping. I strained my eyes to read the title: *Around the World in 2,000 Pictures.*

His name was Hank, and they went to the same school, but he was an upperclassman.

What world had that book sucked him into? What kind of pictures were there? I glanced back at my papa who was paying me no mind. He and two other customers were talking about the war. With no one else my age to talk with, I stood and slowly inched my way to Hank.

Out of the corner of my eye, I saw Papa watching my every move. I peeked over Hank's shoulder. "I've never seen that book in the library before. You going somewhere?"

He looked up and blinked at me. His brown eyes seemed to melt like chocolate, and I liked the milk chocolate chunks Papa would bring me sometimes.

Hank's toothy grin reminded me of when Lily Rae drooled as a baby when she wanted more peas—except Hank didn't need his mouth wiped.

"Yeah, I'm going to travel the whole world," he said as if he was in a trance.

I frowned. "They won't let us Coloreds go too many places after dark. You best be content right here in Little Rock. For an upperclassman, you ain't too bright."

"Watch me. Who's going to stop—"

"Hank, stop babbling and come clean up behind Mr. Fultz," his daddy, yelled.

"Yes, sir." He scrambled to his feet. Hank was tall and muscular like a wrestler. We called light-skinned Coloreds like him high yella. His silky straight curls were "good hair" instead of the woolly-like forest most of us had, even me before Miss Beulah pressed it out.

"What's your name?"

"Beatrice. You should know that. We go to the same school." I huffed, stood taller, and swayed left to right. How could he not notice me? I wore some of the prettiest clothes. I was glad I wore the fancy blouse Momma made me from Mrs. Rothman's hand-me-downs.

A lot of Coloreds used the tailors on Ninth Street.

Not Mama.

She would cut up those hand-me-downs, then create a new garment just as pretty as the ones Auntie Stella bought Lily Rae. Of course, Lily Rae would come to our house to show off whenever she had anything new from a doll to clothes or money.

"You Mr. Tilley's daughter?" Hank asked.

"Weren't you paying attention when I walked in?" I *tsk*ed. "He's my papa."

"I'll see you later, Miss Beatrice, Mr. Tilley's daughter."

Nobody ever called me Miss before and I liked that. My heart raced as I tried to breathe. I blushed as my wobbly legs guided me back to my seat, and I fought the urge to sneak a peek at Hank again until Papa was ready. Otherwise, I would faint and tinkle on myself. That wouldn't be a good thing.

As Papa and I were leaving, Joey, another classmate, was coming inside for a haircut.

"Hi, Beatrice." He grinned and nodded at Papa.

I sighed and waved a hello. Although we were in the same grade, he was too young for me. "It's Miss Beatrice." I lifted my chin and stayed in step with Papa. I felt disrespected.

Papa didn't say anything to me about talking to two boys in one day. On the way home, I could only think about if Hank would talk to me again.

Chapter 5
Pardon the Interruption

Victoria
PRESENT, Ferguson, Missouri, 2023

"Wait a minute." Kami stood and pushed out her hand as if she were stopping traffic. Her manicured nails were dazzling.

Victoria copied her sister's style when Kami convinced her to go to the nail shop with her. The family said that ever since Kami returned after a summer with Queen in Tulsa, she had become prissy like her auntie.

"Grandma BB was younger than me when she met the love of her life, and you all gave me the fourth degree with Tango. He was my first love."

"Don't go there," Parke warned his oldest daughter. "It was all lust for that thug." He growled out his displeasure.

At the time, Kami was the only Jamieson girl in the family, so everyone was protective of her. Victoria was now smothered with that same vigilance.

The big blowup between Kami and her family happened before Victoria and Kami had met. Every morning and every night, Victoria thanked the Lord that the father and daughter had reconciled their differences.

Things might have turned out differently otherwise. Victoria had been in a horrific foster care situation, and it was because of Kami's persistence with her parents that she found a forever home with the Jamiesons through adoption.

She didn't know why bad things happened to innocent people, but God reminded her of His love and the Jamiesons' daily.

Grandma BB huffed and broke into her reverie. "Your daddy and uncles were soft. Me? I was about to handle his smart mouth with a beat down, either by cane or g-u-n," she spelled in front of the small children. It was a three-letter word, so most school-aged children knew it. She let out a hoot of laughter as she slapped her knee.

Pointing her finger in the air and rolling her neck, Grandma BB became animated. "I told him I had a rap sheet too. I wanted the dude to know who he was dealing with without all that testosterone for backup in the room. I had already done my homework on him and let the thug know that I was on to him. His real name was Terrence Jackson Kelly, aka Tango, for that week. I had everything I needed to know about him. I begged him to give me half of a reason to inscribe a permanent tattoo upside his head—"

"That's enough, Grandma BB," Parke said. "We're in a family setting. We all were there. And who are you calling soft?"

"Honey," Cheney said, placing a hand on her husband's arm, "everyone knows you protect your own."

The wow effect her mom had over her dad made Victoria giggle. It was cute. She never knew what love looked like until Parke and Cheney became her parents.

"You're right, dear." He brushed a kiss against her lips as if they didn't have an audience. "We were all surprised you withheld that piece of information about his rap sheet from us—her parents."

"Hey, I'm known to deal with shady people. I found out where he lived, his parents' names, and reviewed his juvy records—"

"Which I'm sure was illegal." Kidd grunted.

"I know people who know people." Grandma BB shrugged, then looked at the purple polish on her manicured nails. "I had him tailed for the past twenty-four hours leading up to the family game night. You never let him out of your sight, right, Chip and Dale?"

Both bodyguards shook their heads and looked offended that she had asked.

"See." Grandma BB sat back and folded her arms, then crossed one leg over her knee and rocked her leg. "I had it under control—until that peon made fun of my shoes." Her nostrils flared with indignation.

"I was going to ask you about the shoes," Deli whispered to Pace, discreetly pointing at Grandma BB's Stacy Adams.

"Tell you about that later." Pace shushed her with a slight nudge, then gave Grandma BB a "sorry" expression.

Grandma BB cut her eyes at Deli, but Pace offered an endearing smile. She had a tender spot for Pace who was robbed of his birthright from his biological mother who died and never told Parke he had a son.

Before he was renamed Pace, his adopted White parents changed his name to Gilbert Junior. When Parke learned all this, he prayed for God to move heaven and hell to regain his parental rights to a son who didn't know him.

God had been on the father and son's side because Parke had the adoption overturned. Impossible. Unheard of. But God did it.

Pace should have been named Parke VII, but Cheney and Parke had a stillbirth, and Cheney demanded the baby be named Parke VII, his birthright, so that he would never be forgotten. By the time Parke got custody of Gilbert, he had changed his name again to Parke VIII. The family called him Pace for short.

Unlike his father, Pace was quiet and low-key, but he guarded Kami from afar, even though she annoyed him growing up. He protected Victoria, too, despite her demands that he keep his distance.

"Anyway," Grandma BB continued, "the little ugly thug underestimated the wrong old woman. My jewel-encrusted cane will whip any would-be robber."

Parke rubbed his forehead. "We know. You not only sent the criminal turned-victim to the hospital, but after giving the police report, you showed up at the ER to finish the job. What were you thinking?" He shook his head. "Bad influence."

"That's old news." She fanned her hand. "For the record, I never touched that thug Tango. I just sweetly told him I was strapped."

Deli sucked in her breath. Her brown face showed a mix of horror and disbelief.

"And dared him to ask about your rap sheet," Cheney chimed in and lifted a brow.

Cheney knew most of her secrets but it took a while. They didn't become fast friends at first. Grandma BB had bumped heads with Cheney days after she moved next door.

Because of her former neighbor, Grandma BB had an extended family. Victoria had spent many nights talking about life's happiness and disappointments. When Victoria cried, Grandma BB had held her in a cocoon of love.

"She's scary," Deli mumbled to Pace. The young woman looked frightened.

Pace took her hand and in a reassuring voice said, "Only to someone who doesn't know her. To family, Grandma BB's the best at what she does. My great-grand loves hard and is fierce when it comes to us and who we love…"

Clearing her throat, Victoria cut her eyes at her brother. "As I was saying before I was interrupted, Henry Beacon stole Grandma BB's heart…"

Chapter 6
Henry Beacon

Henry
PAST, Little Rock, Arkansas, April 1957

Days after Beatrice had been in Mr. Taylor's barbershop, I couldn't stop thinking about Mr. Tilley's daughter.

I, Hank Beacon, was smitten! That's the term Mama would use. I came along one year after my parents, Flora and Jim Henry, were married. Two other siblings followed. Twins, but they died as babies. David died in his sleep. Ana choked to death.

So basically, I'm an only child. Make good grades too. Responsible and spoiled by my grandmother MaDear CC, my dad's mother, who lives with my dad, Mama, and me. Although I had friends, I wasn't influenced by them. I was a good kid, according to my parents.

Not one to become easily distracted until now, I didn't know what to do about this new condition. Dad and I were alone in the barbershop, which he had been saving up money to buy when Mr. Taylor retired in a year or two.

"Beatrice sure is a pretty little dark thing. Reminds me of your mother when she was about that age. It was love at first sight. Nothin' wrong with a woman who has some color to her," Dad said, knowing any mention of Beatrice's name would get my attention.

A grin stretched across my lips. I stopped sweeping and leaned on the broom. "She is. I like her."

I'd seen Beatrice at school, but from afar and never alone up close. I wasn't affected by her beauty until the day she walked into the barbershop Then I noticed everything about her—long lashes that shaded her brown eyes, a few gray strands, and the hint of a smile when she seemed impressed that I liked to read, and how she was confused at my dreams. The next thing I noticed about her was she was shaped like a woman, not a girl.

"But she's too young for you." He pointed his clippers at me as if he read my thoughts.

Standing taller, I asked him, "How young?"

"Too young for you to be serious about a gal." He turned back to finish straightening his station.

"Perhaps." I rubbed my jaw where a thin beard was trying to grow. When it did, I would look more like my dad.

Beatrice was a fancy name. I wondered if I should have introduced myself as Henry instead of Hank. Yes, I'm older, wiser, and definitely better looking than those knuckleheads who think they have a chance with her. "Dad?"

"Yeah, son?" He looked over his shoulder.

"Can you call me Henry from now on?"

Dad squinted. He twisted his mouth as he considered my request, then nodded. He walked up to me and extended his hand. "I sure will, Henry."

Suddenly, I felt like a grown man. I grinned and pumped his hand with a shake.

We closed up the shop and walked home. Beatrice. I held my breath when I recalled her name and then exhaled slowly so the memory wouldn't fade. Her skin reminded me of the pure maple syrup I pour on my pancakes, and her eyes were the darkest brown. She wasn't shy, but she wasn't flirtatious either.

Mama called them fast-tail gals. I had never met any girl named Beatrice before. After that brief moment at the shop, I became aware of her presence in the school hallway, even if it was from a distance. Whenever she did notice me, our eyes connected for the briefest moment. My heart sped up. She blushed, and I couldn't stop grinning. Other girls at school blushed when I looked at them, but none had made my heart gallop.

From that day forward, whenever Mr. Tilley came to the barbershop—without Beatrice—I practiced my best manners. My dad noticed my behavior too.

"What are your plans after graduation, Hank?" Beatrice's father asked one Saturday morning as I swept the floor.

Startled by his commanding voice, I broke out in a sweat but stood erect at attention as I had seen former soldiers do when they entered the barbershop. Clearing my throat, I found my voice, which was in hiding. "It's Henry, sir, and my plans are to go to college and work."

What I would study or do afterward, I didn't know, but I wanted to travel. See the country. See the world.

Mr. Tilley almost nodded his approval, but my dad had a grip on his jaw. Otherwise, his lining would have been crooked. I puffed out my chest in pride. My confidence slipped when he asked about my major. That's when I stuttered, "I'm not sure yet."

"A man's got to know what he wants to do in life if he's going to support a family," he said, and my dad mumbled his agreement.

How did he know how much my heart longed to spend five minutes with Miss Beatrice?

The odds weren't in my favor to get what I craved—travel the world with a girl like her on my arm. I could tell adventure stirred her curiosity despite what she said about staying in Little Rock.

As Coloreds, our world was limited. The Jim Crow line made sure of it but it wouldn't always be like that.

Yet, hearing Dad talk about the world war he served in, he was just as disrespected while fighting for our country, but he saw the world. That's what I wanted to do, see the world without having to go to war.

Grandmother Celia, my MaDear CC—dad's mother—believed in my dreams. "You can do whatever you want. Don't let nobody tell you differently." And she was willing to put up the money for whatever college that interested me and took Coloreds. "Or you can pass as I have for years when the situation called for me to speak and conduct myself as a White lady."

I believed her. My parents said I looked a lot like her, except she had a funny shade of green eyes. Mine were brown.

MaDear CC's grandmother was born enslaved to her father, Michael Crocker, the year before the Civil War ended. As a mulatto, she inherited money and spread her wealth among her sons. One died, and three of Dad's uncles remained.

Mr. Tilley asked him what he was going to study in college. I better make up my mind if I wanted to get to know his daughter.

I saw Beatrice every day in passing for a week. We hadn't come face-to-face, but it seemed like my vision could spy her out, no matter the distance. Something about that one encounter—five minutes tops—made me crave to be in her presence. It was torture.

Determined to build up the nerve to get permission to court Beatrice, I practiced my words, waiting for the next time Mr. Tilley would walk into the barbershop. My chance came the following Saturday morning.

He took a seat and opened the newest copy of Mr. and Mrs. Bates' *The Arkansas State Press* newspaper, which featured Colored folks' news.

With his face hidden behind the paper, I gathered the nerve to speak to him as a man, not a schoolboy. Standing over him, I summoned the deepest manly voice I could muster. "Mr. Tilley, may I have a word with you in private?"

Lowering his paper, he eyed me, folded it, and stood, towering over my six feet by three or four inches.

His breath—fresh butterscotch—made me sweat. He didn't blink. I did several times. I dreaded Mr. Tilley's intimidation. Finally, he nodded, and I exhaled on shaky knees.

"Dad, I'm going to step outside with Mr. Tilley for a minute."

"Don't make it any longer, Hank. Joe is next." He squinted then continued with his clippers.

It's Henry, I wanted to remind him, but I could only handle one battle at a time. "Yes, sir."

Mr. Tilley watched me and waited for me to lead the way.

Once outside, the sounds of Ninth Street's bustle distracted me, and I rubbed my hands together. It's not that in my four years of high school I hadn't asked a girl out or introduced myself to her parents, but this parent was different. Something about Beatrice warned me not to blow it.

"Hank, if you're here to inquire about my daughter, Beatrice, you're going to have to come to me as a man unafraid."

I snapped to attention and met his eyes without a blink. "Yes, sir. Please call me Henry, sir." I wasn't scared to ask for respect. Never had been. MaDear CC drilled that into her grandchildren. All three of them. If respect as a Colored man didn't work, pass as White.

"Either way, demand respect," MaDear CC always said.

Mr. Tilley cleared his throat.

The Glass Front Barbershop's window took up most of the front of the building, and I could feel us being watched by everyone inside, especially Dad. No more hesitation.

"I'd like to visit Beatrice some evenings after school if that's okay with you and Mrs. Tilley." *Breathe.* I stated my intentions.

"I'll think about it," he said as Dad tapped on the window and mouthed, "Time's up."

Mr. Tilley strolled inside first and sat in Dad's barber chair. He didn't even look at me as I grabbed the broom and began to sweep.

Beatrice's father received the services he requested—a shave and haircut. He paid Dad and left, still thinking about it.

Beatrice

I overheard Papa talk with Mama about inviting Hank to dinner. "I guess she's old enough to court."

When he grew quiet, Mama said, "It's all right, dear. She's growing up."

"I know, but I don't like it. Seems like the Lord just gave her to us yes-day." Silence again before he pounded his fist on the table. "He's respectable enough and even told me to call him Henry." That made Papa chuckle. "Plus, he's older than Beatrice. I know what's on a boy's mind at eighteen, so we need to keep an eye on him."

Shaking my head, I couldn't believe Papa was acting like Hank was twenty years older rather than two. *We go to the same school!* I wanted to scream, but that would be childish behavior. The punishment would be not allowing Hank to court me.

"Yes, he needs to know what we expect from him," Mama said. "If he says or does something we don't approve, that will be the end of Henry Beacon."

And just that quick, Papa changed the subject. "Do you want to go to the movies or dancing this weekend?"

Who-wee, wait until I tell Peggy. My heart pounded with jubilation. I'd never had a boyfriend ever. When I turned around from eavesdropping, there stood Lily Rae. She was listening too. I squinted and put my fist on my hip.

"Cousin Beatrice, you're too ugly to have a boyfriend." She stuck out her tongue.

"Well, I'm getting one, so I can't be too ugly."

Putting my happiness on hold, I debated retaliation against my little cousin. If I got in trouble for pinching her until she cried, I would be restricted from receiving company. I weighed my decision, inhaling and exhaling as Lily Rae bated me.

"My mama said so."

The hurt stabbed me through my heart. I blinked and stopped breathing. Auntie Stella had said that about me? Instead of tears, I had the perfect payback. I stormed into the kitchen as a tear fell from my eye. "Mama, do you think I'm ugly?"

Mama frowned. "Of course not. You're beautiful and remind me of your Auntie Stella as a young girl." I hugged and kissed Mama.

Turning to Lily Rae, I held my head up high and grinned. "I'm just as beautiful as your mama."

I walked out of the kitchen into my bedroom and closed the door. I had upped my cousin. My school had pretty brown girls, not just the high yella.

Early Saturday morning, Mama woke me. "Get up, Beatrice, and get ready. You're going with me so Miss Beulah can do your hair."

Wiping the sleep out of my eyes, I scooted up in bed to register what Mama said. Miss Beulah never did my hair on a regular schedule like Mama's—only for special occasions.

Before I could ask, she answered my unspoken question. "We're having company after church tomorrow."

"Oh."

We weren't supposed to question our parents, just do as they say, but Mama also said the only way for me to learn things was to ask questions. "Who's coming, Mama?"

She lifted her eyebrow and her nostrils flared. They were signals that I knew better than to ask, but she answered. "The Beacons."

Excitement and fear battled for dominance in my heart. So, this *was* going to happen. I had wondered what came of Papa and Mama's talk about Hank—or would he want me to call him Henry too?

I freshened up, dressed, and ate breakfast, then the three of us were off to the business district on Ninth Street. I missed Mama when she had to clean Mrs. Rothman's neighbor's house on Saturdays for extra money. Lately, she hadn't since Papa took on side jobs.

As we passed several tailors on the way, Mama stopped at Crenshaw Tailors and admired garments hung in the window. "I'm going to make you some more clothes, Beatrice."

Will they be courting clothes? I didn't ask. Instead, I grinned and hugged her. "Thank you, Mama!"

Papa escorted Mama and me to Miss Beulah's and gave us a kiss on the cheek then walked past the Ninth Street Cab Company to the barbershop where Hank worked.

When Miss Beulah finished with my hair, instead of two ponytails, she cut my hair for bangs, which I stayed calm for like a grownup customer, then Miss Beulah gave me curls. It probably would have bounced if it hadn't been for the pressing oil to keep it straight. The extra service cost more. She didn't mention more gray this time but I knew what to do. Put some of Papa's black shoe polish on them before I went to school and remember not to touch them.

"Beatrice, run down to the barbershop and tell your papa to give you five more dollars for our hair," Mama said.

Horror gripped me. I almost choked as I forgot to breathe. I needed a day to process the "new me" before Hank saw me.

"Yes, ma'am."

I left out the side door of Miss Beulah's white siding house with the yellow door to match the daisies she tended to in front of the porch.

Once outside, I gave myself a pep talk. "You're grown, Beatrice. You ain't scared." My mouth said it, but my ears didn't believe it.

Forcing one foot ahead, I began my trek two blocks to where Hank worked. It wasn't far, but I wished it was. Would he notice? Would he say anything? Questions swirled around in my head until the barbershop's door handle was within reach.

Before I could touch the knob, it swung open. Hank greeted me with a smile as he scanned my head and face.

His words seemed to catch in his throat. "You…you look beautiful, Beatrice." He exhaled as if he was practicing his breathing.

"Thank you, Hank." A blush sprang up.

"Call me Henry, so I can sound important like your name." He grinned, and I admired his nice smile.

"Han—Henry," his father called. "Let Mr. Tilley's daughter inside."

"Right. Ah, sorry." Hank seemed as nervous as me as he stepped back.

"Well, if it isn't Miss Beatrice all grown up," Mr. Beacon said to my embarrassment and Henry's pride, judging by how close he stood next to me.

Even Papa's eyes sparkled. "Beatrice, you tell Miss Beulah she made you as pretty as your mama."

My cheeks started to ache from another blush. "Thank you, Papa. I will." I felt I should curtsy at all the compliments. "Mama says she needs an extra five dollars for our hair."

"Just a minute," Papa said to Mr. Beacon, then angled his hip to reach for his wallet in his back pocket. He counted out the dollar bills and handed them to me.

"Thank you, Papa." I kissed his cheek.

"Dad, can I walk her back to Miss Beulah's?"

His father, an older and more mature version of Henry, seemed annoyed. "Sure, Henry, if it's okay with Mr. Tilley, but hurry back so you can clean the clippers and tools."

"Yes, sir." He appeared to hold his breath, waiting for Papa's answer.

Henry exhaled when my papa consented. He beat me to the door and held it open for me to step out first. The distance to Miss Beulah's house seemed shorter than when I came. Soon, we were one house away.

"You are the prettiest girl at school."

Me? I blinked with surprise at the revelation as he stole a kiss on my cheek and hurried back down the street.

"Then you should have told me before now," I yelled to lessen my shock. Touching my cheek, I tried to rub the kiss into my face like mama did her cold cream. I grinned. My first kiss from a boy. "Whoa." But he was going to have to do better than that next time.

I walked through the back door of Miss Beulah's kitchen and handed Mama the money as if nothing happened.

Chapter 7
Daddy's Little Girl

Victoria
PRESENT, Ferguson, Missouri, 2023

Victoria turned the page in the program.

"*Eew.* You let a boy kiss you?" Lauren scrunched her nose and motioned as if she was about to gag.

The adults laughed at Ace Jamieson's eleven-year-old daughter's theatrics.

"A boy tried to kiss me in my class on Valentine's Day—"

"What?!" Ace whipped his neck and focused on his daughter as he balled both his hands into fists. He seemingly was about to explode, while his wife swung one leg over her knee.

"Calm down, babe." Talise patted her husband's leg.

"Calm down?" He looked as if he didn't recognize his wife.

The mood in the room grew serious as everyone, including Victoria and Grandma BB, waited for the outcome.

"I punched him, Daddy, real good," Lauren said with a fierce expression.

A cheerleader for woman's causes, no matter the age, Victoria couldn't help herself from lifting her hand for a high-five. Lauren smacked it so hard that Victoria's hand stung.

Fair-skinned like everyone in Parke's family, Victoria admired her adult cousins Kidd, Ace, and Queen's rich dark skin tone, which was blemish-free. Handsome and beautiful was how Victoria described them, and their children were a satiny blend of browns with dark lashes, even the boys. The girls had long, thick jet-black hair. When Lauren and Kennedy got older, a lot of boys would try to kiss them. Hopefully, both would punch their way out of unwanted affections.

"Ah." The sighs filled the room.

"Oh—okay." Ace relaxed in his chair, satisfied, then twisted his lips in thought. "Baby, Daddy doesn't want you fighting. If someone in class is bothering you, I want you to tell Daddy, and I'll take care of it. Okay?"

"Mommy already did."

Talise shrugged and offered no explanation as chuckles filtered through the room.

Eva, who was married to Kidd, reached across her husband for a high-five from her sister-in-law. "Moms to the rescue, sis."

"You know it." Talise nodded. "Made my own teacher's conference and informed Mrs. Hicks that my children are not to be touched—ever."

"Alright. Alright." Grandma BB waved her hands in the air. "All I know, ain't no youngun in this room better be exchanging bacteria saliva that could contain infectious mononucleosis, influenza, coronaviruses, gum disease…"

"She's a regular Wikipedia," Deli said in awe.

Grandma BB didn't seem to take that as a compliment as she squinted at the newcomer. "If I keep living and my great-gran is serious about you, you'll hear more."

"O-okay." Victoria cleared her throat. "Back to Grandma BB's life reflections."

Chapter 8
First Boyfriend Woes

Beatrice
PAST, Little Rock, Arkansas, April 1957

Henry Beacon got permission to court me. Now what? I waited the next day for something to happen. Was he going to do more than wave at me in the lunchroom? I was confused.

Finally, it happened. Henry asked me if he could walk me home a few days later. I couldn't stop blushing as Peggy giggled. My friend thought I was lying when I told her about Henry talking to Papa like a grownup.

Now, it was happening. Henry's gait was as confident as a soldier's. I felt like the most important and beautiful girl in the world. No, I was no longer a girl but a sixteen-year-old woman who could wear heels until my last infraction. Where was Lily Rae, the brat, so I could show off my boyfriend?

Henry didn't talk much, and I didn't know what to say.

The silence was driving me crazy as we passed one house after another. He seemed in a trance with each step closer to my house, which came into view down the street.

"You ain't got nothin' to say?" I challenged him.

He stopped and stared at me. A shiver tickled my arms as if it were winter instead of spring. "I like you, Beatrice."

Might as well have said he loved me the way my heart fluttered, but I wasn't easy to win over. I didn't care that he was a senior and I was a sophomore who had never gone steady before. Jutting my chin, I batted my lashes. "I like you, too, Hank, but I like lots of people."

"I'm Henry, remember? It sounds more grown-up like Beatrice."

Right. We were grownups. I wouldn't forget. I'd never make that mistake again.

Henry lifted a silky brow as he twitched his mouth. "Other boys? Who?"

Was he the jealous type? Smug that I had frazzled him, I resumed walking. "Oh, nothing."

"Name them," Henry said as one long step caught up with me.

"Are you plotting to beat them up or something?" I couldn't figure him out. He was quiet, but apparently serious.

"Nope." He slipped his hands into his pants pockets. "Pay them off to stay away from you."

"Why would you do that?" I covered my mouth in shock. Didn't know how I felt about him using his money to bribe people to get what he wanted. I studied him from his shoes to the top of his wavy good hair.

"Like I said, I like you. Maybe one day we'll get married."

"You can't make me marry you." I frowned and squinted. How did I get from wearing heels, going steady, to getting married so quickly? Flattered—yes. Foolish—nope. Then I fumed at his resumption. "I'm going to save you the trouble. My answer is no." I dismissed him, walking the rest of the way home alone. When I stepped onto my porch, I knew he hadn't moved from the spot I had left him, but I didn't look back to make sure no matter how much I wanted to.

Mama didn't let Papa's temper stop her from doing what she wanted to do. She just waited until he calmed down. If Henry was upset, then he had some thinking to do. I had bigger plans than getting married.

I let Henry think I was mad at him, but I wasn't. Peggy said I was teasing him. So what? I didn't care. Mama had sewn me more blouses and skirts. I made sure my hair shined with pressing oil and curled tightly. Joey and other boys in my class took notice, but Peggy and I agreed, they were ugly, even with a good haircut.

The next day after school, Henry was back. "Beatrice, you might as well stop playing hard to get. You can't win, and I won't lose," he said, taking my books from my hands.

Henry smelled good. I wondered if he had sneaked some of Mr. Beacon's cologne.

"*Humph.* Who says?" I shrugged. "What if I don't want to date an older boy?"

The look on his handsome face was funny. "I'll be able to take care of you after college."

He reached for my hand as we crossed Ringo Street in front of the school. Henry had never done that before. I wanted to faint from his touch. "I plan to see the world and want you to go with me."

I loosened my hand, confused by what he was asking me. I wasn't leaving Little Rock with Henry Beacon! Did I want adventure in my life—yes. It wasn't that easy. "You say the strangest things." Once again, I walked the rest of the block home under his watchful eye.

The more I resisted his charms, the more determined he became. I loved it!

Going steady was all new to me. Instead of playing with my dolls or gossiping with Peggy, I thought about fun things to do with Henry.

Peggy said it was cool to have a boyfriend who was an upperclassman. Even more of Henry's friends like Roger Williams started speaking to me while some older girls rolled their eyes at me.

"He's cute," Peggy whispered when no one else was around us. Despite her best smile, Roger didn't pay her no mind. With good hair and light skin like Henry, he was seen with girls who were the same high yella.

Each day, Henry continued to walk me home. He always brought something extra for me for lunchtime—an apple, strawberries, then he gave me a Fry's Chocolate Cream bar. I shared a piece with Peggy; it was so good.

One morning, Henry met me at my locker. His bold statements seemed odd with his shy mannerisms, just like now. "I got this card for you." Either he was acting bashful or it was secretive so no one could see him give it to me.

"What does it say?" A smile lifted my lips as my heart danced with excitement. Papa gave Mama lots of cards.

When I opened it this time, I didn't share what it said with Peggy. *I think of you all day, and dream about you at night. Signed, Henry Beacon.*

Chapter 9
Dating 101

Henry
PAST, Little Rock, Arkansas, April 1957

I was serious about winning over Beatrice's affection, and my parents and MaDear CC knew it.

"What makes a girl like a boy?"

My dad stopped chewing on his stew at the dinner table and gave me one of those "you should know" looks. "Beatrice has your brain all twisted up. You've taken Mr. Boulding's daughter to the picture show a couple of times, then there was Julia, Mr. Porter's niece, and…" He tapped his jaw. "Can't remember the other girls."

Charlotte was the only other girl. She liked me more than I liked her, and she became bothersome by showing up everywhere I went. The other dates were because my friend Roger and another buddy, Ted, were going steady, and I took them as a favor. "Dad, they liked me, but I never noticed them. It's not that way with Beatrice. I like her, and I want her to like me too." I tried to hide my torment.

MaDear CC rested her spoon beside the stew she had prepared for all of us, and she looked at me with an expression softer than my father's.

"Always make sure she feels special, and let her feelings count. Nobody likes to be bossed around just because the person can. Remember that." She was the expert after being widowed twice.

"Listen to your grandmother," Mama said. "MaDear CC did a fine job with my husband." Mama giggled.

Since that day, my curiosity grew about Beatrice Tilley. When I mentioned her name to my mother and grandmother, my dad said she was too young for me. My grandmother had laughed.

"I still think she's too young for you." Dad shrugged and finished his dinner before it got cold.

"Henry don't need an old crow to have babies with." MaDear CC's eyes twinkled with mischief, then she snickered.

"And I want plenty of grandbabies." Mama looked hopeful as she folded her hands in a pleading gesture.

"Well," my father said, standing and puffing out his chest, "a man's got to take care of his family. You have a lot of babies; you've got a lot of mouths to feed. I make a good livin' as a barber. It's a service Coloreds and Whites need. You'll never run out of customers."

Henry swallowed to keep a straight face. He couldn't travel the world tied down to a barbershop. He glanced at MaDear CC. She knew he had bigger dreams.

"All that will come in due time. Instead of working in a barbershop, he might own dozens of them." MaDear CC tapped her forehead with her finger. "Think ahead. Get educated at college."

That Saturday, Mr. Tilley walked into the barbershop. He acknowledged me with a nod but didn't come for a haircut but to speak with Dad. "My wife and I would like to invite your family over for Sunday dinner after church tomorrow."

I swept the same spot, gripping the broomstick so hard that I could have snapped it. Mama and MaDear CC cooked Sunday's dinner on Saturday.

"Have a seat, Joe. Let me finish up with Norman, and I'll phone the wife."

"I can call Mama, Dad," I offered, then swallowed.

Three pairs of eyes watched me: Dad, Mr. Tilly, and Mr. Norman. Dad twisted his mouth, then nodded. I released the broom, which crashed to the floor, then I picked it up and hurried to the yellow phone on the wall.

MaDear CC answered. I repeated Mr. Tilley's invitation with desperation in my plea.

"That sounds like a good idea. We accept. Tell Joe we'll bring dessert."

"Thank you, MaDear CC," I said, relieved.

I hung up the phone and relayed the message, grinning. Mr. Tilley exchanged an unreadable expression with Dad, stood, then left.

We weren't regular church-going folks, but because Beatrice's family had invited us to supper, my mother thought it best to give a good impression. "Folks should know we are upstanding people too."

To prepare for the big day, I asked Dad to give me the best haircut ever and a shave. Although my beard was faint, I wanted to show every effort was made for my grooming. Dad offered his services for free, but I tipped him anyway.

Dad choked and gave me a bear hug. "I've raised a good young man."

The next morning, I said a prayer before church that everything would turn out okay.

Mama and MaDear CC's hats, dresses, shoes, and purses were the same color: pink for Mama and blue for my grandmother. Dad and I suffered through the confines of black suits and ties.

Only for Beatrice.

Bethel A.M.E. Church and Wesley Chapel were huge corner brick buildings within walking distance of each other. The chapel was intimidating with its castle-like skyscraper tower in the front and twin shorter ones in the rear. Two circular stained windows seemed big enough to place the moon. Inside about twenty to thirty pews were between the entrance to the pulpit with the main aisle cut in the middle.

Since the Beacons weren't regulars, we sat in a row that was halfway between the front and back door—MaDear CC's choice. I craned my neck to sneak a glance at Beatrice and her family who sat across the aisle, a few rows up. While her parents listened to the reverend, we exchanged glances. She was even prettier than at school, wearing a light shade of purple.

Was she excited about the supper between our families after the service?

Beatrice's skin reminded me of Mama's perfect blend of chocolate. MaDear CC mentioned babies, and seeing Beatrice now made me think about a family. Our babies would look like the crust of one of MaDear CC's peach cobblers—brown to perfection.

Mama nudged me and without taking her eyes off the minister she said, "Pay attention. There may be a quiz at dinner."

I sat straighter and didn't steal another peek. That didn't stop me from thinking about Beatrice while I tried to focus.

Reverend Greenlee was a short, dark, and round-bellied man whose loud voice announced his presence before he appeared. He also sweated with little exertion.

"In Ecclesiastes four, verses nine and ten, the Bible says, *two are better than one, because they have a good reward for their labor. For if they fall, the one will lift up his fellow: but woe to him that is alone when he falls; for he hath not another to help him up.* If we see our neighbor in need, Jesus expects us to help…"

Got it. "Two are better than one." Proof that I needed to go after Beatrice.

After the benediction, my parents and grandmother greeted friends. A few members raved about the sermon, reminding everyone to help their neighbors. Definitely a mixed message.

I scanned the church for Beatrice, but I saw them leaving. After too many goodbyes, I drove the family car to the Tilleys' one-story-long house near the corner of Cross Street in the opposite direction of our house. We had a second floor that was tall enough for me to turn into a bedroom, giving up my room downstairs for MaDear CC when she came to live with us.

Walking Beatrice home, I had stayed at a distance, watching her open the white picket fence that bordered their property, showing off thick green grass compared to their neighbor's balding lawn. Their long white porch was inviting, with three chairs lined in a row. Plants were arranged in order of height on one side.

We got out of the car, and I inhaled, then held my breath as we climbed the couple of stairs to the porch. I stared at the beige wood door until I could see the even paint strokes.

Dad cleared his throat. I snapped out of my trance and exchanged glances with my parents and grandmother. MaDear CC encouraged me to knock with a nod.

I did, and Mrs. Tilley opened the door. The smell of supper tickled my nostrils.

She smiled and reminded me of Beatrice. "Come in, come in." She moved back as Mr. Tilley appeared but not Beatrice.

They stepped inside the living room where there were three armless bright red chairs and a gold couch in front of a window. Red, green, orange, and yellow floral curtains matched the pillows on the couch. The walls were painted a shade lighter than the grass outside. A television sat across the room.

MaDear CC complimented Mrs. Tilley on her decorating ability. "Your home is lovely."

We followed the Tilleys through one door toward the back of the house where Beatrice stood in the kitchen with a black-and-white square floor, light green cabinets, and a red table with four matching chairs and two black ones added for guests. An apron was tied around her tiny waist. I smiled to myself, conjuring up images of her cooking our meals in our kitchen.

She paid me little mind as she checked on dinner, but she did greet my parents and MaDear CC.

Once the food was ready, we took our seats around the table where the plates, utensils, and glasses were waiting. Mrs. Tilley and Beatrice set large platters and bowls in front of us.

Mr. Tilley said grace then the dishes were passed. I felt all eyes were on my table manners as I unfolded the cloth napkin and placed it on my lap. I coaxed myself: pick up the fork on my right, don't gobble down my food like I did at home, and don't slurp! As a Beacon. I would make my family proud.

Everyone complimented Beatrice's tasty Salisbury steak, green bean casserole, and buttery mashed potatoes.

"You're a great cook, Beatrice." I grinned as my accolades weren't an exaggeration.

"Now," Mr. Tilley said, pushing back some from the table to pat his stomach, "I understand you like my daughter."

Nodding, I grinned first before answering, "Yes, sir."

"Beatrice is finishing her second year at Dunbar High, and you're about to graduate. If you go off to school, you won't see her…"

Her dad listed all the reasons to damper my interest in Beatrice, and I listened respectfully.

To my surprise, my parents voiced their concerns, which I hadn't heard before they turned the conversation around.

"Yes, they are young, but like the sermon today, they will be together to figure things out."

Tapping a finger on the table, Mr. Tilley stared at me, squinting and twisting his lips. With his free hand, he rested it on Mrs. Tilley's. "My wife and I give our consent—"

I exhaled the air I didn't know I was holding.

"Only if your parents agree with us to chaperone whenever you two are in our presence. Beatrice, I will say this in front of Hank— rather Henry—because we mean what we say. You can date her, but don't touch her. Beatrice, you know how you were raised and what type of behavior is expected from you. I never thought I would have to say this…" He paused and swallowed, "but keep your dress down, legs closed, and knees locked."

My jaw dropped. I couldn't describe the mortification I felt from the mention of sex in front of me and Beatrice. The discomfort was painted on her beautiful face too.

"My grandson has been instructed over the years to keep his pants zipped," MaDear CC snapped to defend my honor, but I didn't need backup. I wouldn't disrespect Beatrice anyway.

"Then we have an understanding." Mr. Tilley stood first, then my dad, and shook hands.

My mother and grandmother smiled at Mrs. Tilley.

"The rules are," Mr. Tilley said, clearing his throat, "you can continue to walk her home from school but can't stay so you both can complete your studies."

"Yes, sir." We shook on the agreement.

"I want you to bring Beatrice to our house sometimes, so we can get to know her." MaDear CC made known she and my parents had requirements too. "There are some teas and other events we would like for her to attend with Flora and me."

I rubbed the back of my neck. I had no idea that asking Beatrice out would be a contract, but the sparkle in her eyes and the hint of a blush on her cheeks let me know she was worth it. I had no plans to dishonor her, but I was hoping for a kiss. A glare from Mr. Tilley directly made me wonder if he had read my mind.

Chapter 10
The Fight

Beatrice

PAST, Little Rock, Arkansas, April 1957

"You stole my boyfriend, Beatrice," senior Trudy Pepperidge said through bad breath as she blocked my locker. Next, Trudy planted a fist on her hip.

Tilting my head, I frowned. "Who's your boyfriend?"

"Don't act dumb. You know Henry Beacon wants me."

I sized her up. She wanted a fight. Trudy picked the wrong one. "But he chose me instead," I baited her, squinting. If she swung, I would leave her bald from one good yank on her hair. Next, I would go for both eyes she liked to roll at me.

Intimidation wasn't in my blood. Inches taller than me, a shade lighter than me, hair longer than mine, and more womanly shaped than me, Mama would have called her behavior "fast" and promiscuous.

She stepped forward. I stepped backward then took three steps forward to bump her. "Touch me, and you'll be bald, blind, and bow-legged."

Shock slapped Trudy first. Then her nostrils flared as she gritted her teeth in a growl. "Are you threatening me?"

Didn't I just throw the first hit? "Oh, no." I shook my head and stepped out of her space. "I would never do that."

Trudy had a bad tooth. If she had been nicer to me, I would tell her about Dr. Davis' dental clinic, but she wasn't nice. With eyes locked on each other, I watched her move away from my locker. "Good. You know better. Stay away from my boyfriend."

I grabbed my books and shut my locker. As I walked away, I glanced over my shoulder. "It's a warning."

"You little…" Trudy's two friends restrained her. "Meet me after school."

"What time? I don't want to be late." I didn't back down despite having no backup. I was taught to be peaceful when possible. That's what Reverend Greenlee said one time, but if we have to settle a score, fight dirty, and folks will mess with you no more. That was good advice.

The rest of the day, I prepared myself for the fight of my life and the lie I would have to tell when I got home. All because of Henry Beacon. Was it or he worth it? Probably not, but my family's name was.

Papa hated troublemakers. Mama said Papa was too stubborn and stupid to be afraid, while she avoided confrontations. She refused to argue with Auntie Stella.

Me? I guess I'm more like Papa.

After the dismissal bell rang, I raced out of the building to be the first one at the corner across from the school. Might as well get the fight over with. I might be smaller than Trudy, but I was strong.

Peggy was uneasy all day, looking over her shoulder and jumping at the slightest noise, yet she was my best friend. Reluctantly, she came with me, but Peggy would leave me for dead and go home to tell what happened.

In a military formation, Trudy and her gang marched toward us. I had to calm my nerves to endure punches and give back better licks. All this fuss over a boyfriend who was nowhere to be seen because he had to stay after school for a senior meeting that Trudy had skipped.

Henry knew nothing of this. When he brought me extra cookies for lunch and purposely passed me in the hall between classes, I didn't breathe a word of Trudy's jealousy.

She took off her clipped earrings and gave her sunglasses to Peggy who was about to take them.

"Peggy, she's the enemy, remember? Hold them yourself, Tutti Frutti." I resorted to name-calling as more classmates gathered around.

"Call it," Trudy's cousin Nancy said as she flipped a coin to determine who would give the first lick.

"Heads," Trudy and I said at the same time.

Trudy's nostrils flared like a fire-breathing dragon. I squinted so I could focus on where to land my first punch—her mouth or nose. Who was going to back down? Tired of these shenanigans, I stepped forward and began to swing my arms like I was a windmill at high speed. I went for multiple blows.

Something or somebody gripped me around the waist and lifted me off the ground. I tried to break free but couldn't.

"Beatrice, calm down," a deep voice ordered.

My mind registered Henry's voice, and I began to lose steam.

Henry pushed me behind him and addressed my nemesis. "Trudy, Beatrice gave you a warning, which you should have heeded. She's my girlfriend now. She's never bothered you, so don't bother her. I have snitches everywhere. Don't look at her, breathe, or walk near her. Do we have a gentleman's agreement?" Henry looked deadly.

"As you can see, I'm all woman," Trudy flirted.

"*Hmmph.* Then act like a lady." Henry took my hand and tugged me toward home.

"Wow." Peggy said what I was too shocked to say.

I didn't know how I felt about that intervention. Trudy needed a whupping. If I couldn't deliver, she would at least get a spanking.

He surprised me. While I fumed quietly, Henry had a lot to say. "Don't ever take her or anyone else's bait again." He frowned, looking ahead as he marched down the street.

Silence. I didn't like being told what to do.

He squeezed my hand. "Beatrice?"

Silence. *You're not my papa.*

Henry faced me.

Peggy, who had been trailing us, also stopped mid-step. I ignored her. So did Henry.

The kindness I saw in his eyes made me wonder who this Henry Beacon really was—the handsome senior boy or a protector like Papa?

"Why did you do that? I could have handled her." I had something to prove to myself.

"Because I like you. You haven't been my official girlfriend long. In less than a month, school will be out for the summer, and I want to spend more time together."

"What does that have to do with getting some licks in on Tutti Frutti?"

He chuckled and shook his head. "You get into a fight and get suspended, what does that mean for us? We probably wouldn't be able to see each other because of you getting in trouble." He lowered his voice, "I don't want to see your parents punish you or someone hit you."

He turned to resume the stroll to my house. "When I heard about what was going to take place, I said I had an emergency, left the meeting, and came running. I have no problem using my allowance and money earned from the barbershop to pay for snitches. Peggy is one of them."

I shook my hand free and bent over laughing, then I looked back at my friend and laughed some more. "Peggy? If she's my backup, then I'm in trouble. I may be better off with my little cousin Lily Rae."

"That can be arranged too." He didn't say another word until he said goodbye at my door.

That day, I learned a lesson that wasn't in the classroom. Because of Henry, Trudy would never bother me again. He was more mature than me to think about the consequences of my actions.

He would protect me at all costs.

If this was love, maybe I would marry him...in about ten years.

Chapter 11
What Happens at Senior Prom…

Beatrice
PAST, Little Rock, Arkansas, May 1957

Senior prom was a big deal to a sophomore, even Peggy said so, but she wasn't going. Mama sewed me a pink full tea-length dress with lots of lace. A wide satin belt wrapped around my waist. The taffeta bodice was strapless and heart-shaped with more pink lace on top.

Miss Beulah fixed my hair in a fancy updo. Once she finished, she stepped back and patted her chest. "Where did my little Beatrice go from all those years ago that I had to put you on a phone book to press your hair?"

"I grew up." I didn't know what else to say. "Mama?"

Shaking her head, Mama looked at me as if she had never seen me before. When she tried to speak, her words choked in her throat so she hugged me instead, careful not to mess up Miss Beulah's work.

When Papa came to take us home, he blinked. His eyes watered, and he sniffed a couple of times. "Baby, you look as beautiful as your mother on the day I married her."

From the backseat, I blushed. "I'm just going to prom, Papa."

Later that evening, I slipped on my dress and gloves, and I didn't recognize myself when I stared in the mirror.

Peggy came over to gawk. "Beatrice, you don't look real, you're so pretty."

When Henry arrived, he was speechless, and so was I. The white tuxedo jacket made him more handsome than singer Bobby Freeman. His dress shoes were Stacy Adams. He slipped a corsage band on my wrist and handed me a box. "This is from MaDear CC."

Opening it, I gasped. "A pearl necklace and clip-on earrings?"

Mama smiled next to Papa who wiped his eyes. "I had planned to buy you a necklace, but Henry's grandmother called and asked if it would be all right."

Henry put it around my neck. "You're beautiful," he whispered.

I couldn't stop the chill that tickled my arms from his compliment.

Papa picked up his Kodak Brownie camera from the end table. "You two pose so I can take some photos."

We did as he instructed while he snapped away. When Papa finished, I picked up my purse. Henry covered my bare shoulders with a wrap as Auntie Stella and Lily Rae rushed through the door to see us.

My aunt *ooh*ed and *aah*ed. Lily Rae folded her arms and cut her eyes. She refused to give me a compliment until we were a foot out the door. "I guess you're pretty after all."

When Henry and I entered the high school gym, it was a different world that bared no resemblance to where games were played. Is this what attending grownup parties felt like to my parents? Linking his fingers through mine, Henry kept me close as he doted on me and included me in conversations when he spoke with Roger and his date.

I saw other girls who were underclassmen, too, and they seemed just as excited as me.

As the Andrew Sisters' "I Can Dream, Can't I?" played, Henry smiled and led me to the dance floor. I was hesitant to follow.

"What's wrong?" He frowned.

I was ashamed to meet his eyes. Henry touched my cheek to face him. His warm brown eyes pleaded with me to answer.

Swallowing, I gathered the courage to confess. "I don't know how to slow dance."

He gently lifted my feet off the ground and placed my shoes on top of his. "You will after today." With a secure embrace around my waist, we gently swayed to the music.

Content, I exhaled and rested my head on his chest and smiled. This was the best night ever.

Roger and his date danced close to us when the beat changed. "Henry, there's a house not far from here for private prom parties if you want to take Beatrice." He winked and guided his dance partner away.

"Are we going?" I asked, not sure why anyone would want to leave this party.

Henry looked at me. "Do you want to go? It's probably a motel."

Were we contemplating breaking a promise that we both said we would keep? Yep. I was curious. How would our parents know anyway?

By nature, I was a rule breaker, but that was with petty stuff… If I had fought Trudy, I would have been expelled. That was major. But the catfight might have been worth the risk.

Were we going to cross the line? We could go so far, then I would say no, and he would have to stop. I had it all figured out.

Henry hugged me tighter as we danced. "I'm about to break a promise, Beatrice, so get prepared."

Was his plan different from mine? Did he want to go all the way? I was numb with uncertainty. Was he worth me losing my virginity?

"We're not going anywhere but home after this party because I want us to be together this summer, and if I mess this up, I can't marry you."

Lay off the marriage stuff, I wanted to say, but I was somewhat relieved that I didn't have to pretend that I was okay with going to a motel, I released a nervous laugh as a tear fell. Then Henry broke his promise and kissed me.

When prom ended, Henry drove me home minutes before my one-hour extended curfew, against my protest.

"Did you enjoy yourself tonight?" He glanced at me and smiled.

How could I have not? This man cared about me. If this was love, I wasn't prepared for this emotion. "Yes," was all I could say.

"Me too. Thank you for being my date and girlfriend." He parked in front of my house. "You're special, Beatrice, and I know it." Although he stared at my lips again, he kissed my hand this time, then he stepped out to open my door.

Papa waited in the doorway for us. He nodded at Henry.

"Good night, sir." Henry stepped off the porch and walked back to his car—or his father's car.

Watching him drive away, I smiled to myself. Mama was in the kitchen waiting to hear how I enjoyed it.

I told her about the decorations, the other dresses, and the food, but most of all I thanked her and Papa. "Henry really is a good guy. Thank you for letting us go steady." I hugged them both then went to my bedroom where I didn't want the fairytale to end, so I slept in my prom dress.

On Sunday after church, which Henry and his family attended more often, he took me to Gem Theatre to watch the latest movie.

His grandmother's first invitation to a fancy tea came soon after that. She hosted a party with other ladies in the community Mama called them prominent—people with more money than us.

Mama and I dressed up as if we were going to church. MaDear CC was thoughtful to have a couple of other teenage girls for me to talk with while their mothers discussed fashion shows or other events.

MaDear CC had charm, influence, and money. She treated me like the granddaughter she never had.

I think Mama enjoyed herself more than me, and I was happy to see her happy.

We both looked forward to the next tea party, but Mama couldn't make it because she had to work for Mrs. Rothman's neighbor again. Mama didn't hide her disappointment, and Papa didn't cover up his annoyance that his wife wanted to make the extra money.

"You're in good hands, Beatrice. Mind your manners. Say *yes ma'am*, *thank you*, and *please*." She kissed my forehead.

"Okay, Mama."

On the day of Henry's graduation, Mama and Papa attended with me. For the first time after our "almost fight," Trudy was brave enough to approach me.

"He wasn't worth it anyway." She *hmmmph*ed, rolled her eyes, and joined her friends.

Her snide remark made me want to throw the first punch—no coin toss was needed—but I didn't. If Trudy knew Henry's heart as I had come to know it, she would have regretted those last words because he was worth fighting for.

Papa and Mama valued Henry because they saved up money to buy him a Timex watch for his graduation.

Trudy might not have seen Henry's value, but clearly, my family did.

Chapter 12
What's Love Got to Do With It?

Victoria
PRESENT, Ferguson, Missouri, 2023

"Team Henry!" Cheney shouted, lifting her arm in the air as if she were about to praise the Lord, responding to something the preacher had said.

Victoria chuckled. Her mother was the ringleader when it came to praising the Lord.

"Every woman needs a high school sweetheart like him. He was something! *Whew.*" Cheney fanned herself, then her mood sobered. "You were blessed. My college sweetheart experience turned out to be a recurring heartache."

Parke reached over and squeezed her hand. "That's why God sent me."

"God sent you, huh? Ha!" Grandma BB grunted. "You were jogging down the street and collided with her. Knocked her down. Could have broken her bones." She squinted at Parke with a "dare call me a liar" expression.

Parke took the dare as Victoria had seen her father often do. "I was trying to break the fall of a damsel in distress. She needed a man to do the yardwork she was attempting to do."

Watching their tit-for-tat was the norm. The Jamiesons loved, laughed, and were fiercely protective of their family. They had adopted Victoria without question because her half-sister asked them.

At eighteen and already a college sophomore, Victoria didn't miss not having a high school sweetheart since she dropped out of school and opted to received her G.E.D. When Kami graduated from high school, their father demanded Victoria be allowed to walk across the stage for graduation too. Having a first love wasn't her lifetime goal. Like her young cousin, she would punch any man who thought he could kiss her.

Did you not know I do exceedingly abundantly above all you can ask or think? I know the blessings I have for you, the Lord whispered. *Read Ephesians 3:20.*

I haven't asked for a mate, Lord, Victoria thought.

But I know your heart's desires, whether you ask for one or not, Jesus whispered.

She cleared her throat. This moment wasn't about her thoughts but Grandma BB's life. If only everyone would stop interrupting, she could get through this. "Mom, Dad, I'm supposed to keep the program running smoothly. You two interrupted the story Grandma BB wrote out for me, and it's long."

"You mean mini-series," Parke joked and looked to others to agree. There were nods.

"Everybody already knows how you and Cheney met, but shall I remind you…" Malcolm reached for his wife's hand. "Hali and I were together first."

"And broke up first after she dumped you, bro," Cameron, the youngest of the brothers, added with a laugh.

Malcolm turned and gave Cameron his best deadly "I will hurt you" look. It didn't work. "Oh, you want to go there? Your wife almost didn't give you a chance."

"Oh boy." Victoria closed her eyes and slapped her forehead. "Here we go again. What have we started?"

Kami bumped Victoria's hip. "Our uncles act like our brothers. Juveniles," she mumbled.

"Daddy," Camille said with trembling lips, looking at her father with teary eyes, "Mommy didn't like you?" She sniffed.

Cameron lifted her onto his lap and kissed her cheek. "Of course, your mother loved me. I was irresistible—" He ducked when his wife, Gabrielle, playfully tapped him on his head. "Okay. She was the irresistible one that I couldn't live without." He looked into her eyes and leaned over. She met him with a kiss.

"All I have to say," Cheney said, "is I'm glad none of my children had high school sweethearts. Well, we still have two left at home, but I'm weary about college sweethearts, especially for my girls."

"College is a good place to meet the woman who you want to spend the rest of your life with, Mom," Pace spoke up, and Del glanced down, blushing.

"Okay, okay! Break it up. This is my story, remember?" Grandma BB straightened her shoulders. "Victoria was getting to the good part about that summer."

Chapter 13
A Storm is Brewing

Beatrice
PAST, Little Rock, Arkansas, May 1957

During the last week of school, the principal, Mr. Edward Hawkins, sent a letter home for my parents.

As I tucked the envelope inside one of my books, I was quiet, anxious about what it could contain. Letters being sent home to parents were never good. I didn't think I was in trouble for anything. Henry had saved me from possible detention or expulsion.

"What could it be?" I asked Henry after showing him the envelope.

Although he had graduated a few weeks earlier, I could count on him to be outside when the dismissal bell sounded so he could walk me home. He never showed up empty-handed. He always had fruits, trinkets, or daisies, which was becoming my favorite flower.

"Hey," Henry took the school books out of my arms, "you're smart and a good student, so there's nothing for you to fret about. Since my family has been attending church more regularly, I'm learning that we need to have faith and trust in God. I need you to do the same." He wrapped his arm around my shoulders and squeezed me closer to him. That wouldn't happen once we were near my house.

Henry always made sense. He was smaller than me, which was good enough for me. "So, what are you going to study at Philander Smith?"

It was one of two colleges for Coloreds in Little Rock. Henry was smart too. He graduated with top honors. I was proud of him. As Henry looked ahead, thinking, I admired his facial hair that he was growing thicker into a beard, which made him look older.

"*Hmmm.* Anything that will make me a lot of money so I can take you places." Whenever he talked about the future, Henry had memorized his thoughts because the answer was already about the future.

Although I was comfortable with him, it was what he talked about that scared me, so I changed the subject. "Mama says I can work this summer, but she doesn't want me cleaning White folks' houses or their dirty laundry."

"You're too smart for that. But I was hoping we could spend a lot of time together this summer too."

Grinning, I inhaled his compliment. "I'm glad you're not going away to school."

"*Ah,*" he said loud enough that a neighbor on a porch looked up, "I can't, not with you here and me somewhere else."

"Why me? What's so special about me and not others at Dunbar High?" It never mattered to me in the beginning and really didn't now, but the more he wanted to include me in his plans, the more I wanted to know.

Henry took my hand and stopped me in my tracks. "You're special. Something about you feels right to me. Plus, you're beautiful like my mother."

Mrs. Beacon was brown-skinned like me whereas Henry and his father were very light-skinned like MaDear CC. I was glad he thought I was beautiful.

He squeezed my hand. "It's hard to explain because my heart took notice before I did. I want us to do more things together, like picnics and go to dances at the Masonic."

"I don't know if I'm old enough for that." Those conversations were reminders I wasn't grown enough to do everything.

I've got to respect you, and I do," he was quick to say, "but I'd sure like to kiss you like a man kisses a woman he loves." He didn't hide the yearning.

Love? "Mama says kissing leads to making babies, and Papa said he would go to jail after killing you if you try anything."

Henry's jaw was set as he looked away. Was he afraid of my Papa? "We're going to have to get married."

Sure, I wanted to be grown so I could do things, but being a wife wasn't one of them. Not yet. I feared I would break his heart if I told him that.

The slow stroll to my house seemed to get shorter every day. On the porch, Henry handed over my books so we could part ways. He slipped his hands into his pants pockets and waited until I was safe inside. As I was about to walk into the house, I looked over my shoulder and blew Henry a kiss.

"*Whoa.* I'm telling unless you bake me some cookies," Peggy teased.

She had trailed us from a good distance. Our families expected us to walk to school together and come back home together. Most of the time, she was so quiet, I forgot she was there.

Cupping both hands, Henry leaned forward as if the kiss had the wings of a butterfly and landed in his palms. He grinned. "That was a good one."

After the school year for the freshman, sophomores, and juniors ended, I'd be permitted to have company other than Peggy when Papa or Mama wasn't home.

We could sit on the porch but not go inside until my parents were home. That way, all my neighbors could monitor our activity. I was convinced Mrs. Paddock, two doors down across the street, was a spy because she knew all the latest gossip, which turned out to be true.

Of course, depending on what was in that letter, my happiness might be on hold. A few hours later, Mama arrived home and kicked off the nursing shoes that she wore to clean houses, even though she wasn't a nurse. She dropped to a chair, leaned her head back, and closed her eyes. Good thing I'd prepared a ham casserole, and the Jell-O in the mold should be ready by the time Papa got home.

I hated to disturb her peace and my peace when I uttered, "Mama?"

"*Hmmm?*" She moved her head from side to side but didn't open her eyes.

"Principal Hawkins sent a letter home with me."

Her eyes popped open, and she sprung forward as I handed her the envelope. I wished Henry was there with me.

Accepting it, Mama groaned. "I thought after our meeting with Miss Holland, I wouldn't have any trouble out of you. Beatrice, it's too close to the end of the school year for any foolishness. Please tell me you didn't say anything to the school cook about her seasoning like you did last year. You somehow find a way to come up with your shenanigans. Henry might lose his girlfriend all summer." She examined the sealed envelope, then lifted her left brow. "Your Papa and I will open this together."

Mama stood and picked up her shoes. "Wait in your room until your father comes home."

"Yes, ma'am." Lowering my head, I did as she ordered. Since my bedroom window was on the right side of the house, I craned my neck to watch out for Papa's blue-and-white Chevrolet Styleline.

I never remembered looking out of the window so much. I opened my door and walked back to the kitchen where Mama was checking on the casserole. "Can I wait on the porch for Papa to come home?"

She consented, so I gathered my books to study for the last of my final exams. It had been hard to concentrate banished to my room.

Papa was like clockwork.

Predictable, except for today.

Finally, his car was in sight. I jumped up but didn't run down the stairs to greet him. He would suspect I was in trouble.

Papa parked and hiked our steps to the porch. In one hand, he held two bouquets. In the other hand was the unmistakable candy bag for us to share.

Traces of grease were under his fingernails from working on cars at the shop all day. "I bought M&M's peanut chocolates for my girls." His wide grin was a comfort many times that everything would be all right.

I fell into his arms and hugged him tight, then looked up into his eyes. "I love you, Papa."

His chuckle rumbled in his throat before it came out. "Love you, too, my baby girl…" He slowly untangled me, and with a stern expression asked, "What did you do?"

"I hope nothing," I said as I trailed him in the door.

"Nellie! Nellie," he shouted all the way to the back of the house.

Mama appeared and told him about the letter from the principal before my parents exchanged their routine hugs and kisses.

She accepted the flowers and grabbed the bag. Mama reached inside and pulled out a piece of candy in a black wrapper. When Mama popped an M&M in her mouth, she closed her eyes and enjoyed the sweet treat. It probably would make me nauseous right now because of the uncertainty of what was in that letter. My stomach was unsettled.

But the torture of not knowing what the principal said in that letter was killing me anyway.

Papa patted his stomach. "I'm starving. I'm ready to eat, then we'll discuss your punishment."

"Yes, sir, but whatever the principal said I did, I didn't do it, but if I'm going to be on punishment, I probably should have done it." I had to defend myself ahead of time.

Dinner was torturous. For a starving man, Papa ate as slowly as Lily Rae when she was a baby. I picked at my food that I'd cooked. How could I be hungry, yet my stomach registered as full?

When Papa and Mama placed their forks on their plates, I exhaled. "Honey, is that Jell-O ready?" Papa asked as Mama stood to check.

Why would he want Jell-O when he brought candy? To my relief, Mama said it was still watery.

"Okay. Let's go into the living room." Papa led the way.

Mama sat next to Papa, and I took the chair as she opened the letter and read it aloud.

I closed my eyes.

Mrs. and Mrs. Tilley…

"I didn't do it!" I gritted my teeth and balled my fist. Tears began to sting under my eyelids.

Beatrice has been selected to be one of the Colored students to integrate Central High…

"Huh?" My head shot up, and I blinked the waiting tears away. Sinking back against the chair, I didn't care what the rest of the letter said as long as I wasn't in trouble.

Unfortunately, Dunbar High School and Junior College did not receive the much-needed state funding for improvements to our building. All funds were directed to the completion of Central High School.

This is a rare opportunity since the Supreme Court's ruling on Brown vs. Board of Education of Topeka.

Be that as it may, the Little Rock School Board has approved twenty-five Colored students to enroll at Central High School this upcoming school year, so I am recommending Beatrice because I feel she would thrive in the advanced academic environment.

My heart celebrated the good news. Not for being picked, but because Henry and I could spend the summer together. I couldn't wait to phone him. Not only would he be attending a new school, so would I at Central High.

Papa had a faint smile as he and Mama exchanged a glance that I couldn't decipher. Neither one of them seemed moved by the good news. As a matter of fact, Mama looked concerned. "Do you want to go, Beatrice?"

"Of course, Mama! They have all new stuff—tennis courts and a stadium—plus I can join the choir." Henry had told me I had a lovely voice when I was singing along with some of the tunes at prom. I looked at Papa for support.

He sighed and twisted his mouth as if something pained him. "Nellie, if Beatrice wants to go, we should support her. She knows how to act when she crosses the Line."

"I can't wait to tell Henry. He'll be happy for me." I ran into the kitchen and lifted the receiver off the phone on the wall and dialed his number, JE 1-8388.

"Hello?" he answered with a baritone that I liked.

"Henry, it's me, Beatrice."

He chuckled. "I know your voice." He paused and lowered his. "Is…is everything okay?"

"Yes!" I breathed a sigh of relief, then I told him what Principal Hawkins' letter read.

"Congratulations. I'm so proud of you. If I was close, I'd sneak a kiss."

I giggled.

"But I hope the White students treat you nice. It will be harder to get bodyguards to watch out for you over there, but I'll figure something out. MaDear CC may have to ask some of her White friends for help."

Rolling my eyes, I dragged a chair from the table to the wall to sit. "Henry, I'll be fine."

The next day as Henry walked me home, I talked about the things that Central High had.

"I knew you were smart." He linked his fingers through mine.

"I'm glad I didn't go away to school, so I can be here to take care of you because we're going to get married."

The sacrifice Henry was willing to make for us left me speechless. But I was unsure if I was a good fit to be a wife.

That summer, Papa and Mama watched more television news. Integrating Central High was all over the local news. Whites were mad and threatened protests. Colored folks' excitement turned into concern.

"The United States has decided to give Coloreds the same education as Whites. To continue to segregate the students makes it unequal," President Dwight Eisenhower said on television and in the newspaper.

Our Arkansas governor, Orval Faubus, was angry. He hated the idea of mixing Coloreds and Whites at school and said the federal government was invading our rights to force us to integrate. Not my rights, because I wanted to go to a better school. I wish Peggy and my other friends could go too.

None of that mattered to me. Nobody was going to deny me a chance to better myself.

One Sunday after church, we were about to enjoy the dinner Mama and I had cooked for Papa, Auntie Stella, Lily Rae, and Henry when the doorbell rang.

Papa threw down his napkin and stood. One thing he didn't like was having his eating interrupted.

"Hi, Joe. Sorry for the intrusion."

"That's okay, Daisy. C'mon in. We were about to have supper."

Mrs. Bates' heels clicked against our wood floor as she followed Papa to the kitchen doorway. She and her husband owned the *Arkansas State Press* newspaper. Mrs. Bates attended the other church in the Dunbar neighborhood and hadn't changed out of her church clothes.

Her pearls and earrings resembled the ones Henry's grandmother gave me for prom. Mrs. Bates was a pretty lady with jet-black hair styled like Mama's when they returned from Miss Beulah's. But Momma's didn't last in the summer because of the housework at Mrs. Rothman's house.

"Oh, I'm sorry. I didn't realize you had company too. I'll come back another time."

"Nonsense, Daisy. If you're here, it must be important. Why don't you join us for dinner, and we can talk?" Mama said.

Papa dragged an extra chair from the corner for another guest, waving off Henry's attempt to help while I added another place setting.

Mama said Mrs. Bates was the president of the Little Rock chapter of the National Association for the Advancement of Colored People. I'd be glad when we advanced so I could go anywhere I wanted.

"Actually, I'm here to talk about Beatrice attending Central High. I'm visiting all of the students who were selected."

Though she spoke seriously, her lips seemed to wear a smile. "Although Arkansas wasn't one of the five plaintiffs in the Brown vs. Board of Education lawsuit, our school board came up with a plan for gradual integration beginning with the high schools, and to accept twenty-five Coloreds, I'm concerned that number may be too ambitious starting off because of the hostility Governor Faubus is stirring up."

Everyone stopped eating except for Lily Rae.

"What are you saying, Daisy?" Mama asked.

Mrs. Bates shifted in her chair. "Beatrice was selected because of her brilliance and academic performance, but according to her school records, her behavior may not work in her favor at Central. She's had a total of ten incidents at school within two years that sent her to the principal's office. They were minor infractions at Dunbar but could be considered major at Central High," Mrs. Bates said with an apologetic look.

"Mr. Hawkins picked me," I blurted. Henry patted my hand, and Papa and Mama frowned at my outburst.

Mrs. Bates sipped on her glass of iced tea.

"I'm aware of that, and we're proud of you." She paused. "But it's going to take more than intellect to attend Central High. I've dedicated my life to make sure our children succeed. That's why those chosen will receive special training to survive."

"Survive what?" I demanded. "I know how to take care of myself."

Papa frowned and Mama lifted her brow,

I didn't care of the punishment that was due me. Now, I was getting mad. No one would deny me what was due me.

"Hate, Beatrice," Mrs. Bates said.

Even Lily Rae looked up.

"Hate?" I repeated, and Henry took my hand under the table and didn't let it go.

The word didn't strike me with fear. It was the way Mrs. Bates said it that made me shiver.

Mrs. Bates reached inside her purse for a notebook and began to ask me a series of questions. After she had recorded my answers, she closed it. "Joe, Nellie, may we speak in private?"

I looked at Henry as I strained to hear. Hushed tones carried in our house.

"Beatrice is smart and has a great measure of confidence," Mrs. Bates started off.

"Those are good qualities," Papa said in my defense.

"Yes, and this is an experiment. Governor Faubus doesn't want Coloreds and Whites in the same building. All it takes is one incident, and we've lost the battle and may never get another chance again to integrate the schools. We need to prepare students to be quietly strong, resilient, and wise in that environment."

"I overheard Mrs. Rothman talking about Central High School with another neighbor." Mama *tsk*ed. "They were horrified about the idea, and both backed the governor."

"Our children are our future; they're going into war here in Little Rock, not across the world. They'll need prayers and mental and emotional conditioning to stay disciplined to win this challenge for all Colored students."

Silence. Were they about to pray already? I wondered.

"This summer," Mrs. Bates began, "I want to prep the students who I think can withstand the attacks. A team of us will mentally condition them for what they most likely will encounter. If someone hits one of them, they can't hit back."

Like I had planned to stand up to Trudy, I'd stand up to them too. Mama always said Coloreds were just as good and smart as Whites.

"You beat me up all the time, BB" Lily Rae blurted out between licks on her ice cream cone, loud enough for the others to know we were eavesdropping. I cut my teary eyes at her.

Mama and Papa didn't sound like they were changing her mind. I stood to go and defend myself when Henry pulled me back. He shook his head to stay and listen.

"I asked Principal to compile a list of about twenty-five of the brightest candidates for me to talk to, then I plan to narrow the choices to nine.

"Stupid people," Mama said with a huff. "The board should have put money into Colored schools like they promised." She lowered her voice. "I guess I won't get fired now."

Fired? I frowned and looked at Henry, then Auntie Stella. What was Mama talking about? Why would Mrs. Rothman fire Mama? She had worked for the woman for years and never missed a day of work. That made me mad.

"Unfortunately, we don't know how far the retaliation will go and to what extent the damage will be. The parents who do send their children to Central High may be harmed, lose business, employment, or be attacked. This is very serious. Believe me, any way White folks can get their way, they will try it, and they don't care who gets hurt in the process. It's sad."

"Yes, it is. After hearing what Mrs. Rothman said, Joe and I were putting aside money in case she fired me. No one is going to stop Beatrice from getting a better education."

Although I fumed, secretly I grinned that Mama would stand up for me against mean old Mrs. Rothman. I was mad...at Mrs. Bates for turning me away.

Mad at Mrs. Rothman for wanting to fire Mama.

And mad at the prejudice that was part of my world. When our guest left, I raced to my parents. "Papa, Mama, I'm going anyway. She can't stop me!" I stomped my foot as a tear fell.

"Beatrice, you're worth more to us alive than dead. Somebody may get killed before this is over." Papa sighed and walked away, mumbling, "And it won't be my only child."

Chapter 14
Fighting Words

Victoria
PRESENT, Ferguson, Missouri, 2023

"I'm scared." Little Gabriel's lip quivered. "Grandma BB, did you get killed?"

The story frightened Victoria, too, but she kept that to herself. When she attended high school, Whites and Blacks attended together. It was no big deal.

"She's alive talking to us, dummy," Chance told his younger cousin.

"Son…" Parke waited for his youngest boy to look at him. "That is not the way to speak to anyone, especially in our family. You're the big cousin. Apologize, and I don't want to ever hear you call someone out of their name again, or there will be consequences. Do you understand me?" When it came to discipline, her dad was stern and didn't have to repeat himself.

Chance bobbed his head.

"Talk to me," Parke demanded.

"Yes, sir." Chance looked like he was on the verge of tears as he held up his head.

"Now, go and make it right. You see he's scared." Parke folded his arms and waited for his son to follow his instructions.

Twisting his lips, Chance stood and climbed over other family members. "Sorry," he said to Little Gabriel who was sitting on his father's lap. He reached for his cousin, lifted the boy, who wasn't much smaller than Chance, and hugged him. "Come on. You can sit with me."

Little Gabriel leaped into Chance's arms.

Victoria smiled. Reconciliation came easily with her family. In gratitude to them, she planned to make them proud. "I'm so glad to be a Jamieson."

"We are too," many of the Jamiesons shouted back at her.

"That's sweet," Deli said to Pace.

"Yeah. We're a tough act to follow." Pace chuckled. "For a minute there, I thought you were about to tell us you were part of the Little Rock Nine."

"Stranger things have happened. Nothing surprises me with Grandma BB anymore." Cheney shook her head. "Sounds like she was unmanageable as a child and in her old age."

"Some people never change. Grandma BB had a stroke when I came here but managed to escape from a rehabilitation nursing home facility." Kidd snorted.

"But God changed you, dear, and I will be forever grateful," Eva, his wife said. "Hallelujah!"

The other adults joined in for an impromptu praise break. Parke joked that Kidd and Ace were the bad boys from Boston. Victoria never learned what dirt everyone had on them.

"But wait a minute," Cheney said, barely composing herself, "stealing a would-be thief's getaway van tops all of her shenanigans."

"You haven't heard nothing yet," Grandma BB said smugly, then nodded for Victoria to continue.

Chapter 15
This is Not a Drill. Repeat:
This is Not A Drill

Beatrice

PAST, Little Rock, Arkansas, Summer and Fall 1957

"Don't get mad at me, but I'm kinda glad you're not going to Central High," Henry said one evening as we sat on my front porch. We watched children play a few doors away while my neighbors monitored what was happening on our porch.

I whipped my neck around and glared at my boyfriend as if he were my ex. "What? I was qualified to be one of the nine students Mrs. Bates chose." I gritted my teeth just thinking about the injustice.

"I gave you a warning not to get mad at me." He waited until I calmed down. "All nine classmates have been prepping for weeks at Philander Smith College. They may be subject to mind games and physical harm at Central High. I can't let anybody hurt you, Beatrice." The determination on Henry's face was mixed with sadness. "I would take my dad's shotgun and go hunting, and I don't mean for rabbits."

What would her classmates Melba Pattillo, Ernest Green, Elizabeth Eckford, Minnijean Brown, Terrence Roberts, Carlotta Walls, Jefferson Thomas, Gloria Ray, and Thelma Mothershed face?

At that moment, I knew. There was no more wondering if my emotions were real. I was one hundred percent in love with Henry Beacon. "Do you love me?"

His lips curled into the widest smile across his face. "Haven't you been listening?"

"As a matter of fact, I have, and all I heard were hints." I looked to my left and right for neighborhood spies. "I'm not about to tell you I love you first."

Henry blinked and did his own survey of the street. "You love me?"

I wagged my finger. "No, no, no. I'm not saying it first."

Mrs. Darling across the street and Mother Chatman to the left of us stepped outside on their porch at the same time as if they were waiting for Henry's declaration too.

I waved, so did Henry.

"We're being watched." He reached for one of my hands and studied it as both of his large, strong hands held mine, then he looked at me. "And someone will probably tell on us, but I have to hold your hand when I tell Beatrice Tilley that I love her."

All my senses seemed to freeze. The wind, the birds, and even the sound of cars ceased. The sweet smell of Mama's roses dulled the faint scent of his cologne. My lids couldn't blink as I stared into his brown eyes, which revealed he was telling the truth.

"Now, do you have something you want to say to me?"

"I love you too." I exhaled as Mother Chatman's screen door slammed shut.

Whether or not my neighbors would tattletale to Papa and Mama didn't matter. I was in love.

It was the best summer ever, despite not being able to go to Central High as I had planned.

We packed in as many activities as we could between Henry's job at the barbershop a few days a week and working part-time at Mrs. Bates' newspaper. Henry was in the loop of information. I worked part-time at the church, helping the secretary.

The news leading up to the first day of school wasn't good. There was an eerie tension everywhere—in the neighborhood and the grocer, even at church. Reverend Greenlee changed his sermon to Scriptures in the Old Testament about God fighting our battles. In Exodus 14:13–14: *And Moses said unto the people, Fear ye not, stand still, and see the salvation of the Lord, which he will shew to you today: for the Egyptians whom ye have seen today, ye shall see them again no more forever. The Lord shall fight for you, and ye shall hold your peace.*

Henry sat beside me while his family preferred sitting on the other side of the aisle. Mama and Papa were next to me. I wondered what they thought of the message. Would the Lord rescue my classmates and destroy all the Whites who hated us or what?

On Monday evening, September 1, the day before all students in Little Rock were supposed to attend school, and my junior year, there was breaking news on the radio and television.

Governor Orval Faubus was making an announcement: "I have activated the Arkansas National Guard to surround Central High School and block the entrance in the morning to prevent integration, ostensibly to prevent the bloodshed desegregation would cause. This is for the safety of the nine students."

I gasped as tears fell from my eyes. "Are they going to kill my classmates, Mama?"

"No, baby. We're praying the Lord will fight this battle." Her worried expression wasn't convincing.

Papa said nothing as he paced the living room. Whenever he did that, Papa was mad and trying to calm himself down.

Henry phoned me. "Did you see the news?"

"Yes." I was slow to answer.

"Beatrice, it's going to be okay."

"I hope so," I said quietly before I said good-bye. All I wanted to do was go to sleep and wake up, and this would be a bad dream.

Colored people were going to die. That's what happened in the Jim Crow South when Coloreds stood up for their rights.

Papa was about to drive me to school and Mama to Mrs. Rothman's home on Louisiana Street near downtown when I had a request.

"Can I see what's going on at Central High School?" I asked as I slid into the back seat.

"That's not a good idea," Papa said. "There's trouble over there, and we need to stay as far away as possible from it."

Folding my arms, I had to think fast. "Papa, you and Mama tell me stuff that happened when you were kids. How can I tell my children anything that I don't see?"

My parents were quiet as Papa drove away from our house. My school was five minutes away. I thought I had lost the battle until Papa passed by Dunbar. He was going to Central High School despite his protests. Triumphant that I had spoken up, but fearful of what I might see, my heart pounded.

As we approached the formerly all-White high school, I heard the noise before I saw the students, the troops, and the madness.

"White people really do hate us."

Mama sniffed. Papa cursed, and that was the first time I ever heard him use bad language. I ached inside as Papa turned the car around and drove back to Wright Avenue to Dunbar High School. For the first time since I learned I wouldn't be attending Central High, I was glad to be coming back to my old school.

Once I arrived at Dunbar High School, I felt no excitement to see old friends. A hush filled the halls despite them being crowded with students.

In the classrooms, the first question asked, "Why was this happening?" followed by, "Why did an angry White mob jeer at our former Dunbar High students? Why didn't our governor want Colored students to get a better education?"

My heart was aching when I raised my hand in homeroom.

"Beatrice, you will be the last question," Mr. Boulding said with sadness in his eyes.

"Why is everyone against us? Are Little Rock Negroes at war against the National Guard troops?"

He was a short man with black hair and a long mustache, which twitched before he answered. "Students, Coloreds will always be at war. Be smarter, do better, and run faster."

The principal announced the teachers could bring their classes to the gym to watch the television coverage. My classmates and I sat in horror for Elizabeth who was outnumbered by hundreds as she walked toward Central High School's entrance.

I was afraid for Elizabeth as White girls walked behind her yelling. Who would protect Elizabeth from an attack? We cheered as Elizabeth's willpower kept her going. She was more restrained than me because Papa hated bullies, and I didn't tolerate them. I would have been challenging them. I might not win round one, but there would be more rounds to the fight.

Where are the other eight? I wondered. I was getting sick to my stomach. I wished Henry was there with me. Things always seemed better when we were together. Always.

The rebellion played out for weeks for my nine classmates. I had already taken two tests at Dunbar High while our Colored classmates were still trying to get inside Central High.

One evening, as I ate my supper, I told Mama, "There has to be a place where people don't hate us."

She stopped eating. "We all want to go there," she said, then scooped up a mouthful of peas.

My church kept praying for God to fight our battles, then three weeks later, the Lord answered. President Eisenhower signed an executive order that sent federal troops to integrate Central High School. That was the first day my former classmates walked through the doors. Everyone at Dunbar cheered.

The jubilation didn't last long as Mrs. Bates' newspaper reported the abuse the students suffered—pushed down a flight of stairs, barred from extracurricular activities, and more. Minnijean was expelled for retaliating against those who hurt her. That would have been me.

All of us at Dunbar High stopped complaining about broken equipment. We got a chance to learn despite what worked and didn't work in our outdated building. Our classmates at Central had new everything but couldn't use it. My junior year was stressful.

Chapter 16
Surprise Attack

Beatrice
PAST, Little Rock, Arkansas, Summer 1958

I didn't begin to breathe again until the summer before my senior year when Henry and I spent as much time together as possible. I had a job at the library on Ninth Street. Henry still worked at the barbershop, but he also worked a few hours a day at the printing shop when I worked at the library so he could drive me home.

I spent a lot of time with his mother and MaDear CC at functions. They never bought me anything without checking with Mama. They had more money than we did, but they weren't showoffs.

"Mama, you don't have to work extra days to buy me things for school. I saved my money from the library, and the Beacons gave me gifts," I told her as she collapsed on the couch. She looked exhausted.

"That's fine, dear. Thank you." Her lids fluttered before they closed, then I heard a soft snore.

I didn't know what I wanted to do with my life, but cleaning somebody else's house as a domestic worker was not on my list—ever.

The upcoming school year was bittersweet. It brought me closer to my high school graduation. I didn't talk to my former eight classmates over the summer. Did they look forward to their senior year at Central High?

One evening, Henry asked me as we were sharing an ice cream sundae at the drug store, "Are you looking forward to joining me at Philander Smith?"

"I don't think I want to stay here and go to school."

"Really? Why not? Where do you want to go?" Henry studied me.

I shrugged. "I don't even know if I want to go to college. This year has made me doubt everything I thought I knew about people. I don't think I like people."

We finished our ice cream in silence.

Chapter 17
Arranged Marriage

Beatrice
PAST, Little Rock, Arkansas, September 1958

Two weeks into my senior year, the unthinkable happened. Governor Faubus closed all the Little Rock public high schools for Coloreds and White students for the school year because he said it was for the safety of Colored students. Papa called him a segregationist. Mama said the governor was hateful. I thought he was a monster.

Emotions stirred in my head as if I were mixing ingredients to bake. Frantic. Anger. Revenge. "Mama, what am I supposed to do now?"

She and Papa exchanged bewildered expressions. They always held the answers to my probing questions, yet they were speechless.

"Even if we could afford to send you to a private school, the Catholic schools won't take Coloreds," Papa said then chewed on the creamed corn Mama had cooked as if it were horse grain. "I don't know if those White folks will act any different."

"Maybe Mrs. Higgins at the library will hire you full-time until we can figure this out," Mama suggested.

"That might be the best solution." Papa wouldn't look at me.

"No!" I blurted, then covered my mouth as I darted my eyes between my parents. "What about my senior prom with Henry."

Seemingly forgiving me for my outburst, Papa sighed.

"I'm sorry this has happened." Mama rattled off places on Ninth Street that might hire me, but I wanted to go to school. Get my diploma. Go to my prom. Get on with my adult life.

This was not happening to me. Papa and Mama both said they wished they could have gone to college. I had to think fast or I could be scrubbing floors. "I just have to move to a different state and finish school."

"Not by yourself, young lady. You ain't grown yet." Mama frowned.

"Guess I'll have to get married, and my husband can take me." I jutted my chin in defiance but not high enough to get slapped.

Mama squinted, shocked that I dare say such a thing. They didn't know I wasn't serious. I wasn't ready to be anybody's wife and have babies.

"Has Henry asked you to marry him?" Papa squinted.

"No." *He's hinted though*, I kept to myself. "But he will." I acted like it was no big deal.

Papa wiped his mouth, stood, and walked over to the wall phone, then called Henry's dad. "Good evening, Jim. I'd like to talk to your son if he's there." There was a pause. "Oh, I'm glad I caught him before he returned to campus."

What was going on? I glanced at Mama, and she didn't seem to know either.

"Just kiddin'," was on the tip of my tongue when Henry probably got on the line and Papa said, "Do you want to marry Beatrice?"

I almost choked on air. I tried to get Papa's attention to stop him from proceeding as a result of my foolishness.

Judging from the stern look on Papa's face, Henry must have said yes. My jaw dropped. Wait a minute. I talked myself into being a wife? I groaned. Suddenly, my appetite vanished.

Papa nodded to whatever Henry said, then looked at me. His serious expression meant that once again, I spoke my mind without thinking someone would call my bluff. "See you tomorrow for supper." He hung up the receiver.

I swallowed. What was Papa planning?

The next day at home, my schooling started on my kitchen table. During my lunch break, I began dinner. "Okay. It's either chicken pot pie or tuna casserole." I scanned the ingredients inside the refrigerator. I was still experimenting with copying Mama's fluffy crust, so tuna casserole was the winner. For dessert, I baked a cherry angel food cake.

With the food baking, I returned to my studies, this time in my bedroom. Soon, I took a nap. When I woke, I straightened the house since Henry was coming to dinner. An imaginary bell rang when I spied the time on the checkered wall clock in the kitchen. Day one at home had ended.

I called Peggy since Mama told me I couldn't be on the phone during school hours, even if I was at home.

"Mama's so mad at the governor. This is our senior year! I saw on the news that the teachers still have to report to the schools," Peggy said.

"For what?"

"To teach lessons to empty classrooms."

"I don't think he's smart at all. That's the dumbest thing I've ever heard." We were quiet. "We should sneak outside the school and listen."

"You go by yourself. I'm scared one of the national guard men will shoot me or put me in jail. I'm too young to go to prison." Peggy began to whine.

"I'm too young to get married, but I suggested that to Papa last night so I can go somewhere to school."

"Beatrice Tilley, stop playing. You're barely seventeen."

"I'll be eighteen next year." I gnawed on my lips. Maybe I shouldn't have said that to Papa, but it was too late. He called Henry, and now my boyfriend was coming to dinner.

"Yeah, but I've got to do something. Staying at home is like being in prison." We hung up the phone so Peggy could get her added housework done.

The phone rang, and it was Henry. "I'm calling before my next class. How was your first day in school without your teacher?"

"Strange. I don't like it."

"I don't like that it's happening either. Mr. Tilley had an idea, and I guess we'll discuss it at dinner. I love you."

My anxiety, which was building, began to dissipate. I closed my eyes and soaked up his declaration as if I'd inhaled fresh flowers. He told me he loved me more than I told him, and that's the way it should be.

"Someone wants to use this payphone. I'll see you and your Papa later." Then Henry threw me a kiss, and he was gone. My cheek felt the kiss and tingled.

Henry arrived with flowers for me and Mama. We both blushed and thanked him. At dinner, Papa blessed the food, and we ate in relative silence. They complimented my cooking, then Henry insisted he help me clear the table and wash the dishes.

Papa and Mama seemed impressed, especially since Papa only cleaned the kitchen when Mama was sick and I was too young to reach the sink.

"Nervous?" he asked, running dishwater with too many suds.

"Yes!" I didn't hide my concern. "I didn't know Papa was really thinking about forcing us to get married when I'm not even pregnant!"

"Of course, you're not, Beatrice," he said, lowering his voice. I stared at his facial features, which I imagined our children would possess. "I've never disrespected you, and I've tried to show you how much I've wanted to get to know you before I fell in love with you. No one can force me to do anything that I don't want to do. That's the Beacon way."

"Too much talking in there," Papa yelled from the living room.

We smiled and hurried through our tasks. When we joined my parents in the living room, they were glued to the television.

"The Little Rock School District is discussing an option for White teachers to provide lessons on TV for their students," Newton Crane, the anchor, said. "Details on when that will happen are forthcoming."

Papa shook his head. "Orval is an idiot. He didn't even have a plan. I wish the President could make the governor open them schools. How can three thousand public students teach themselves?" Disgusted, he stood from the couch to turn off the television.

Shaking his head, Papa *tsk*ed before noticing Henry and me. He pointed to the chair for Henry to take a seat. "Nellie and Beatrice, give us some time."

"Beatrice needs to finish her education and she can't do it in this state. She can go elsewhere, but not my herself. That's where you come in if you love her. If you can't provide for my daughter, then she ain't leaving this house to marry you if you ask her," Mama and I heard Papa say from my bedroom.

"If you consent, I'll ask her. I'll take care of my wife," Henry defended.

"Mama?" I waited for her to face me as we sat on my bed. I hugged my teddy bear Ted to my chest for comfort whenever I was nervous. "Can I be a good wife?"

Tilting her head to study me, so many expressions crossed her face before she smiled. "If you put God in your marriage, you can learn how to be a good wife. You have a habit of speaking and not thinking about the consequences, which is why your papa is in there talking with Henry now about marrying you. Be faithful, and you two can grow together." Mama switched subjects to keeping a clean house, hot meals, and raising children. "Trust Henry to make good decisions for both of you."

Papa questioned Henry for hours before he called for Mama and me to come out of my bedroom.

When we reappeared, Papa and Henry stood, then Henry walked up to me, towering over me with an intense expression. I frowned, trying to read his thoughts. He took both of my hands in his then slowly knelt before me. Henry smiled and released me.

"I've loved you from the first day in the barbershop and more every time we've spent together. I have something for you." Henry dug in his pants pockets and pulled out a ring.

He has a ring. I blinked. That quick?

"I want a wife, and only you can be Mrs. Henry Beacon. Will you marry me?"

Mama sucked in her breath. Papa folded his arms while I thought about being a wife and mother.

I swooned, recalling these scenes play out in movies, and the woman always said yes, but my emotions were frozen.

Henry smiled as he waited for my answer. "I love you and will take care of you and make sure we finish our schooling."

"That's right," Papa said, reminding me Henry and I weren't alone.

"Are you sure?" I finally stuttered.

"I'm not doubting anything at this moment. Mr. Tilley and I discussed what is expected from me as a husband. Part of it is for us to leave the state so you can finish your senior year, but the main reason is because I love you." He held the ring up for me to examine. "I went to MaDear CC and told her of my intentions. She wasn't surprised and gave me her wedding ring for you with her blessings."

I sniffed, but a tear fell. As Mama was about to wipe my cheek, Papa held her back. "Let Henry do the honor."

"Yes, I'll marry you." He slipped the ring on my finger and stood. I've never seen him look so happy. "But—"

My parents groaned.

"I know I'll be your wife, but I happen to like my name better than yours—"

"Beatrice!" Mama gasped.

"I want to be introduced as Mrs. Beatrice Beacon, not Mrs. Henry Beacon."

Henry laughed. "That's why I love you so much! May I kiss my fiancé?" he asked my father.

Papa twisted his mouth. "Make it a quick one. Real quick."

Excited, I was in a daze, but I trusted Henry to take care of me as his warm lips sealed the promise of our happily ever after.

Chapter 18
No Refunds or Returns

Henry
PAST, Little Rock, Arkansas, September 1958

I can't believe I'm scared, but Beatrice trusted me. It was in her eyes. I couldn't disappoint her or our families.

MaDear CC was waiting for the news. My home was my first stop. She was in the living room in her chair, watching *I Love Lucy*.

"Well?" she asked, not taking her eyes off the television.

"She said yes." I grinned. My happiness drowned out my fears. I loved Beatrice.

"I'm going to be a great-grandma soon." MaDear CC waved me over to her chair and hugged me, then shoved me away so she could finish her program.

Dad and Mama were in the kitchen finishing their dessert when I walked in. Unlike the Tilleys' checkered floor design in her kitchen, Mama's favorite color was pink—her fridge, stove, and metal cabinets. The floor was a mint green color.

They looked at him but said nothing.

"I'm engaged." I smiled and took my seat. It was becoming real.

Mama clasped her hands and smiled. Dad didn't.

"Are you sure, son, that Beatrice isn't expecting?" Displeasure was building on his face. "Is that why Joe called last night?"

I explained the solution to Beatrice's finishing high school because of the governor's new law.

"This is a forced marriage?" Wrinkles began to set in Dad's forehead. He shifted in his chair.

"No." I shook my head. "This is about me loving her so much that I want the best for her. She needs to finish high school to go to college." I pleaded for him to understand.

"And you haven't touched her?"

"No, Dad." But I thought about it and I sensed Beatrice was willing.

He was concerned for good reason. My uncle in Detroit had two sons who were bad news. The secret was that one son had gotten two women pregnant, but he refused to marry either. The other son, five years older than me, was married and miserable. That wasn't a secret.

Mama stood and gathered the dessert plates off the table. Her face glowed with happiness. "I like Beatrice. I think she is delightful and would make a wonderful wife and mother. I'll call Nellie in the morning so I can offer my help to plan the wedding."

"Mom, school is underway. We don't have a lot of time," I tried to reason with her, but she was happy and humming.

I stood, and so did my father. We shook hands. "Then it's settled. Treat her right, Henry. You're my son, and we take care of our families. She's young, so you'll have to be more understanding and patient as she matures."

"Yes, sir." I headed toward the front door to return to campus for the night.

MaDear CC called out to stop me. Now, she was watching *The Honeymooners*. She thought the actor Jackie Gleason was funny. "Henry, if you ever need any money, you call."

I kissed her. "Thank you." But I had no plans to take her up on her offer as I left.

Roger was my roommate at Philander Smith College in one of the new dormitories that resulted from a $500,000 endowment to the school. He knew I was going to see Beatrice. Roger thought I was checking on her because of Governor Faubus' edict.

I strolled into our dorm room with the biggest smile. Roger looked up from his desk and stared at me. "What's got you so happy?"

Removing my jacket, I didn't answer right away as I hung it on the back of my desk's chair. "Oh, I have a fiancée."

"What? I know Beatrice is pretty and all, but she's barely a woman." He folded his arms.

"And I'm barely a man. Beatrice and I will be fine. I want you to be my best man."

"Really?" Roger's eyes grew wide as quarters. He cleared his throat. "Well, of course. I've been your best man since my first haircut at the barbershop." Shaking his head, Roger couldn't stop grinning. "When are you two planning to get hitched?"

"As soon as possible. Her family and I don't want her to miss the school year."

The next morning, I called Beatrice early before she started her home classes to make sure she hadn't changed her mind.

"I haven't. Peggy's excited too."

After reminding her that I loved her, we said our goodbyes and hung up. I went to class with a happy but heavy heart. I was responsible for taking care of whatever Beatrice would need in the future.

Once my science class had ended, I left campus and drove home to speak with MaDear CC. She was a good listener, and I looked to my grandmother for advice. She possessed the beauty of a young woman despite her aging years. No one could discount her wisdom. Although she needed assistance when walking to keep her steady, she was an independent ninety-three-year-old. In a way, I was glad to marry young, so MaDear CC could see her great-grandchildren.

"I made the decision to marry Beatrice, but I don't know where to go so she can finish school." I sat across from her in the living room. She was in a trance-like state as she watched *Guiding Light* on television.

Maybe this isn't a good time, I thought.

MaDear CC blinked and leaned toward me. "Both your uncles are doing well. One lives in Missouri. The oldest brother, Willie Earl, moved to Michigan. Buddy is a little better off in St. Louis and has been known to pass whenever the occasion calls for it."

In the South, passing could get us killed or run out of town whenever White folks thought we were trying to take away benefits that belonged only to them.

Throughout the years, I had heard stories of one uncle's escapades. Behind closed doors, Albert Chestnut, known as Uncle Buddy, was smooth in playing the role of getting a job or entrance to where the "haves" deemed the "have nots" didn't belong.

If exposed, my uncle would move on to the next opportunity as a White man.

"St. Louis is closer. I'll call Albert. My son has connections and can help you and Beatrice get settled."

"Thank you, MaDear CC, for whatever you can do." I was relieved.

Although I worked with Dad at the barber's a few times a week, my grandmother gave me a stipend. Whatever she needed, I took care of it—not for the money, but because I loved her.

"This is why the good Lord has kept me around, so I can be a blessing to the next generation."

I hugged her, inhaling her signature scent of gardenias, then returned to campus.

Days later, I learned that the ladies set Saturday, October 11 at six p.m. as our wedding date.

Until then, Beatrice studied the best she could, and the school district had more than a dozen teachers on television teaching various subjects for a certain number of hours. Beatrice tried to pay attention but complained to me and her parents she couldn't focus.

For the next month, I worked a part-time position in the college office and studied hard but rarely saw Beatrice the way I wanted as I made plans to drive to St. Louis. On the day of the journey, something was wrong with my car, and Dad needed his. Even my soon-to-be father-in-law who was a mechanic couldn't fit me into his schedule.

I wouldn't be deterred. I took the railway. When I arrived in St. Louis, Uncle Buddy met me at Union Station downtown.

"Nephew, I haven't seen you since you were a boy." He pumped my hand in a shake. "Come on. I'm not far from here."

Older than my father, Uncle Buddy favored him with fair skin, height, and eyes. That's where the similarities ended. Uncle Buddy's tailored suit hinted at prosperity. I detected intellect in his speech pattern. MaDear CC said he was a businessman. Whatever he did paid well, and that's what I needed, a well-paying job.

We turned onto Clark Street. A row of houses stood at attention for blocks as if waiting for inspection. Not the shotgun houses in the Dunbar neighborhood back home. These were three stories tall. Most were different shades of color.

Uncle Buddy stood next to me as I craned my head back so I could take in the structure. The front double doors were arched and twice our six feet in height. There were three long arched windows that extended into the front yard in a bay shape. The second floor, which had three windows, reminding me of a crown, also had a wrought-iron porch. Even the roof had its own windows. Two large ones.

"This is impressive." I hoped Beatrice would love it.

"Yep." He grinned. "I'll put you on the top floor where there are two rooms. A large, combined bedroom and a living room area. The other is a kitchenette. I won't charge you much until you get on your feet. I put out the man who was barely paying his rent when Mother phoned me. I have two boarders on the second floor—they have wives—and one male boarder in the basement. The first floor is my dwelling because I like to entertain."

We walked inside, and I blinked at the lavish furnishings. The parlor had bay windows. Across the hall was another sitting room adjacent to a formal dining room, and the bath was off the kitchen. So much space for one person.

We stepped out the back door onto a porch where a stairwell climbed to the other floors. "Make sure you use this entrance from the side of the house."

"Yes, sir."

Our first home was an attic with a view overlooking the city. The two rooms he described were furnished. An exposed brick interior wall separated the larger room. I hoped Beatrice would like it, and if she didn't, we would move as soon as I could afford it.

"Thank you, Uncle Buddy." I stuck out my hand for a shake. "Do I need to give you a deposit?"

"You're welcome, nephew. But from here out, refer to me as Mr. Chestnut. People here don't know my business, and I don't know theirs. It helps when you pass to make a living," he said in a hushed tone. "I rent this property and use the boarders' rent to pay mine, and then I put the rest aside so I can buy this place. Save your money for now. Mother wired me two months' rent for you and your bride."

It was humbling how much MaDear CC loved me and helped me. I wouldn't disappoint her or Beatrice.

Next, we enjoyed supper at a nearby restaurant where the cook's menu reminded me of home. We caught a service car to Harris Stowe Teachers College where I planned to enroll and complete my education. "Beatrice needs to finish school."

Uncle Buddy *tsk*ed. "It's a shame about that hard-headed racist..." He used language that I hoped Beatrice never heard to describe Arkansas' governor.

"Yeah." I folded my arms. "He's a loose cannon. He might do it for another year, who knows? He's hurting the White kids too."

"Beatrice will be fine here. We have two high schools for Coloreds. Vashon High School is the closest on Laclede Avenue. Sumner is the oldest, but it's farther north."

"Good." Things were working out. What a relief. When we walked past a phone booth, I stepped inside and deposited my coins to call Beatrice.

"I miss my fiancé,'" she said after hearing my voice.

Touched by her admission, my heart swelled, and I smiled. "I miss you too. We'll be renting the top floor of a big house from my uncle, Mr. Chestnut."

"Huh?"

"I'll tell you about that later. I hope you're not disappointed. As soon as I earn enough, I'll move us to a bigger place."

"If you like it, I'll love it. Mama says we're just kids, so we're not going to have much stuff like adults do starting off. I'll be glad when we are adults."

I chuckled. "Me too, my sweetheart. I'd better go. I love you."

"Love you, too, fiancé. I'll make a good wife, Henry, and give you a lot of babies."

"And I'll be the best husband I can be to my wife." We hung up. Suddenly, I didn't want to wait until October. Maybe I could convince Beatrice to marry me sooner.

Chapter 19
Jumping the Broom

Beatrice
PAST, Little Rock, Arkansas, September and October 1958

I couldn't believe Henry wanted us to get married the day after he returned from St. Louis. Mama was sewing my dress in the evenings after she worked for Mrs. Rothman all day. I didn't budge on the date, even if I wanted to.

"Mama says a woman only gets married once, and every detail is important and can't be rushed. Don't rush me because I might change my mind." I folded my arms.

"About what?" He eyed me suspiciously.

"Marrying you, Henry Beacon," I teased, keeping a straight face.

"You already said yes. You can't back out." Henry looked wounded at the thought of us not getting married.

Grabbing his hand, I smiled. "I'll marry you in thirty days."

The days sped by as I studied with Peggy so we could quiz each other.

On the morning of Saturday, October 11,, I was nervous. "Mama, I'm really going to become a wife like you."

Mama hugged me. "You'll be happy. If your papa and I didn't feel that Henry would love you and take care of you, you wouldn't become Mrs. Henry Beacon today."

I sobered and shook off the doubt like it was a piece lint on my wedding dress. After mustering up the courage I needed, I smiled. "I'm ready to become Mrs. Beatrice Beacon, Mama."

"Don't give Henry a lot of trouble." Mama squinted, then helped me get dressed, and Papa had the car cleaned and polished so he could drive us to the church.

A lot of people filled Wesley Chapel, including some of my classmates.

Peggy was my maid of honor. Roger was Henry's best man.

Lily Rae insisted on being the flower girl. She was about to turn thirteen. Mama said to let her because she was family. How did my cousin get what she wanted at my wedding?

Everything was beautiful. The church was filled with so many flowers as Papa escorted me down the aisle to the altar where Henry stood. He looked so handsome, and as soon as he saw me, Henry didn't look to the left or right.

It seemed like a fairytale as Henry and I exchange our wedding vows. But when Reverend Greenlee pronounced us husband and wife, and Henry kissed me for the first time, it was very real.

MaDear CC paid for the top floor of the Mosaic Templars Building on Ninth Street as our reception. Henry said MaDear CC was close friends with Mr. John Bush, chairman of the Republican party in the state and co-founder of the Mosaic Templars of America. Not only did his family build larger homes in the same neighborhood where we lived, but they outshined the repetitive order of shotgun houses from one end of the street to the other. Mr. Bush also built and owned this building that housed many successful businesses for Colored folks.

At seventeen, I was suddenly a grown married woman as my handsome husband twirled me around on the dance floor, except on the slow songs. I hiked my shoes on top of his Stacy Adams and allowed my husband to guide me across the floor.

"I'm scared," I whispered close to his ear before the music stopped.

He frowned. "About tonight?"

"No, silly." Mama had said the honeymoon is fun. "Moving away from our families. I guess that doesn't sound real grownup, does it?"

"We're young, Mrs. Beacon." He grinned. "We'll figure it out together."

Our parents made toasts and wished us well, then the advice came.

"Beatrice, you and Henry don't make no babies before you finish school," Mama said. She frowned at Henry. "No babies before Beatrice finishes school."

"You've been a good son. Finish school and take care of your family," Mr. Beacon said and invited me to call him Dad if I was comfortable. I wasn't. Yet.

"If you two need money, I'll wire it through Western Union," Papa said.

As a gift to Mama, since I was getting married, Mrs. Rothman offered Henry and me her cottage in the back of her house to use for our wedding night.

Thinking about how that rich woman threatened to fire my mama if I had been chosen to integrate Central High School made my blood boil. Mama urged me to accept graciously. "White folks have taken a lot away from us. Accept it, Beatrice. Besides, I've cleaned and dusted that cottage for years. My daughter and son-in-law might as well use it."

After I danced with Papa, Henry danced with his mother, then he swayed a few steps with MaDear CC before we were off to Louisiana Street where the mansion's cottage awaited us.

The next morning, I admired the diamond ring on my finger when I woke. It wasn't a dream. I was married! I never knew I could fall so deeply in love with a man. Our wedding night taught me otherwise. I was glad Henry was my husband and my first love.

We packed up our things and tidied the cottage. I didn't want to leave a mess for Mama to clean the next day.

With Henry's trunk stuffed with our meager belongings and wedding gifts, we began our five-plus hour drive to St. Louis after stopping by our parents' homes for tearful goodbye hugs..

"You're going to have to teach me how to drive." I smiled then looked out the window. I was married. I crossed my arms over my chest and sighed.

Henry glanced at me. "What are you doing, Mrs. Beacon?"

"I can't hug you because you're driving, so I'm making believe."

He took my hand and kissed it. "I'm real, but it's best I drive to get us to St. Louis before dark. Dad gave me a recent copy of the *Negro Travelers' Green Book*, so we'll know where we'll be safe if we have to stophave."

I flipped through the pages. "I see two tourist homes in Cape Girardeau, Missouri, about two hours from St. Louis where it would be safe for us to stop. The other places aren't close."

"Thank you, sweetheart," Henry said as he kept his eyes ahead.

His endearment made me blush.

We followed the map's route and arrived in downtown St. Louis with no delays. Henry turned on Clark Street from Vandeventer and parked in front of a monster of a house. "Wow. We're living here?"

He stepped out of the car and walked around to help me. Henry looked worried. "You don't like it?"

I kissed him. "I love it!"

"Whew." He exhaled and twirled me around before he wrapped me in his arms and hugged me. "Our space isn't that big inside. I'm warning you."

"It's you, me, and a bed. There's room."

"Oh, so now, you're a sassy woman." He kissed me again.

"Well, you can always give me back," I teased.

"No way."

The door opened, and a fair-skinned man stepped out and waved. It was Uncle Buddy, or Mr. Chestnut as Henry said he preferred to be addressed. He was as handsome as Henry and his father. The only difference was his attire this late afternoon. Slacks and a shirt weren't everyday wear at home.

"Welcome home, newlyweds."

His arms were open in a grand gesture as he stepped off the stairs.

Mr. Chestnut showed us our accommodations. They were meager but furnished. I had a home with a loving husband.

"You wait here, Mrs. Beacon, while your husband and I get your things."

I blushed and couldn't help but giggle. "I am a Mrs." My heart fluttered, and Henry crossed the space and hugged me, pulling me into his loving stare. "My Mrs. Be right back."

They unloaded our bags and gifts from the car and brought them inside. Once we were alone, Henry grabbed me in his arms. "Let's dance." He grinned as I rested my feet on top of his and waltzed to our own tune.

"Wife, we better call our parents and let them know we arrived safely. Mr. Chestnut says we can use his phone until we get ours installed."

Funny how I had forgotten about them so soon.

Holding the phone receiver between our ears, we called Mama and Papa first. We didn't talk long because of long-distance charges. "You sound happy," Mama said, "but remember, try not to have any babies until you finish school, Beatrice.

Henry and I shared a silent grin. "Yes, Mama. We'll try."

"Call every week collect, and we'll accept the charges," she admonished us.

"Okay. Love you. Bye."

The Beacons were next. The first thing MaDear CC wanted to know was if I was satisfied with the accommodations.

"Yes, I am. They're perfect," I told her.

Mr. Beacon came on the line. "Remember, Henry, you treat Beatrice right because she's our daughter now, and get a job sooner than later, son."

Henry hugged me tighter. "Yes, sir."

"Get settled," Flora, his mother, said. "Expect us to call and check on you every week. If you need something, we'll wire you the money, but I expect my son to take care of his wife."

"Yes, Mama," Henry told her, then they hung up the phone.

"Whew." We exhaled together.

Our new landlord treated us to dinner prepared by his cook who made extra servings in anticipation of our arrival.

"Mrs. Papin is an excellent cook. You'll see her three times a week. Sometimes she will cook something for my other tenants—at their expense, of course."

"Understood." Henry devoured the beef stroganoff.

Afterward, we returned to our place and began to unwrap gifts. We were amazed at our friends' generosity and the cash we received.

"Tomorrow, we need to open a bank account, enroll in school, and get a newspaper for me to look for jobs."

"I can work," I offered. "I like having my own money."

Henry frowned, pulled my chin closer, and kissed my lips. "My wife will not work. I'm the husband who vowed to take care of you. Plus, you're still in high school." He kissed me. "Will you let me take care of you? I'll give you the money. All you have to do is ask."

My driving lessons began the next day. Under Henry's patient guidance, I drove to Jefferson Bank on Market Street and Jefferson, not far from our new home to open up a savings account. Mr. Chestnut said they were one of a few banks that accepted Colored account holders.

I was a pro on the road, except for the parallel parking. Papa made it look easy. It wasn't, *and* I was smart.

"That was fun." I beamed after Henry helped me out and linked hands to walk inside the bank. Once we finished our business and left, Henry said he would drive the rest of the day.

We bought the morning paper, *Globe-Democrat*, then visited Harris Stowe Teachers College and Vashon High School.

He signed up for three classes so he could take me to school and pick me up. Although Vashon was within walking distance, Henry refused to let me walk.

We were set to resume school in a week. Exhausted and hungry, we stopped at the corner market to stock up on groceries.

While I cooked, Henry scanned the want ads. Both the *St. Louis Dispatch* and the *Globe-Democrat*, the evening and morning paper respectively, ran classified ads for job openings, none of which my husband was qualified for yet. He would find something. Until then, we could enjoy married life.

Chapter 20
The Big Adjustment

Henry

PAST, Near downtown St. Louis, Missouri, October 1958

I was the master of our house with a wife to take care of but no job yet. The money in our bank account was from the wedding. I didn't want to voice my concerns to Beatrice and cause her to worry. I had choices. If I worked as a laborer, I would earn a decent salary, but then I couldn't go to school.

Southwestern Bell had left our apartment that morning, and our phone rang for the first time. It was MaDear CC on the other end.

"I guess Mr. Chestnut gave you our phone number."

She huffed. "You don't have to call Buddy that when you speak to me. Yes, he gave me the number, and I didn't know when you were going to call. How's everything going with my grandson and granddaughter? Do I need to wire you money?"

"Thank you, MaDear CC, but I should have a job soon. I'm surprised at the companies that will hire Coloreds."

"Really?"

"Yep." I chatted as I watched Beatrice stir up dinner in our kitchenette. "There's Royal Meat Packaging Company that's within walking distance. Laclede Christy is another. They mold clay pipes for the sewers."

"Sounds like they're looking for skilled laborers."

Although MaDear CC wanted me to have a profession, I had to think about right now.

"There's the Scullin Steel plant and Liberty Foundry, which is also close. See, I can take care of my wife."

"I knew it was a good decision for you to go to St. Louis!" She seemed pleased with herself.

"Yes, Mr. Ches—I mean Uncle Buddy—said jobs are plentiful for Blacks."

MaDear CC was chatty as Beatrice distracted me from the kitchen. She had stopped cooking and began to tease me dancing and giggling.

"Ah, I have to go. Beatrice is calling me. Love you. Talk to you later." I hung up without waiting for MaDear CC to say goodbye.

With measured steps, I approached Beatrice as my prey. When I captured her in my arms, we danced together. "I think you need a break."

"If you think so." She wrapped her arms around my neck, then I scooped her off her feet.

We were running out of time. Next week, Beatrice and I would be students again, and I hadn't applied yet to any of the companies I'd told MaDear CC about.

I didn't mind getting my hands dirty, but these were day jobs that would interfere with my classes and prevent me from taking and picking up my wife from her school. Not that Vashon was far from our house on Laclede, but this was a new city, and her safety was my responsibility despite Mr. Chestnut's assurance of the city's low crime rate.

There was another option to provide for my family *and* to get an education. Take a janitor job at one of the hospitals or department stores downtown. The drawback was Beatrice would go to bed at night without me.

When we discussed my plans, we had our first argument. Beatrice was downright mad.

"My mother cleaned Mrs. Rothman's house and others'. I hated it, and so did Papa. My husband is too brilliant to be a janitor. That isn't the only job for us."

I grabbed her in a hug. "I love you so much, but I can't let you go to school unaccompanied in a city we have lived in for a few weeks."

"And I'm not willing for you to forgo your education to do the dirty work." Beatrice wiggled out of my embrace and folded her arms. "Want to call our families for advice?"

"No. We won't get them involved. This is between Mrs. Beatrice Beacon and Mr. Henry Beacon."

My wife blushed when I called her legal name. "Mama would probably ask if we prayed about it. We haven't even picked a church to attend."

I folded my hands. I'd forgotten that was something else we needed to do. I asked Mr. Chestnut for recommendations. "There's a church on almost every corner. Pick one and have a seat."

Beatrice and I did exactly that. On Sunday, we saw a "Christ Saves" sign on the roof of a building. We walked inside, and an older, short, dark-skin female usher greeted us with a big smile, then we took a seat. The sermon on Sunday didn't help ease my mind about keeping the peace in my home by taking the janitor opening. It was "Live Your Life so People Can See Jesus in You."

The following Monday, we started classes. I was still jobless.

Chapter 21
The Fear Factor

Beatrice
PAST, Near Downton St. Louis, November 1958

St. Louis was colder than I was accustomed to, and Henry bought me a wool warm coat, gloves, and boots. I also made him warm gloves and socks since he had been a construction worker for weeks as the city began demolishing houses and businesses in the Mill Creek Valley neighborhood near downtown.

Henry walked me to Vashon, went to work until it was time to pick me up, and took two courses at night at Harris Stowe Teachers College. Something my husband didn't want to do, leave me at home alone, but I convinced him I would be okay. Mr. Chestnut assured Henry he would keep an eye out for me too.

When Henry returned to the apartment at night, I had a hot meal prepared. Once he rested, we did our homework together.

Mama didn't have to worry about us having a baby yet. My husband was too drained.

Every Sunday, we called home and gave our parents updates on how we were faring.

"Mama, he's taking good care of me. I'm the only married gal in my class," I boasted. "The girls think Henry's handsome."

"*Umm-hmm.* He is. You look out for them women. There's a difference between stealing a boyfriend and stealing a woman's husband. God heard your vows to each other, and we did too. Be careful making friends. Everybody's not Peggy, and you tell Henry the same about any new men friends."

"Yes, ma'am." I giggled because, with one look, my husband put fear into the boys at Vashon High.

Even without Mama's repeated warnings, I wanted my female classmates to keep their distance from my husband.

Nosey Rosie—as I had begun to call one girl—asked me if I got married because I was pregnant.

"Don't you know that grown folks' business is between the husband and wife? I did not invite you into my bedroom." I gave her one of Mama's "don't ask me again" looks, and it worked.

I called my new attitude "the fear of Beatrice Beacon." I had been so looking forward to enjoying my senior year back in Little Rock. Now, living in St. Louis, I couldn't wait until spring next year for it to be over.

Another time, the captain of the football team approached me. The girls thought Headie Eddie—another nickname I came up with because his head swelled with conceit—was cute.

To me, Headie Eddie was annoying. He cornered me coming out of the ladies' restroom one afternoon. His sly grin showed bad teeth. "I bet your old man hates to see you go in the mornings."

I reached inside my purse and pulled out my nail file. Anything could be used as a weapon if applied enough pressure. "Mr. Beacon knows I will *always* come home to him. Now, if you step into my space again, one of us won't make it to graduation. I know how to cut ya in multiple ways."

He backed off.

Henry and I didn't make many friends besides the older couple on the second floor. Mr. and Mrs. Grady were our parents' ages and treated Henry and me like their son and daughter.

One evening after Henry walked me home from Vashon, he didn't kiss me goodbye to go to classes. I grew concerned. "What's wrong? Don't you feel well?" I touched his forehead. I turned to go into our kitchenette to make him some chicken soup. Henry grabbed my wrist.

"Have a seat, sweetheart." He smiled, but it didn't reach his eyes.

I didn't understand his contradictory tone. I sat next to him. My tears were on standby. "What's wrong?" I swallowed the lump of fear in my throat.

Rubbing his forehead, Henry exhaled. He looked serious like Papa. "Why didn't you tell me you were having trouble at school with Eddie Russell?"

Shocked, I blinked. "There was nothing to tell. I scared him off with my nail file." I nodded, lifted my chin in satisfaction.

"A nail file, huh?" He grunted.

"How do you know about that anyway?" I frowned.

"I have people watching out for you." Henry seemed calm about his admission.

Questions swirled in my head. Before I could ask him to name one of them, Henry stopped me by placing a finger on my lips to shush me.

"You're my wife. Mrs. Henry Bea—"

"Mrs. Beatrice Beacon," I corrected, but it didn't earn me a smile like it usually did. I shifted and folded my hands. "Sorry."

Henry squinted. "From the day in that barbershop until my last breath, I will protect you."

"This isn't Dunbar High. We don't know anyone here—not really."

"But I know people Mr. Chestnut has introduced me to. I work with older men who have sons and daughters at Vashon. I have classmates at Harris Stowe Teachers College that recently graduated from Vashon."

My Jaw dropped. "You're paying them when we could save that money?"

"You're worth more to me than money, and I won't leave you unprotected when I'm not there." He frowned and guided my lips to his. He got no further arguments from me.

From then on, whenever I walked the halls at Vashon, I didn't know who my friend was or my foe. But big old Headie Eddie seemed to avoid me. Too bad, I was looking forward to taking him down with my nail file.

On my Sunday call with my parents, Mama asked, "How do you like the city? I can't wait for your Papa and me to come visit."

"I like it. Mr. Chestnut says the Polish immigrants live in the north part of the city, and the Germans live on the Southside, so most of us are squeezed in between them in the downtown area near the Mississippi River. I guess Grand Boulevard is our invisible line."

"Are you enjoying yourself, baby?"

"Yes, Mama. When Henry and I aren't studying, we go to the movies at Strand Theater by Union Station, not far from here." I didn't mention when he was rested up.

"*Hmmm*. What about church, Beatrice? That's important. It will keep Henry away from loose women and liquor and you from temptation."

I withheld my chuckle. Mama wouldn't see the humor. It seemed like every corner had a church across the street from a liquor store and a pharmacy next to it. Sometimes, a mortuary was nearby. "We joined Washington Tabernacle. Tell Papa I love him, and we can't wait for your visit next month."

The Tilley and Beacon families arrived in St. Louis a few days before Thanksgiving. We were so glad to see them. The Beacons stayed downstairs with Mr. Chestnut, since they were kin, while Papa and Mama stayed with us. Henry had purchased a folding roll-away bed, and we slept in the kitchen.

Papa and Mr. Beacon praised Henry for taking care of me. Mama, MaDear CC, and Mrs. Beacon showed me how to put fixings together for a Thanksgiving meal.

MaDear CC asked her son to give her a tour of the city. They had been gone for a couple of hours. For ninety-three years old, she moved around well, albeit slow. When they returned, she suggested that a small home in the Ville neighborhood would be roomy enough for Henry and me when we started a family.

A family. At first, I was excited about becoming a mother, but the way Henry was working, I didn't want to put more burden on him. I had a plan and was certain Henry wasn't going to like it.

Chapter 22
Life Ain't No Fairytale

Victoria
PRESENT, Ferguson, Missouri, 2023

Cheney *tsk*ed and wagged her finger. "Poor Henry. You were scheming early in your marriage. Why am I not surprised?" A tease danced in her eyes.

"Wait a minute." Pace blinked. "I'm still trying to wrap my head about Grandma BB married in high school and your mother telling you not to get pregnant."

"If only she knew." Grandma BB's eyes seemed to wander and focus on a memory none of them were privy to. "We didn't pay them no mind. Love was in the air. Looking back, I almost wished I had a baby while in high school since most of the girls there thought I was pregnant anyway. Them hussies."

The room grew quiet. As Victoria was about to continue reading from the script, Grandma BB spoke.

"I knew that man loved me, and if I could get the time back, I would marry him again..." She glanced down at her Stacy Adams shoes. "We were committed to each other."

"You were blessed. They don't make men like that anymore," Victoria said. She had seen the ugliness of men.

Deli cleared her throat, and everyone whipped their heads toward her. "I don't know about the other Jamieson men in this room, but I can speak from experience that this one right here…" She covered Pace's hand. "He's handcrafted. A good one."

The way her brother looked at Deli, Victoria surmised it had to be love. The question was why any of the family hadn't known anything about her.

Queen stood, and in her signature runway walk, came to Victoria's side and hugged her. "Your brother, dad, uncles, and cousins aren't the only good guys. I got one, and he's a Dupree. You're young—"

"But not too young to find love," Grandma BB interrupted. "If you need a matchmaker, I'm the one. I'll run the usual criminal background checks, active child support warrants, and see how he treats his mama. That's important."

Victoria inwardly groaned. How did she lose control, not of the meeting, but her emotions that the funeral drill turned into an "about Victoria" moment?

"Honey," Victoria's mother said gently, "we all came into our relationships with baggage." She scanned the room. The aunties and uncles nodded.

Ace raised his hand. "I was on the do-not-fly list after federal marshals removed me from a plane, and someone recorded it, and I became a viral sensation for the wrong reasons."

His wife, Talise, shook her head. "Despite his baggage, I kinda liked him, so I married him anyway." She chuckled, and Ace kissed her cheek.

Would someone want to marry me, knowing my baggage? Victoria wondered if she would trust a man to get close enough to find out.

Cheney was transparent about her abortion. Parke had fathered a son he didn't know he had. Kidd and Ace struggled with abandonment issues from their father. Ace's wife, Talise, was pregnant with his child and wasn't going to marry him. Plus, Grandma BB had landed in jail. And the list was long.

"Victoria?" Grandma BB came near. "Baby, you will overcome. It might take a while, but you'll be okay. You hear me?"

Nodding, Victoria looked up in embarrassment. "Sorry."

"You have no reason to be sorry. You're among family, and we—"

"Take care of each other," practically every Jamieson in the room said as if it had been rehearsed.

"I just don't know if any man will want me because of my childhood past," Victoria mumbled.

"Humph." Queen stood. "Have I not taught you anything?" She rolled her neck. "When the time comes, you're the one who decides if he makes the cut."

"Whew." Philip put his arm around Queen's waist. "My wife was ruthless, but I'm glad I met her requirements."

"As a matter of fact, I may hold off dying until I tend to that," Grandma BB said with a determination that Victoria didn't want.

"Grandma BB…" Philip, the family minister and Queen's husband, stood. "First, I'm glad you were active in the church."

"Huh?" An audible chorus went around the room with Grandma BB being the loudest. "No, I said we joined the church—showed up, gave them money, had our names on the church rolls in case our families asked. Nothing more."

Everyone waited for Philip's response. He seemed to listen for God to tell him something. Nodding with a warm smile—he gave the best smile of all Victoria's uncles. "Grandma BB, unless you join the Body of Christ through the baptism in His name, you're not in His Book of Life. The buildings we call 'church' are meaningless unless the leaders point you to Christ."

"Amen, preacher!" Kidd said.

Philip gave his brother-in-law a smile. "I said that to say this. We can't choose our death date. In a blink of an eye—" he snapped his fingers—"our life can be over."

Grandma BB gripped both sides of her armrest and snarled. "I can tell you a thing or two about losing someone in the blink of an eye. Hold me back, hold me back." She shook her head as Chip and Dale came and placed their hands on her shoulders. "I don't want to fight with the minister at my own funeral like I wanted to do at Henry's…"

She started removing her bobby pins. Next would be her clip-on earrings. If she slipped off her Stacy Adams, after that she would be going for her Smith and Wesson.

"Oh no. Isn't beating up on God's anointed an automatic 'going to hell' judgment?" Deli said, talking to herself, but everyone heard her.

Victoria led the chorus of *uh-ohs* around the room. Pandemonium broke out among the children.

"I don't want to go to hell!" Little Camille bawled. "And I don't want my Grandma BB to go either."

"Say one more word," Grandma BB said between her gritted teeth, "and you're out of here." She shot daggers at Pace's guest.

Deli took the threat as intended and stood to leave, but Pace restrained her. he coaxed she sit back down and wrapped his arms around her.

"If Grandma BB likes you, insults are the norm," Pace said.

Humph. Grandma BB folded her arms. "Who said I liked her anyway?"

Chapter 23
Oops. Change of Plans

Beatrice
PAST, Near Downtown St. Louis, May 1959

I did it! Mrs. Beatrice Beacon was scheduled to graduate from Vashon High School with honors and on time despite my late enrollment.

Our families were ecstatic at my achievement and planned to drive up to St. Louis for the commencement.

"Then we made the right decision to send you there." Mama sounded relieved.

"And to marry Henry. He protects me—" No need to tell her about his hired snitches. "He provides for us, and he studies with me." I glanced at Henry who was stretched out on the couch asleep with a book resting on his stomach. "He's been a wonderful husband, Mama. I love him."

"Your papa and I love him too, sweetie." She yawned. It was late. The rates for long-distance calls were cheaper if placed after eleven at night. Mama had to get up early to go clean Mrs. Rothman's mansion-sized house, so we said our goodbyes.

I stood over my husband and watched the rise and fall of his chest, admiring his features and physique. His jet-black beard was now thick and full and framed his jaw to perfection. His biceps were built as a result of hard labor at the construction sites all day. My cooking was responsible for his slight pouch where his schoolbook rested on his stomach. I closed his book and gently nudged him.

"Hey. Let's go to bed."

"Got to study," Henry murmured without opening his eyes. He smacked his lips as if he had a taste of my apple pie.

"We'll get up early to finish." I wrapped my arms around his waist when he stood. I pulled out the sleeper, helped Henry undress, then we slipped under the covers together. I drifted into a peaceful sleep with my husband.

"It's not the career I envisioned, but it pays a decent salary, and it's a respectable profession," he said early the next morning while we studied.

"I know you want to travel and see the world. We will. I promise," I said with all the love in my heart because I believed him.

The hard work paid off for Henry. He passed his finals and was halfway toward his teaching certificate.

Two weeks before my graduation, Henry wanted to take me downtown to shop instead of Wellston that was across the city line where many Coloreds were welcomed to spend their money. We caught the streetcar to Stix, Baer, and Fuller on 6th and Washington Avenue. Outside the glass and brass doors, Henry held out his elbow for me to rest my hand, and we strolled inside with a purpose.

Mr. Chestnut said that Stix was pricier than Famous Barr. That didn't deter my husband. He didn't know I overheard him on the phone with his grandmother the other day.

"MaDear CC, I love you and appreciate everything you've done for us, but as her husband for more than six months, I've learned how to take care of my wife. I put aside money to buy her a nice dress for her graduation."

He had paused while she spoke, then he said, "If you want to give us money, give it to Beatrice for her to keep or do whatever she wants."

That's when I had stopped eavesdropping and smiled. I had the best husband, and I wanted to be the best wife to Henry.

Although I admired several garments in the women's clothing department, I was determined to choose the least expensive.

Henry watched as I walked out of the dressing room each time to model five dresses for his inspection. His eyes twinkled, he smiled, and he even blew me kisses but wouldn't offer an opinion.

The decision wasn't easy. A peach dress with white polka dots and a flared skirt had soft fabric. It had six buttons on the bodice with a white collar. It would make my brown skin glow.

If Mama were here, she would sew me one. The other dress was yellow like daffodils, and its skirt flared too. The sleeves ended at the elbows, and a crisp bow was tied at the waistline. Then…I thought I'd look sophisticated in a two-piece mint green blazer and pleated skirt.

"Henry, I can't make up my mind. Help me." I became flustered, gnawing on my bottom lip. Polka dots were popular but the most expensive.

Henry came to me from his post leaning against the wall. "Whichever one you want, Mrs. Beacon."

My heart melted as I looked into his brown eyes. "I want the yellow one."

Henry folded his arms. "No, you don't."

Looking both ways to ensure we had privacy, I whispered, "It's the cheapest."

"I did not bring you to Stix to buy you the cheapest thing on a hanger. You are graduating, and you're my wife. Make me happy and get the polka dots." He grinned.

I frowned. "How–how did you know?"

"Before we married, my father had a long talk with me. Dad said to learn your ways and what makes you happy. I've been watching you, baby."

I blushed at the endearment. "Okay. The polka dots, please."

He kissed my nose. "Do you need shoes?" I shook my head without thinking about it.

"Look anyway," Henry said and headed to the checkout counter.

I glanced at the shoes on display from afar. I was afraid to go any closer for fear I would find something I liked. Plus, I still had the shoes

I wore on my wedding day. No. I couldn't do it. I trailed him to the register.

The clerk gave Henry the total. "I would like to pay a deposit and put it in layaway until next week."

I looped my arm through his. "Thank you."

He kissed my forehead. "You're welcome."

The evening before my graduation, Henry and I stood at the curb outside our place, waiting for our families to arrive. When they drove up, there was an extra person in the car.

"Peggy!" I cried and scrambled to get to her. We hugged each other tightly.

My parents had to break us up to get their hugs and kisses. We had spoken a few times but not often because of the long-distance charges, and she went out of state to live with her aunt in Mississippi for school.

Our Arkansas governor had separated friends and families. Before I complained too loudly, I thought about what I got in return—Henry Beacon.

Mr. Chestnut invited the men to come downstairs to visit while Mama, Mrs. Beacon, MaDear CC, and Peggy stayed with me.

"It hasn't been a year, but you look so grown up, not like my friend I played with," Peggy teased, staring at me as if to make sure it was really me.

"You look mature too. We did what we had to so we could graduate on time." I squeezed Peggy's hand and grinned. "I've missed you. I've made some friends, but it's not the same."

One girl I had let into my friendship circle was Helen. The rule of our friendship was she couldn't ask about my husband. Her first question was, "Why? Has he been in jail?" I later learned she was a paid informant too, but we became acquaintances anyway.

"Plus, I'm married, so I don't do the same things as they do. One girl thought I married because I was pregnant."

"Are you pregnant? Because you're glowing," Mama butted in as she opened one cabinet after the other, making sure we had food on the shelves.

"How would I know?" I shrugged.

"You could be nauseated or tired," MaDear CC said. Her eyes twinkled.

I shook my head. "Mama told me not to get pregnant until I finished high school." Sometimes, Henry and I were careful. Other times, it didn't matter to us.

After Mama took a seat, satisfied Henry and I wouldn't starve, she folded her arms. That had been her concern on some of the weekly calls, whether we had enough food.

"Tomorrow you'll be out of high school, so we'll be waiting for news about a grandbaby," my mother-in-law said.

Henry walked in the door, and we paused our discussion as if the air was sucked out of our lungs. He looked at each of us suspiciously. "Ah, Mr. Chestnut says come downstairs. His cook made supper for us."

He assisted MaDear CC first then kissed my cheek and led the way.

My graduation the next day was bittersweet. I had achieved what Governor Faubus tried to stop—an education for Coloreds. After the program, we went out to dinner to celebrate.

Too soon, the day after that, my friend and our families went back to Little Rock.

As the summer rolled in, Henry and I enjoyed our marriage without so many distractions. He worked long hours since he didn't have to escort me to school while I stayed home, cleaned, cooked, and searched the newspaper for jobs.

"Just think, honey, you can work earlier, get off sooner, and take summer classes." I tried to convince him by preparing his favorite meal for dinner. I would help my husband whether he wanted me to or not.

"And how will my wife get to work? Your driving is improving, but you're not safe to be alone on the road yet."

Hmmmph. I'll have you know, Mr. Beacon, if there's a problem with my driving, then it's my teacher who's to blame."

He kissed my lips. "And I promised to make you happy. If you want to work for the summer and see how you like it, I'm behind you.

If you feel you want to make more money, then join me at the teacher's college to earn your degree, or you can go to nursing school at People's Hospital."

Choices. That's what I was looking for. But I wasn't really ready to study to become a teacher or nurse. I hadn't thought that far ahead as an adult yet.

When I called the department stores downtown about an opening, I was asked, "White or Colored?"

"Colored."

"We don't have any openings for you." The call ended but not my determination to earn money without cleaning someone's house.

Henry didn't work on the weekends, so that was our time. On Saturday afternoons, we explored the city's attractions for Coloreds. The Fox Theatre on Grand Boulevard near our church wasn't one of them. There weren't any "No Colored Allowed" signs, but an invisible line that flashed "Not for you."

Sometimes Henry and I would sit on a park bench across the street and watch the White folks dressed in their Sunday best go to see the latest movies. St. Louis also had movies for us—the Comet, Strand, plus two others.

One day, we saw a familiar face.

"Isn't that Mr. Chestnut?" I whispered to Henry even though we were across the street and couldn't be heard.

"And he has a lady friend," Henry stated as we watched him buy a ticket and escort his date inside.

"I'd like to go inside just because they say I can't." I turned and looked at Henry. "You can go. You could pass too."

"Maybe." He shrugged. "I never tried. Why would I want to go to a place where my wife would not be acknowledged? Despite my White bloodline, I'm comfortable in the colored skin I'm in."

Me too, which is why I decided I would apply for jobs in-person instead of looking through the newspapers to call personnel to be asked if I was White or Colored. I wanted to be seen as my husband saw me—a beautiful young woman—although more of my hair had silver strands.

I wanted to challenge the unfair system at Famous Barr or Scruggs department stores where Coloreds could spend their money but had to stand up to eat their food at the counter. I wanted to copy what Miss Rosa Parks from Montgomery, Alabama, did on the bus, but at their food counter. Time to either insult me verbally or recognize me physically at the stores' cafeterias.

After Henry left for work one morning, I rode a service car, which was cheaper and driven by a Colored man versus a bus or streetcar. It was amusing to see how many people could fit inside the service car, which was roomy, before the driver would say, "Wait for the next one."

I walked into Famous Barr downtown to apply for a summer job. It would be a wonderful place to work. I admired the beautiful clothes, perfumes, and other expensive merchandise that was meant to be seen rather than touched by us.

Stopping at the jewelry counter, I became impatient being looked over as White customers were serviced before me.

"Oh, sorry. I didn't see you."

Ummm-hmmm. "With my rich brown coloring, how could I be missed?"

Stunned, the woman was quiet. The White woman beside me sucked in her breath, yet no more challenged me. I walked away with dignity and not the cufflinks I could afford for Henry. My purpose was to make money, not spend it.

The lady in the personnel department at Famous Barr stood to greet me—or dismiss me—when I walked into the office. Her name plate read Louise Downer.

"Good morning, Miss Downer. I'm here to apply for the perfume counter position."

The woman, with pale white skin, red hair, and a thin frame stood eye-to-eye with me. "Those positions are…not available to Coloreds."

"Since I have White in my blood somewhere, I should be considered." I wished I had known my history because I would have told her exactly which relative was raped while she was enslaved. Teachers should have taught that class in school.

She stuttered, "Well, that's not the way it works. I have something in housekeeping—"

No, she didn't. "I am not a maid. Otherwise, I would make a living cleaning your house. I'm a recent graduate of Vashon—"

"Yes, I'm familiar with the Colored schools here." Miss Downer seemed bored with me.

Keeping a pleasant expression, I masked my annoyance at her interruption. "I excelled in my studies. Although I transferred from Dunbar High in Little Rock, I was accepted into the National Honor Society…" I continued to toot my horn. When she didn't seem impressed with my scholastic ability and accomplishments, I went for the physical attributes. "I'm very attractive. My husband tells me my brown eyes and perfect smile are my best assets, and my hints of gray in my hair give me the maturity to converse with customers."

The woman spied my hair, which had been freshly shampooed and pressed. The beautician did just as good of a job as Miss Beulah back home and had her own shop, too, instead of in her kitchen.

"*Hmmmph*. There's more gray than hints." She snickered.

"My husband is working hard to provide for us and taking classes at night to become a teacher. You have openings. I saw the sign, and I am available."

Her attempts to dismiss me with sly remarks made me refortify myself and not take no for an answer.

Fifteen minutes later, I had talked myself, a brown-skin Colored girl, into a job. Not at the perfume counter like I wanted but as an elevator girl. Anything but housekeeping. Papa and Mama wouldn't want that.

"I must say, you have a winning personality, Beatrice. You're not the type we usually allow in that position—"

"You mean because I'm not fair-skinned or near-White looking. That's okay. My husband is light enough for both of us." I smiled.

After I completed the paperwork, Miss Downer walked me to where I would work from nine to four-thirty. "The pay will start at sixty-three cents an hour. If your service is exemplary, you'll get a raise to one dollar an hour in three months."

"Thank you." I would have to work past the summer because I was going to get that raise. A dollar an hour would help more than sixty-three cents.

My plan worked. Like Miss Rosa Parks who refused to move, I refused to work in housekeeping. Now, Henry could cut back his hours for summer classes. With my head held high, I, Mrs. Beatrice Beacon, had my first real job. Working at the library back home didn't count. I took a bus ride the short distance home.

Henry stopped pacing in front of the bus stop when he saw me stepped off. "I didn't know how long you would be, but I wasn't going home without you." He kissed me, then linked his fingers through mine, and we strolled to our apartment together.

Soon, we began to meet other couples, more at social events than at church. We were happy, but to keep our parents, especially Mama, happy, we attended church so we could tell them about the sermon in case they asked.

Enjoying my freedom at Famous Barr, I convinced Henry that delaying college was a good thing since it cost. "At least until you graduate, then I can enroll."

One afternoon, I strolled past the men's shoe department as I was leaving work, then backtracked. Shiny black, brown and black-and-white shoes caught my attention. Henry needed a new pair. He seldom bought anything for himself.

Henry had two suits. One for when we went dancing a Club Riviera and a church suit, but he wore the same pair of shoes from our wedding day. I went to the counter to inquire about the price. No one waited on me. Even from the White salesmen who had rode on my elevator.

If they didn't recognize me, I planned to make them not forget me. Tired of standing, I took a seat and nodded to the handful of male customers looking at me. Removing my shoes, I wiggled my toes. I had painted my toenails pink. Perplexed, a salesman approached. Now, I had gotten some attention.

"Young lady, you're in the wrong department. The ladies' shoes are on the other side." He seemed annoyed with his feigned politeness.

"I'm aware of its location, and I'm familiar with the departments." I folded my arms. "I'm the elevator operator."

"These seats are for paying customers. I must insist you leave." He lifted his chin in a superior manner and turned as if he was about to dismiss me.

"I would like a size twelve in that black-and-white pair of Stacy Adams." I pointed to the display table. Smiling, I gave him an "I'm waiting" expression.

Once Orville, as it read on his name tag, registered my demand, he spun around and disappeared behind the curtains. He returned with the box of shoes and a smirk. "Would you like to try them on?"

"No," I said, then I changed my mind just to annoy Orville. "As a matter of fact, I do. Yes, please."

He put them in front of me, and I slipped into them and clunked my way to the mirror. I looked back at him. "Great fit. I'll take them. Please put them on layaway and use my employee discount."

From that day forward, Orville remembered me when I begrudgingly greeted him on the elevator. One day I said to him before he got off at the lower level for lunch, "Please let me know if you get any new styles in the Stacy Adams collection."

Orville huffed and stepped off when I opened the door. I snickered until I let out a belly laugh. When another customer stepped inside, I had to sniff away my tears.

By the end of the summer, after three months of employment, I earned my raise, paid the balance on my layaway, and had Henry's shoes for his birthday.

He was overcome with happiness. "Baby, thank you for the gift."

The shoes were worth the money for the joy I brought him. He swept me into a hug, then released his hold long enough to kiss me.

Grinning, Henry slipped his feet into the shoes. "They feel good. Let's dance."

I laughed and was about to get my heels from the corner armoire, but he took my hand.

"No. Put those pretty feet of yours onto my new shoes, and let's go."

We didn't play music on the radio as I closed my eyes and swayed with my husband.

The next morning over breakfast, we discussed our finances.

"The money you're bringing in has allowed me to cut back hours to have more time to study. MaDear CC says the Ville is a nice place to live with black businesses, and the oldest black school is there. The college is half the distance. Are you ready to enroll for the upcoming semester?"

I shook my head. "I'd rather work until you finish your degree, then I can go to college."

Henry squinted. "I don't like the sound of you supporting me. Our families are going to have a fit." He sighed and rubbed his head.

"High school was free. We can't afford two tuitions. Since we're moving, why can't we do what Mr. Chestnut is doing, rent rooms to pay for our rent?"

He frowned, giving it some thought. "You are one smart, beautiful woman. I'll explain that to our parents, especially MaDear CC. It's not like I'm not working, and the extra income will be great when our baby comes."

We both grinned.

We discussed our plan with Mr. Chestnut, and he was pleased at our desire for ownership. "One caution: You're going to have to move after dark."

"Why?" Henry and I asked at the same time.

"There are Blacks north, but many Whites don't like to share their block or neighborhood with us. It's best they're surprised."

A few weeks later, Henry and I made a move to our own two-story house on Garfield Avue near North Newstead Avenue in the Ville neighborhood.

When construction work slowed down, Henry had more time to study, but there was less money coming in. While we advertised in the newspaper rooms for boarders and waited, Henry offered barber services on the back porch for extra money. That was another trade he didn't want to do.

Although our money was tight, Henry took me out to dinner for our first wedding anniversary, and he insisted I have a new dress. He wore the shoes I bought him.

Before dessert came, he handed me a gift. "I asked my mother what to give you for our first anniversary, and she said paper. Here's some stationery for us to write each other love letters."

"Are you planning on going somewhere?"

"Never." He covered my hand. "We can write our family instead of making long-distance calls. I wrote you the first letter." He grinned.

I unwrapped the paper and smiled. The box was colorful blues, pinks, and greens. The stationery was pink. An envelope was on top.

"Open it." His eyes sparkled.

Dear Wife,

I love you. I always have, and I always will. Thank you for agreeing to marry me, although it wasn't under the best circumstances. There is so much I want to give you. Love me as I fulfill all your dreams.

Your loving husband,

Henry Beacon

I cried, and Henry dabbed at my tears with his handkerchief.

We went home and celebrated our union for the rest of the night. I was on clouds when I strolled into Famous Barr the next day—until a customer said she would slap me if I didn't hold the elevator door long enough to help her drag her cart inside. Images of the hostility toward my nine classmates in Little Rock surfaced. I dared her. I wouldn't be humiliated. She didn't call my bluff, but she did contact the personnel department.

Miss Downer fired me without listening to my side of the story.

Chapter 24
No Regrets

Victoria
PRESENT, Ferguson, Missouri, 2023

"*Woo-wee.* I remember that." Grandma BB grinned. "It was liberating to speak my mind and to stand up for myself against a White person." She sighed as if she was enjoying a bubble bath. "Of course, Henry wasn't happy about me losing my job."

Parke grunted. "He never questioned you losing your temper?"

"Why would he?" Grandma BB removed her glasses. "I spoke the truth. If I had known I would get terminated, I would have gotten a lick in."

Groans circulated around the room.

"That's not a good example to include in an obituary," Cheney spoke up.

"Why? Everybody needs to know their self-worth, and I wasn't a punching bag. After living in Little Rock as a girl and being denied basic rights, I was done with being disrespected. Now..." She shifted in her velvet high-back chair and nodded for Victoria to continue.

"Moving on, back then, the better jobs for Blacks were in teaching or nursing. Grandma BB turned her career aspiration to education after a White patient didn't want our grandma to help her bathe while she was a candy striper at a hospital." Victoria shook her head.

"*Whew,*" Deli said, patting her chest. "I thought you were going to say a stripper." She chuckled to herself because no one else saw the humor. "They're called certified nursing assistants now."

"My funeral is rated PG, so keep it clean." Grandma BB twisted her lips. She had more to say, so everyone waited. She mumbled some choice words under her breath.

"Your words," Cheney baited her. "Let's keep the pre-funeral shindig clean."

Grandma BB nodded. "Victoria, don't forget to mention that part I added in the footnotes about the up-and-coming lawyers during that time."

"You have footnotes in an obituary?" Parke threw up his hands in disbelief. "Who does that?"

"Grandma BB can do anything, Uncle Parke," Little Camille said with a determined nod.

"Never mind. I'll tell you myself that I missed my calling as an attorney. Frankie Muse Freeman—a Black woman lawyer—was a powerhouse back then. She fought for education and housing equality right here in the Lou. For me, the best part were the protests that landed some of us in jail. I was able to argue our rights a couple of times, and the police let us go."

Pace frowned. "I can't fathom being denied opportunities if we're competent."

"The master plan by Whites in charge was for Blacks never to become competent. Money wasn't always pumped into Black schools for Coloreds, Negros, Blacks, and even now African Americans to learn. While White schools were given distinguished names, Black schools were known as Colored School #1, Colored School #2, and nonsense like that. They eventually were renamed Dumas, Dessalines, and L'Ouverture Elementary."

As a retired teacher, Grandma BB gave them a brief history lesson. White students had Hadley Tech, and Blacks had Washington Technical High. Courses weren't offered at Washington Technical for aircraft mechanics. It was at Hadley. With McDonnell Douglas' aerospace company headquartered here, three Black brothers wanted to take those classes. Attorney Freeman represented them and won her first civil rights case.

"I tell ya, ignorance must be hereditary. Instead of offering equal access to those classes, the school dropped the course from the curriculum. Ornery just like Governor Faubus shutting down Little Rock's schools that would've bettered everybody. I thought I left the stupidity behind when I moved to St. Louis." She *hmmph*ed and folded her arms.

Victoria watched as her surrogate great-grandma worked herself into a frenzy. Deli's off comment didn't help. They needed a cool-down period. "How about a potty break?" Everyone scrambled from the room.

Chapter 25
The Ups and Downs of Any Marriage

Beatrice

PAST, The Ville Neighborhood, St. Louis, Missouri, late summer 1959

After the fiasco at Famous Barr, my husband was disappointed that I was spoken to in such a rude manner and I took the bait and lost my job.

"Beatrice, you tried it your way. Now this is the way it's going to be." Henry wasn't harsh, but he wasn't giving me any options either.

As a dutiful wife, I submitted to my husband and enrolled for fall classes at Harris Stowe Teachers College to our parents' relief. Plus, I knew it was just a matter of time before Henry wouldn't let me have my way. Still, I tried one more time to convince him to let me find part-time work. Our income had suffered.

With his fists at his waist, he towered over me with a concerned expression. "Lord, help me to have some control over my pretty little wife." He frowned, then kissed me. "Maybe we should go to church more often and get some spiritual intervention."

Until then, I saw Jefferson Bank had a classified ad in the *Globe-Democrat*. When I got there to apply in person, Nancy Walker, who worked in the stockroom at Famous Barr, had shown up for the only opening for a Colored girl. Nancy had gotten fired, too, because of what her supervisor called insubordination. A storage room was in disarray, and Nancy couldn't find an item in a timely manner.

Neither of us was hired at the bank, but we became friends. Nancy was two years older than me at twenty.

We both had brought sandwiches from home since Coloreds couldn't eat at the counters where they purchased the food at department stores.

We walked to the park on Market Street and sat on a bench. Nancy and I watched the buses and street cars pass by.

"My husband is seven years older than me and working two jobs," Nancy said. "Milton is a doorman at the Chase Park Plaza Hotel through the week. They don't pay well, so he sells papers on the weekend. We're trying to save up money to get a place of our own instead of boarding."

"Henry, my husband, is a construction worker and is going to college," I said. Chatting with Nancy, it hit me how much I missed Peggy when we used to sit on my front porch as little girls. We could talk about anything. Could Nancy be my next best friend?

Mama taught me to be cautious with women folks.

Nancy was a pretty lady. Medium brown. Really tall compared to my stature—at least seven inches over my five feet. Her hair was thick like mine, except it was black. Getting grayer faster, I feared my hair would make me look older than my handsome husband. Henry never complained about it.

I exchanged numbers with Nancy, and we planned to invite each other over for dinner. That didn't happen for weeks, but we did talk on the phone.

It was probably for the best since more potential customers inquired about Henry's barbering service, including men at Washington Tabernacle and some of the White neighbors.

On Sundays after church, we drove to Forest Park where we could visit free attractions. Sometimes it was simply to get relief from the heat.

"I hope it won't get as hot as it did four years ago—July 1954," Nancy said when she called to check on me, and I had the kitchen window open, wishing for a morning breeze. "It reached one hundred and fifteen degrees, and more than a hundred folks died. It was just that hot."

The fall ushered in cooler temperatures and finally two boarders upstairs! Mr. Chestnut had been right when he said boarders help pay the rent. We now had extra money. And I was a college student.

The following summer, Henry took a week off from work to go back to Little Rock to visit our families.

We stayed a few days at the Beacons' house and the rest at my folks'. Now that I had graduated high school, Mama asked when they would have a grandbaby.

"Soon, I guess." She and Henry hadn't discussed extending their family.

Peggy had returned to Little Rock from Mississippi after graduation. She had a boyfriend, James. He attended Philander Smith College, so we went on a double date. I missed the old times.

Afterwards, we sat on my parents' front porch. We weren't ready to retire. Henry had his arm around my shoulders and pulled me close. He kissed my forehead. "I can tell you're happy."

"I am. This is familiar. Family, friends, places."

"Do you want to move back home?"

I whipped my head around and stared at my husband who looked ahead like he used to when he walked me home from school.

"If I said yes, would you be willing to move?" He nodded. "And if I said no, would you be disappointed?"

He didn't answer, so I asked him the same question. Henry shifted in the swing and squeezed my hand. "I married you to make you happy, and we can live everywhere, but I like the independence we have to make our own decisions. I still want to explore the world with you, and I don't think we can do that from here.

"Well, Mr. Beacon, it looks like St. Louis is our home." He hugged me tightly.

The next day, we packed up and drove back home to St. Louis.

Mr. Beacon was proud that Henry had decided to become a barber like his father. MaDear CC still possessed warm smiles and tight hugs.

She was glad we had followed her advice to move to a different neighborhood and rent to boarders for income.

Our Little Rock families were happy for us.

The next big celebration would be Henry's college graduation.

Chapter 26
All News Isn't Good News

Beatrice
PAST, the Ville Neighborhood, 1962

On May 13, 1962, my Henry graduated from Harris Stowe Teachers College with plans to teach at Samuel Cupples Elementary School in the Ville in the fall. It had taken him a year longer because he worked full-time and went to school part-time as me because we couldn't afford two tuitions.

I purposely shopped at Famous Barr to buy Henry another pair of Stacy Adams shoes for the occasion, hoping Orville would be my salesman. My old coworker wasn't there for me to boast that my husband was graduating from college.

My next gift to him, our parents, and even his ninety-seven-year-old grandmother who was determined to make the car ride to see her grandson receive his degree, was that I had all the symptoms as if I was expecting.

"I'm going to the doctor to confirm it." I rubbed my stomach as if I was swollen with a baby.

"We're going to have a baby!" Henry was beyond himself with excitement.

I hadn't seen my husband smile so wide since the day we were married.

It was a festive time. MaDear CC gave Henry three hundred dollars for the baby—if I was pregnant—and his graduation. He thanked her and immediately turned the envelope over to me for safekeeping.

At the beginning of June, our happiness was short-lived when Henry opened his mail after work. "It's an induction notice to report for duty." His jaw dropped, and torment was etched on his features. "I'm being drafted to Vietnam."

Henry put his arm around me, and we cried together. It was the first time I saw my husband shed tears.

"I don't want to have our baby without you."

"I don't either. The war has been going on for years, and since they didn't draft me after high school, I pushed it to the back of my mind. I'm twenty-four, so it's my time to serve."

Three weeks later, I said a tearful goodbye to my husband of four years. Mr. Chestnut said he would check on me to make sure I was okay. I'd never be okay without Henry. I wanted my husband.

I was lost without Henry. I couldn't return to school in the fall without my study partner. We always studied together. Even after I graduated from high school, I would quiz him. As a college student, he helped me with my homework.

Mama stayed with me for the first month that Henry was gone.

"You can always come home, Beatrice, while Henry is away," Mama suggested.

What would Henry want me to do?

What do I want from you? God whispered. *Stay.*

Why would God ask me that? Henry had become more involved in church than me. I showed up for attendance purposes.

"Plus, if I keep taking off, Mrs. Rothman might find someone else to clean her house, but you're more important than the money." Her kind eyes backed up her words.

"Thank you, Mama. I'll be all right."

The following month, I was admitted to City Hospital #2. Doctors said I had miscarried in the first trimester. No baby. No Henry. The nurse called Mr. Chestnut, whom I listed as next of kin because he was local. He sent a telegram to Henry's unit with the unfortunate news.

Mama came back before I was discharged from the hospital.

"What about Mrs. Rothman?" I didn't want Mama to lose her job because of me. I teared up and cried. I did a lot of that for days.

"I told her my daughter needed me, and I would be back as soon as you were okay."

Good for Mama because I hated that job for her. She stayed for two weeks.

Henry's mother, Mrs. Beacon, arrived to take over. I cried again with her. "MaDear CC sends her love and prayers. She wanted to travel, but she can't tolerate the ride anymore," my mother-in-law said.

They kept me from being alone, but all I wanted was my husband.

Chapter 27
Baby News

Victoria
PRESENT, Ferguson, Missouri, 2023

Deli's sniffs were louder than everybody else in the room.

All eyes zoomed in on Pace's guest as he wrapped his arm around her shoulders to comfort her.

Even Victoria was teary-eyed. She knew Grandma BB didn't have any children, but reading about her loss made her heart ache. Deli didn't know Grandma BB, so why was she crying?

Pace's consolation was as tender as their parents, aunts, and uncles.

Victoria had never seen Pace so protective of another woman outside of their family. Built like their father, he was tall and muscular. Pace possessed a quiet strength. Deli had to be special.

"Son," Parke's voice was steady, "is there something you want to tell us?"

Turning his attention away from Deli, he met their father's stare. He didn't blink with intimidation as their younger brothers would. "No, sir."

The room was still.

"All right." Grandma BB sliced the air with her booming voice. "I lost my baby, and she's crying. Somebody is going to have a baby, and it ain't me." She squinted at the aunties who said nothing.

Victoria exchanged looks with Kami. They weren't dating. Kami repented and rededicated her life back to God during her senior year in high school. Her sister was determined to stay in the safety of the Lord's arms and not go out with any man who didn't practice a Christian walk. Victoria, having surrendered to the Lord, too, tried to mimic Kami's footsteps, except for the dating part. That was not a temptation for her.

"Pace, if Deli isn't pregnant, what is the meaning of her emotions all over the place?" their father demanded.

Their father had stressed that none of them were to become single parents. They knew better than anyone about the consequences of unplanned pregnancies.

Getting to his feet, Pace didn't back down. He commanded everyone's attention. "Dad, I told you that I never wanted to father children outside of marriage. I've kept myself clean—"

Chip and Dale gasped in horror at Pace's admission.

"What?" Chip said. "No!"

Their eyes seemed to cross in disbelief. Dale began to stutter, but no distinguishable words came out. Chip had been married with three children. Per Grandma BB's gossip, Chip's wife kicked him out because of his cheating. Dale had never been married but had several children. They both were barely making a living because of child support payments, and they earned a ridiculous amount of money. During a trip to Las Vegas with a red hat society group, she met them while all three were playing slots in the casino.

Grandma BB had won big, but they had emptied their bank accounts. Feeling sorry for them, she befriended them, learned about their hardships, then she'd hired the pair as a widow's bodyguards. They lived in the guest apartments behind her house.

She said Henry would approve of them for her protection.

Pace slipped one hand in his pocket, a gesture he picked up from their father when he was about to impart wisdom or say something of importance. "I know it's a sin against God, but if I ignored that and indulged, how can I know whether I had produced a child if that relationship fell apart? What happens when the mother dies in a car crash and the boy has never met his father? What happens to the child? I won't have that." His voice cracked as he described his story.

Her brother wasn't showing disrespect as he continued, ignoring their father's pained expression. "I'll take care of my family like you have taught me, Dad, but if any woman carries my child, she will be my *wife*." He sat again and rested his arm over Deli's shoulders. The room went wild with applause. Their uncles Philip, Malcolm, and Cameron patted him on his back. Older cousins like Kidd and Ace were considered uncles too.

Kami, Victoria, and Pace were in the foster care system. Kami was rescued first. Pace next, then Victoria. If only Victoria had been rescued sooner, she might not have suffered at the hands of foster dads.

Parke waited his turn to show his affection. Once Pace was within reach, he wrapped him in a bear hug and kissed his jaw until her brother broke away, embarrassed.

"I'm sorry for what you experienced, son, but I'm glad you're mine. I can't change the past, but I plan to be with you until God takes me home."

With his emotions transparent on his face, Pace nodded and composed herself. "Deli," he said, reaching for her hand, "is doing her nurse residency in obstetrics and gynecology. She's had days when she has to comfort women who suffered trauma through miscarriages and stillbirths."

Deli's eyes were glazed. She faced Grandma BB with a gesture of a slight bow, and she said, "I'm sorry, Mrs. Beacon, for your loss."

"It's all right, chile. You call me Grandma BB."

Nobody called Grandma BB that endearment unless she instructed them.

"If you must know…" Queen stood with flair in her movements. With the grace of a dignitary, she lifted her chin. "Philip and I are expecting."

Grinning, Philip got to his feet and slipped his arm around her waist. Where Philip was a humble pastor, Queen was fierce and took no prisoners with people's nonsense. She was Victoria's hero as a strong Black woman.

They blushed from the round of congratulations that went around the room. Ace and Kidd hugged their sister and shook Philip's hand and slapped him on the back. The little ones immediately ran to pat her stomach.

Talise handed Ace their sleeping two-year-old daughter, Diamond Queen, and stood. "Ace and I are expecting too."

More congratulations were given as the sisters-in-law hugged each other.

"Ace and I are hoping for an Aaron Junior," Talise said.

Ace snaked his free arm around his wife's waist. "I'm not going to be the only Jamieson without a son."

Talise grunted. "I hope you get him this time because you might be."

A chorus of "whoas" filled the space.

This wasn't a sad occasion, after all, Victoria thought. The pure joy on Auntie's face made Victoria smile. Kami left Victoria's side to hug and kiss the expecting couples.

"How far along are you?" Cheney asked. "You're glowing, although you're not showing."

"Four months!" Queen beamed.

Cheney asked Talise the same.

"I'm almost three."

"That means I've got to wait five more months before I can die." Grandma BB squeezed her lips. "Yep."

Victoria burst out laughing. "I want you to live forever." She meant it. Once Queen had some breathing room, Victoria walked into her and Philip's embrace. "Congratulations, Auntie and Uncle."

There were lots of them in the Jamieson family, but she was the closest to her dad and Philip. They had impacted her life in ways she couldn't express.

Parke was patient while Victoria acted out her anger. Not once did he reject her, but she overheard him pray for her scars to be healed.

Philip knew the perfect words to say, being a pastor. Whenever she needed him to listen to her internal confusion, Philip was there to work through her anxiety and self-doubt. Queen was there, too, because Victoria avoided one-on-one with any man, even though she trusted him ninety-nine percent.

Her younger brothers, Chance and Paden, twelve and fourteen respectively—the only biological children of Parke and Cheney—spared her no mercy. They were annoying, but let someone try to disrespect her, and the two were ready to defend.

Victoria was about to get the program back on track when Chip brought in glasses of milk for Queen and Talise. Dale followed with cookies.

"It is not time for my repast," Grandma BB griped then grinned.

Chaos erupted again. This time it was among the little cousins who scrambled for their share of refreshments.

Victoria called for a thirty-minute intermission this time.

"At this rate, my funeral will take all day." Grandma BB huffed and snatched a cookie.

Chapter 28
Love Letters Are the Best Medicine

It was weeks before I received Henry's letter. The paper was puffed as if it hadn't been shielded from the rain. When I opened it and saw his smeared handwriting, I wondered if it had been soaked with his tears.

*I'm sorry, Beatrice and my unborn baby. I'm sorry...*He wrote *I'm sorry* ten times. And I cried each time.

The army will pay the hospital bill. Save the seventy-eight-dollar check they mail you every month, and when I come home, we'll buy a big house and have lots of babies. Take care of yourself, and write me every week. And I'll write back when I can.

I believe God's been whispering in my ear at night that I'll make it home. I hope so. Pray for me, Beatrice. Pray.

Love,

Your Husband

Henry's letters were comforting and heartbreaking. His absence made time stand still like a broken watch. How could I pray? How could I eat and sleep without him? If it weren't for my boarders who paid for Sunday dinners, I wouldn't cook.

Nancy called one morning after I ate my breakfast of juice and toast. I couldn't stomach more. "Hey. How are you feeling?"

"Better. Lonely. I decided to look for a job again. I know I should go back to school, but I can't. It's not in me. Henry was my motivation to study because we did it together."

"Beatrice, if you go to college, you can get a better job," Nancy insisted.

"I know, and I've been praying for my husband to come home whole. Some ladies at my church have husbands—or brothers and sons—away in the war. They've formed a weekly support group, and I go. It helps, but there are countless hours I need to fill with something of substance. At least you're working. Are they hiring?"

"The job at the insurance company was cut. I couldn't find anything else, and we needed the money, so I'm cleaning houses for now. You should see the inside of some of these homes. They're mansions."

Disgusted at our options, I bit my tongue not to offend my friend. "I have seen them. My mother has been cleaning one or two of them in Little Rock for as long as I can remember."

Closing my eyes, I could recall the tiredness in Mama's eyes and her swollen feet some days when she left Mrs. Rothman's house.

"It's been this way for Coloreds for a long time. I read in the newspaper a few years ago students at a North Carolina college protested segregation for Blacks and Whites at Woolworth counters. The sit-ins changed the policies. That's what we need is change everywhere," I said.

"Dr. Martin Luther King has been here twice telling Negroes to demand our civil rights. He spoke at two Baptist churches, even the Kiel Auditorium. Thousands packed the place to hear him. I went with my mother. Have you seen the weather lady on KSD-TV? I'm proud to see her—Dianne White, a Colored face—on television. The newspaper is starting to call us Negroes, probably because of Dr. King, I guess."

Miss White, who could pass as White like my Henry, was the exception to Coloreds getting good jobs. We were relegated to janitorial positions or peddling our wares up and down the streets, ringing bells.

Whatever it took to survive, we did it—selling fruits, vegetables, wood, coal, and even ice during the summer up and down the streets. "I was surprised to see her on television when I got here. I can't remember what she said because I was so busy looking at her. Little Rock wouldn't dare have that."

"During an interview, Miss White said it took four auditions before she was hired, but she gets angry calls at home and at work. I'm praying for her to keep that job."

I grabbed a piece of fruit from the bowl. Talking with Nancy was giving me an appetite. I washed it and took a bite. It was surprisingly tasty. "You sure know a lot of what's going on in the city," I joked.

"Can't afford to go to college, so I read everything and listen to White folks' conversations. Reverend John Hicks was elected to be the first Negro on the St. Louis school board. That could mean better education for us. Since city officials tore down our communities in Mill Valley Creek, then squeezed in more poor Negroes into Pruitt than it could hold while the poor Whites had Cochran projects, Attorney Frankie Freeman sued the St. Louis Housing Authority. We're making noise, sis."

Despite her circumstances, Nancy was encouraged and hopeful that better days were coming.

"My life is on hold until Henry comes home," I said.

"Your husband loves you and would want you happy while he was away. Do something that makes you happy. I hear Milton coming through the door now. Let me go and fix his lunch."

After I hung up the phone, I stared at it. What made me happy besides my husband? "Being busy, making money…"

I reminded myself how I got the job at Famous Barr. In the morning, I'd do the same.

The next day, I added determination to my bacon and eggs. I dressed in a suit I had purchased while I was an elevator girl at Famous Barr and had ten copies of my résumé done.

I caught the streetcar because Henry wouldn't want me to squeeze into a service car when there were possibly more men than women, especially without being able to sit on his lap.

The utility companies were my first stop: Southwestern Bell, Union Electric, and Laclede Gas Company. But I couldn't get past the security guards at those places without an appointment.

So, I left my résumé. Now I was glad I had some college coursework that amounted to one-and-a-half years. Mama and Henry had been right. I needed to finish and make them proud.

I returned discouraged and had three résumés left but no interviews.

No one was hiring us despite the want ads in the paper or posted in the windows. My mood changed when I got the mail and there was a letter from Henry.

I kicked off my shoes and stretched out on the couch to savor every morsel of Henry's letter as I carefully opened the envelope.

Hi Wife,

Thanks for your prayers, which are keeping us safe. Ted Kimble was injured today. He's from St. Louis, but he'll be okay. Fred Cummins graduated from Vashon before you. He helped save Ted. I'm okay. I love you and miss you so much. Thank you for your long letters. Try to be happy. I hope to get a leave for Christmas. That's a maybe.

You mentioned going home for Christmas, so you probably should go in case I can't make it.

Love you. Keep the letters coming.

Your Husband

I counted down the months until Christmas, I attended the support group at church and talked to my parents and Henry's family more often because they would accept my collect calls whenever I became lonely. But I never talked long.

For Thanksgiving, Mama and Papa drove up to spend the holidays with me before it got cold. The Beacons stayed behind with MaDear CC who wasn't feeling well.

Until Henry got drafted, I was never more curious about Papa's time in World War II. I needed to know what my husband was experiencing.

"But Papa, will Henry be okay?" I wanted to pull the curlers out of my hair in desperation to know. "I watch the news every evening, and all I hear about is more Americans have been killed. Were you scared? I know that's a silly question, but you're the only one who knows what war is like."

I was on the verge of tears as I pushed my dinner plate aside.

Papa rested his fork after finishing up a helping of pecan pie. "You feel alone, baby, even though you're surrounded by comrades. In Vietnam, I understand it to be you don't know who to trust. You question whether your life has meaning. You ask yourself if what you're doing will make a difference." He swallowed and looked past me. "You try to forget the death and destruction your eyes have recorded."

"My poor Henry." This time, I sobbed as Mama held me. Drained, I sat there quiet while Mama fixed up the couch for me to sleep. Papa had gone to my bedroom for the night.

"He'll be home, sweetie." Mama patted my hand.

During the rest of their stay, we shopped downtown, and they met Nancy and her husband, Milton. Mr. Chestnut and a lady friend came to visit too.

On Sunday morning, I hugged and kissed them goodbye.

I stopped applying for jobs but saved the money Henry sent home. The boarders helped to pay the bills. Come next year, I would go back to college. I would.

The week before Christmas, I cleaned our small house, put up decorations, and purchased coal from a street peddler to have plenty to heat up the rooms in preparation for Henry. I counted four days, three days, and finally two days before Christmas, and no husband.

Every day, I prepared dinner as if he would walk through the door. I went to bed every night bathed and perfumed after I prayed for Henry and other soldiers to come home safe.

Hours before Christmas, I heard the lock turn on the door, and it startled me. If someone was breaking in, I would scream, and my two upstairs boarders would come to the rescue. That was the agreement they made with Henry before he left in exchange for reduced rent.

My heart pounded with fear. There had been a few break-ins down the street. I wrapped my robe around me. I didn't have many options for weapons and I didn't have time to think. Grabbing my lead crystal jewelry box, which was heavy and a wedding gift, I cracked the door and peeked down the hallway. If I aimed right, I could knock him unconscious, blood his eye or crack some teeth.

A shadow.

I opened my mouth to scream loud and long.

Then I saw him—a man in uniform.

Our eyes connected at the same time. I threw the jewelry box on the bed and leaped into his arms. Henry cried, and I hugged him and whispered soothing words.

"I've missed you, Beatrice," he said over and over.

I peppered him with kisses as I patted his face, examining each inch. My handsome husband looked weary.

With all my strength, I squeezed his neck. "I've missed you so. Welcome home. Are you hungry? Want a hot bath—"

Henry silenced me with a kiss. "I want to dance. That's the first thing I want. Every night I went to sleep thinking about our dances."

He lifted me in the air and rested my bare feet on his army boots. Right there in the hallway, we danced until exhaustion hit him.

There was no strength for a hot bath or food. I undressed him, and we both slid under the covers.

That was the best night's sleep I'd had since before he left. Henry's tossing, turning, and mumbling "enemy" painted a picture in my mind of what my husband had experienced.

The next few days, he rested, and I didn't leave his side. It was the best Christmas ever as we wrote each other love letters.

Henry returned to his post a week later, and I hoped I was pregnant.

On Valentine's Day, it was confirmed when I experienced the same symptoms as before. I couldn't be more excited. I wrote Henry a love letter and drew babies all over it. I called my folks in Little Rock.

Mama came to see me. MaDear CC had been sickly of late, so she sent her love, and Mrs. Beacon stayed behind to see about her. I called MaDear CC with the news. She was happy, but her voice was weak.

The following month in March, MaDear CC passed away. I cried. She had become a part of me, calling me sometimes to check on me, sending gifts, and of course, wiring money that I didn't ask for. I loved her as if she were my own grandmother.

I wanted to travel to attend her funeral, but my parents forbid it, and the Beacons advised against it because the weather was cold, and I couldn't afford to get sick because of the baby.

The Beacons sent a telegram to Henry, and I wrote him a letter.

My Loving Husband,

The baby and I are doing fine. But I have sad news about our loving MaDear CC. She passed away. She lived a long time. I'm heartbroken. I loved her so much. Thank you for sharing her with me.

I listed the many things she'd taught me and gave me until I was tired.

A week later, I was admitted to Homer G. Phillips Hospital from the emergency room. Our baby didn't make it. Emotions swirled in my head as my vision blurred from the tears. My roommate on the other side of the curtain prayed for me.

The what-ifs began to twist my heart. What if I hadn't waited until I finished high school, would I have children by now? What if Henry knew I would lose his babies, would he have married me? What if he had gotten more rest?

By day three in the hospital, Mama was there.

Chapter 29
Looking for Trouble

Beatrice

PAST, the Ville Neighborhood, St. Louis, Missouri, Summer 1963

Henry's letters inspired me to live my life despite the disappointments.

I love you, babe, and I miss you. I don't think we're going to win this war. The enemy could be anywhere in the jungle or nearby. They hit us and run before we see what's coming.

I'm sorry to hear about losing our second baby. Neither time was I there to hold your hand. I'm sorry you had to be in the hospital longer this time. The military will pay the bill. I can't thank your mother enough for being there for you when I should be.

I don't know when I'll have another leave, but I'm praying it's soon. I have one more year to serve, and then I'll be discharged honorably.

I think stress is taking a toll on your body, Beatrice. Try to get some rest. Rest. Do something that makes you happy until I can make you happy.

Love you,

Your Husband

Not long after that, Nancy called early one morning with excitement in her voice that made me chuckle. "Beatrice, I took a day off from cleaning houses to go somewhere. Want to go with me?"

She had two children by now, and her mother-in-law loved to spend time with them.

"Sure. How should I dress?"

Nancy laughed. "Always with dignity. I may clean houses, but I don't have to dress like a domestic worker. I ride the bus looking as if I'm going to Famous Barr. When I get to Mrs. Bliss' house, I change. She's uppity and laughs at me. But that is my dignity. Can you drive?"

"Yep." I'd perfected the task and did well, but I usually caught the streetcar or bus downtown.

My friend arrived almost an hour later dressed in a brown suit, lipstick, and coiffured hair.

I drove to Cardinal and Franklin avenues to an old house next door to Peoples Undertaking Parlor. I parked and looked at Nancy. "Who lives here?"

She smiled. "It's a meeting place for Young Democrats. This is the Jordan Chambers' Democratic Club headquarters."

"Wow. That's a mouthful."

"Yep. It also has meeting rooms, a lounge, a bar, entertainment, and a kitchen where they sell food in case we get hungry while we're here."

Nancy opened her door, but I hadn't moved. She turned back and looked at me. "What? Aren't you coming?"

"We're both married." I took a deep breath and then exhaled. "I'm not going into a lounge or a bar while Henry is away."

She laughed. "I love Milton too. He's been here when he wasn't too tired. We're going to the meeting room where newly registered Democrats are struggling to get other Negroes to register. Speaking of, have you registered to vote?"

I shook my head. "Henry and I never discussed it, so I hadn't given it much thought."

"Then I'm getting you registered. It's time." Nancy clapped. "Yay."

We got out and walked inside. The street was quiet. Once the doors opened, a different world came alive with a whirlwind of activity. Music played inside a bar to our right, but Nancy looped her arm through mine and steered me to the left where there were indeed people who looked younger than my twenty-two years.

I connected with the passion I saw on their faces. "Wow."

"Yep. C'mon." Nancy continued to drag me into a room that was the size of the combined rooms Henry and I rented from Mr. Chestnut.

Nancy introduced me to people she knew. The first question a woman asked me was, "Are you registered to vote?"

I was ashamed to say, so my quietness spoke for me.

"You've come to the right place. We'll tell you what you need to do." Her name was Peggy, and she reminded me of my friend back home.

Everyone took their seats as a man about my father's age tapped on his microphone. "Good afternoon, troops. Let's start off with roll call. How many people has everyone registered since last week?"

"That's Jordan Chambers. He's in charge of this group," Nancy mumbled. "We call him Pops Chambers."

"Four," a young woman yelled.

"Eight!" A young man jumped up.

From there, it was a pep rally of sorts, and I felt a charge.

"Remember, every Negro should register on their twenty-first birthday. If we can go to war over there, we should have a voice *here*."

The cheers were deafening. Nancy laughed as I stood next to her and clapped.

"Somebody should be at Harris Stowe Teachers College every day. Knock on doors. Wherever you see us, get the message out to go register to vote. Ask everyone, young or old."

Speechless, the only thing I could do was breathe.

Nancy nudged me. "You okay?"

"Yes. Hearing him speak and seeing people around my age, is breath-taking. It's jumpstarting my emotions."

"Do we have our assignments?" He scanned the room to make sure he had their commitment. "Remember, stay in school. If you're not in school, go to night school. We have to be overqualified for the jobs we want."

When the meeting ended, Nancy made a personal introduction to Pops Chambers. "Welcome, Miss Beacon." He smiled.

"It's Mrs. Beacon."

"Mrs. Beacon, I apologize." He nodded. "Are you registered?"

"She will be after today," Nancy answered.

"Good. Are you in school, or do you have little ones who need you?"

I swallowed the lump in my throat. I was at the age when everyone assumed I had a child or two. Maybe I'd have one late like Mama had me. "No…no babies yet. I started college but didn't finish."

He frowned, not hiding his disapproval. "Go back and finish what you started. I don't care how long it takes.." He excused himself and turned to others vying for his attention.

The last time I started back to school, I miscarried. That won't happen this time with Henry worlds away.

Nancy and I walked back to my car. She was non-stop chatter as I drove her to her apartment. "What do you think?"

Grinning, I glanced at her. "Thinkin' I'm re-enrolling in college."

"And?" Nancy leaned closer and cupped her ear.

"Register to vote." I sighed at my new commitment. "I'll come back."

After Nancy celebrated with a hearty clap, she listed Pops Chambers' impressive résumé. "He owns the undertaking parlor next door to that building. He's the Democratic committeeman for the Nineteenth Ward, owns a club, and gets jobs for Negroes in state and city offices." She ran out of breath. "Girl, my head is spinning."

Pops Chambers' accomplishments had me speechless. I parked in front of Nancy's apartment, and we hugged goodbye.

Walking into my home, I was too excited to eat leftovers. Within the hour, I sat in the kitchen to write Henry about my day at the Young Democratic building. Four pages later, I ended with, *Your Loving Wife.*

The next day, I did what I said. I registered for three classes in the fall. Henry wrote he was excited for me and that the army would help pay for school, even for spouses. I had no excuse now. Then I took the streetcar downtown to the Board of elections building. There were more Negroes filling out paperwork to vote than Whites. I stepped up to the clerk and requested my paperwork too.

Pop Chambers would be proud of me. I was proud of me.

At the next Young Democrats meeting, Pops Chambers introduced a White man as the national chairman of the St. Louis Committee for Racial Equality.

A tall, slender man, Attorney Charles Oldham, appeared to be in his forties. He spoke about the group's past efforts to integrate lunch counters at Stix, Baer, and Fuller department stores. "We must continue to battle discrimination with civil disobedience."

Not only was he an eloquent speaker, but he was fighting for causes that would help Coloreds, or Negroes. He was captivating.

"A few days ago," Attorney Oldham continued, "the media reported a quarter of a million people marched on the Washington Mall for civil rights for Blacks. My question for you is what are we going to do here in St. Louis?"

I had just adjusted from being called Colored all my years to becoming a Negro. Now, we'd advanced to Blacks. I guess that is our color, but the different terms to describe me was confusing. I was an American.

The room was quiet as we stared at him for the answer.

Slipping his hand into a pants pocket, his stance reminded me of one of my college professors during a lecture. "We're planning for nonviolent demonstrations at area businesses we patronize who won't hire more Blacks."

Nancy would hate that she missed this because she didn't have a babysitter after work. I was a regular myself, but I had made friends with others besides Peggy #2.

My mind drifted to my husband. When Henry answered my letter about the Young Democrats meetings, he simply said, *Have fun, but don't get into any trouble.* After reading my four-page letter, I was surprised that was all Henry had to say as he wrote about Viet Cong being guerrilla fighters and how dangerous it had become.

Thanks for your prayers, sweetheart, because I can hear God's whispers in my sleep and you keep writing me.

Love Your Husband,

Henry

"If you're available to participate," Attorney Oldham stirred me from my musing, "join us tomorrow morning at ten a.m. in front of Jefferson Bank and Trust where many of us hold accounts. Our demand is to hire more Blacks besides the receptionist and a male messenger."

Jefferson Bank? That was Henry's and my bank. I had seen protesters on television, but it was exhilarating to be one as I marched in front of Jefferson Bank and Trust.

That same bank wouldn't hire me or Nancy.

Sorry, Henry. I'm about to get in trouble.

School didn't start for a week, so I had seven days to protest. The next morning, I rode the streetcar to Washington Avenue. Riders were staring out the windows at the commotion. I stopped off Jefferson and Washington and hurried across the street where organizers had large poster board signs for protestors. I accepted one and joined the line that quietly walked from one end of the bank to the other.

Black doctors and lawyers were among the protestors. "This is serious," I mumbled as I thought about what Pops Chambers had said about helping others get jobs.

Day one brought no changes. Day two brought reporters. Day three drew an even bigger crowd of demonstrators and the police.

Our demands were simply to hire bank clerks. I thought back to when Nancy and I became friends. It was after applying at this bank on the same day, only to be turned down. Our protest grew larger and spilled inside as we blocked entrances. Resistance should have been my middle name because I felt I was born for this—making demands.

Dr. Martin Luther King, Jr., had us fired up with the March on Washington. He made us believe that as Americans, we had rights.

I was impressed with this Alderman William Clay, a Negro, who sent a survey to major employers throughout St. Louis. The letter asked for the headcount of Negroes on their payroll, and the information would be used to form a fair employment policy.

The companies' honesty caused a fallout that showed their prejudices and proof on paper of what we were denied.

More than thirty thousand employees worked in breweries, department stores, insurance companies, banks, and phone and utility companies, but less than a thousand Negroes were on their payrolls. Janitors and a sprinkling of receptionists were the exceptions.

Companies had to scramble to ease the damage caused to the image they tried to portray.

Nancy joined me on the picket line when she was off.

The protests continued as I started my classes. While on campus, I encouraged my fellow classmates to register to vote. When my classes were over for the day, I protested. I believed in the cause of making a change.

Mr. Clay and others, including me, were jailed as the demonstrations continued. It was liberating in a way. To speak up and be heard regardless of the consequences.

I don't know if it was retaliation or not, but Alderman Clay was jailed the longest of all of us. I only spent two days before Mr. Chestnut bailed me out but I was willing to do more time. For me, contempt was my taste for freedom.

I expected a tongue-lashing, but Henry's uncle only had kind words. "You're young. Prepare to fight for your civil rights for the rest of your life," he said and drove me home.

Chapter 30
More to Lose Than a War

Beatrice

PAST, the Ville Neighborhood, St. Louis, Missouri, Spring and Summer 1964

When I wrote Henry that I had been jailed for a cause that I believed in, he wasn't so supportive. Actually, he was downright mad.

Mrs. Beacon, my wife, I should have known that I was in trouble when he addressed me formally like a bill collector.

Beatrice, my heart dropped when Mr. Chestnut sent me a telegram that my precious, beautiful wife had been arrested and jailed for two days!!!

Being away from you is a form of punishment, a prison. I don't want you locked away. I'm trying to stay alive so I can come back to you in one piece. Please. Please. Please...

I counted the number of "pleases" too, and my heart softened.

Continue to fight for our civil rights because we need it, but from afar. DO NOT put yourself in harm's way, love. I know you paid Mr. Chestnut back, but don't use any more of our money for bail!!!

Henry had a lot of exclamation points in that letter too. He reprimanded me like Papa had when I was a child with the number of exclamation marks.

My husband fussed at me in that letter from many worlds away. I wrote him back that I loved him despite his yelling at me. I also told him jail time was worth it because Alderman Clay did a survey that exposed the truth. Blacks made up forty percent of the city's population, and about the same percentage of Black males were unemployed. *When you come back home, I want there to be jobs for you.*

I almost promised him I wouldn't get into any more trouble that would land me in jail again but I didn't. We had rights. I had rights and I planned to exercise them.

The protests lingered for seven months from the heat of summer, the snow of winter, to the spring rain into1964. Congress for Racial Equality, known as C.O.R.E., had accomplished its goal. More Blacks got better-paying jobs.

Three months later, in July 1964, exactly two years after Henry was drafted, he came home with an honorable discharge. We hugged and kissed through my tears of pure happiness.

His return was a reason for me to put that last semester of college on hold again.

I know I had changed while he was gone, and Henry seemed to be a different man too. Although he was only two years older, the war had aged him. Gray strands were sprinkled above his ears. New frown lines across his forehead never relaxed, even when he was asleep.

Something happened to my husband. He was broken.

He had seen the death of Vietnamese men. "Some of our soldiers had chopped-off heads and heaped them in a pile as if they were souvenirs. Disgusting." Henry scrunched his nose. "I hope this war ends soon because the United States has the firepower, but those fighters on the ground and in the jungles are ruthless. They used women and children as guinea pigs to defeat us." He choked and held his head down. "We had to kill them, too, to keep them from killing us."

I didn't interrupt while he processed the war, but I rubbed his back slowly in rhythmic strokes. What were the right words to say? I called my mama many nights when the rates were cheaper, despite knowing she had to rise early to clean Mrs. Rothman's house.

"Beatrice, listen to him, but don't judge him for his actions. Your papa and Henry are peaceful men. They were under orders to kill or be responsible for the death of dozens in their unit. The middle is a hard place to be in." She yawned. "Keep praying for him and be patient. He may never be the same, but you are his safe place."

Henry may never be the same? I took her words to heart because Papa said very little about his time in World War II until he went to the barbershop where he and other men boasted of their bravery.

Me waiting for Henry to come home so we could mourn the deaths of our precious two babies together didn't seem as important anymore. We both had mourned enough, even though we were apart.

I rose early to fix big breakfasts and pamper him like he was my baby. He loved me for the treatment, and I loved him back.

"I want us to move on because despite being on the same side to win a war over there, here I can't win any respect for my bravery. Slaves who fought in the Civil War and Revolutionary War earned their freedom. I heard the protests got more companies to hire us, but I think I'd rather work for myself. Those businesses were forced to do right, but it wasn't in their hearts."

When I questioned him, he explained, "I'm going to open a barbershop on Grand, train barbers to work for me, then open another here in this area."

"That's the Henry Beacon I know." I squeezed his neck and kissed his cheek.

He swung me around to sit on his lap. "Thank you for managing our money and taking care of our boarders. I like what you did to our home, but it's time to move."

"Huh? Move? We live in the Ville where Black doctors, lawyers, and teachers are our neighbors. Homer G. Phillips Hospital is here to treat us. Most White hospitals won't. Tandy Community Center and Park is here. While you were gone, I'd walk to the park and sit to think and pray you would come home soon. I feel safe here. Our world is here," I tried to reason with my husband.

Henry wouldn't budge. When had he become so stubborn? Now he was too eager to have it his way.

"White folks were moving out, and Blacks are moving across the Grand bridge to live. I saw a mansion on Washington Boulevard near Sarah for sale. Whites are fleeing around here as if they're in a war against us, and we're buying it! We'll have more rooms to rent to more boarders. And we're going to travel. Life is short. First, I want you to finish school. If anything happens to me—"

I pressed my finger against his lips to shush him. They were soft. "Nothing is going to happen to you. You've served your time for our country. Now, it's our time to catch up on our anniversaries."

Henry kissed my lips. "That's what I want too—to give you the world and see the world."

One thing he hadn't shown excitement about was having a baby. Had the war affected him so much that he didn't want a family? I didn't ask because I feared his answer.

When I returned to college to complete my teaching degree, like before Henry left, he helped me study and quizzed me.

"This feels right. Maybe that's why I wasn't committed to school because you weren't here with me to study."

He kissed my nose. "I'm here now."

Henry rented an abandoned storefront to set up Beacon's Barbershop and hired three barbers. My husband charged them a commission on their weekly earnings as he had seen done at Taylor's Barbershop, which his dad eventually bought. When his father offered to come help for a couple of weeks, Mrs. Beacon tagged along too. It was good to see my in-laws happy that Henry had come back safely, but it felt odd for MaDear CC not to be with them.

Within a month, the barbershop had a steady flow of customers, and Henry had to hire two more barbers.

For our sixth anniversary, Henry gave me an expensive box of assorted chocolates.

He shrugged. "You're supposed to get chocolate on our sixth anniversary, and since I've given you chocolate before, I wanted this to be special." We shared a kiss, then he took me to the three-story house on Washington Boulevard that he raved about. Could we afford this?

The foyer was twice the size of our first place, which consisted of two rooms. My heels echoed against immaculate oak wood floors as we walked through the hallowed halls. Henry folded his arms and grinned as I spun around. "This *is* a mansion. The crystal chandelier had to weigh a hundred pounds. The banister was thick oak wood. The railings were an endless coil climbing to the upper floors.

"Who lived here?"

"Some rich White man. It has thirteen bedrooms and fourteen baths. It's three floors. We can live on the first floor where we'll have a kitchen, two bedrooms, dining…" Henry gave me a tour.

"This is bigger than Mr. Chestnut's."

"It's almost eleven thousand square feet."

"Wow. Who lent us money to buy it?"

"Can you believe Jefferson Bank and Trust? We can do this, Beatrice. MaDear CC willed us money, plus my military pay, and we can live off the rent from our boarders."

We laughed. The same bank I had protested in front of had given a Black man a loan for a house that was meant to be cleaned by him, not owned.

"Wait right here." Henry left me and disappeared into one of the rooms.

"Okay." Since there was no furniture, I sat on the stairs. This place was eerily huge.

Henry returned with a picnic basket, and we retraced the path back to the living room where a large rug was the sole occupant. We sat on it. "To you, Mrs. Beacon." We toasted, then he pulled out a hot container with fixings for two.

He said grace, and as we ate, we came up with a plan to hire a cook to supply meals to at least eight boarders.

When we were about to share dessert, I said, "I have a surprise for you, husband. I don't need to write a letter and tell you…I'm pregnant."

Tears fell from both of our eyes. The time had come for us to mourn as we cried for the babies we'd lost and the one that was growing inside of me. We decided not to tell our families yet, because of the prior miscarriages.

Six weeks later, we moved into our boarding house mansion. We planned to celebrate Thanksgiving dinner with a party for our families and friends.

The celebration didn't happen.

I miscarried for the third time.

Since our mothers didn't know, Henry and I accepted children weren't for us.

"I know you wanted babies that look like you."

He held my hand as I laid in the hospital bed. "I want you more. Children grow up and leave, but you and I have each other until the end, BB."

My husband had never called me BB before. It reminded me of MaDear CC, except I might never become a mother or a grandmother. The nickname was an endearment.

"And we're going to travel across the state—the country—and see the world. I heard some of the fellas in my unit talk about Paris, and it's the place for Negroes—Blacks—to go. They'll treat us with respect." His handsome face lit up with wonder. "We are going to do things most couples can only imagine."

His dreams comforted me as my womb healed for the third time.

Our families drove to St. Louis for Thanksgiving. There was plenty of room. We had bedroom furniture on layaway for each boarder's bedroom but opened a charge card to buy new furniture for our living area on credit.

While the women prepared dinner, Henry gave the men an extensive tour, including Mr. Chestnut who boasted that he taught us well.

And he had. Boarders filled the city as the population swelled from folks moving away from the Jim Crow South.

I was relieved that Mama and Mrs. Beacon didn't ask about whether there was baby news. Maybe they sensed my recent loss and that I was mourning behind my smiles.

Henry opened the second Beacon Barbershop in our old Ville neighborhood.

The boarders were filling up rooms in our new place. Life was good for us despite the losses we'd suffered.

In the spring of the following year, I graduated from Harris Stowe Teachers College with my teacher's degree. It had been a long process with many starts and stops in between.

I didn't want to make a big fuss about it, but Henry said we had to celebrate what I had accomplished. What had I accomplished? The one thing Henry and I both wanted was a baby. How could we fill the void without one?

Henry seemed to be okay with our fate. I doubted I ever would be. For my husband's sake, I pretended to move past our heartaches.

Funny that Henry didn't teach but preferred to open a business. I had tried to work as a business professional, but my tolerance for stupidity was low. Maybe nurturing other people's children would better suit me.

The St. Louis Board of Education said I couldn't teach at Vashon or Sumner High School without an advanced degree and more experience. The elementary or middle schools were my options. Fear gripped me. "Would the small children remind me of what I didn't have?"

Henry must have picked up on my hesitation. "BB, those children that come to school need nurturing. You give them much more than love." He prayed for me. That was the first time I'd heard him do that.

I slapped fear in the face and applied for a position at one of the middle schools.

Turned out to be a perfect fit in the fall. There were so many of them. They were eager to learn and looked to me to have all the answers.

Seemed like my hair turned grayer after each miscarriage. Now, most of it was silver. Henry loved it and called me BB more. Nancy always complimented me, but behind my back, some of the students called me Grandma. It was hurtful from those children who were unruly while an honor from the children who gave me hugs as an endearment when I welcomed them to class in the mornings.

Some of those children were pranksters, and it seemed like every school had a Trudy Pepperidge, and I had today in my sixth-grade class.

Donna Coleman was mean-spirited and influenced others to follow her lead. When I got wind that she planned to beat up another student who was smarter and shorter in stature, I had a plan.

Before the final bell rang, I walked into the principal's office. "I need a folding chair." The woman looked older than MaDear CC and was stern with the children.

"Why?" Mrs. Thomas asked.

"There's going to be a fight after school, and I want to referee." I shrugged.

"What?" Mrs. Thomas became frantic, which was surprising because she was not easily rattled. "Mrs. Beacon, we are supposed to intervene, not encourage aggressive behavior."

"That's exactly what I plan to do."

Mrs. Thomas frowned and rubbed her temple. "I may have to retire after this school year."

"It's about to go down soon, so I don't have much time to explain," I urged the principal who did everything by the book.

"Go, but I'll be watching you!"

The crowd was forming in the back of the school grounds. Taking off my heels, I hurried toward them, dragging the chair.

"Let me through." I nudged my way to get a front row seat. I unfolded the chair and sat. I should have brought popcorn. "So, what's going on here?"

"I was just talking to Christy." Donna gave me an angelic smile with her hands behind her back.

Her victim, Christy Bailey, didn't hide the fear in her eyes. "No, she wasn't. They all were going to jump me." Her lips trembled.

"Don't worry about it, honey. If she or anyone touches you, they will return to their elementary school on Monday," I bluffed but they didn't know that. Folding my arms, I crossed one leg over a knee. "All right. Who wants to take a swing?"

"That's stupid!" Donna stomped her foot. "I'm going to tell my mama what you said." She marched away with only a handful of her friends following her.

"You do that." I *hmmmph*ed.

"Thank you, Grandma BB," the girl said with tears in her eyes. Only students who stayed after school were granted permission to call me that.

"You're welcome." Standing, I folded my chair, then led Christy back to school and called her mother.

Mrs. Thomas met me at the door. She patted her chest. "What did you say?"

I shrugged. "Oh, that whoever gave the first lick will go back to elementary school. I hope that wouldn't have been Christy. But you never know with them quiet one when they're back against the wall."

The principal laughed. "Clever, but you know we can't do that."

"They don't know that. BB is the queen of dares but sometimes, I wish someone would challenge me so they can see what I'll do."

It wasn't the end of the story. The next morning, Donna's mama, a short heavyset woman, came to the classroom with her. I welcomed the challenge.

"Mrs. Beacon, my daughter tells me you threatened to send her a grade back. Why?" Her nostrils flared.

"Middle school is not for bullies. It's childish behavior that needs to be addressed at home and in younger grades. Donna is struggling anyway because her attention is not on the lesson. I suggest you speak with her at home. Otherwise, I am that teacher who will send her back."

Mrs. Coleman's mouth dropped, and she blinked but said nothing, so I continued, "I'm a pro at conflict resolution and have the jail record to prove it."

The mother turned to her daughter. "Donna, do what she says, because if what she says is true, I'll whup you myself." She lifted a brow, and Donna blinked a tear away.

For the rest of the school year, I had the best behaved classroom. I had found my calling.

On the weekends, Henry and I frequented Pops Chambers' Riviera Club. Sometimes we double-dated with Nancy and Milton. Whenever Henry became withdrawn about the Vietnam War, which was still raging, I suggested he visit his army buddies. He did. Henry would come back with a smile and chocolates.

Sundays were reserved for church where Henry was more active. He and other veterans seemed to bond. Washington Tabernacle Church served its purpose while Henry was away. Now that he was back, my prayers were answered.

Drives through Forest Park led us to venture out to White neighborhoods that were forbidden to anyone who wasn't White or domestic help.

Finally, we were able to buy tickets to see a movie at the Fox Theatre, which was even spelled differently from our Black theaters. The majestic structure that hosted venues was a reminder of segregation in the South, which symbolized the nicer things in life were for Whites versus Blacks could only dream about them. But here we were inside and we didn't care what was showing.

Soon, we set our eyes on the large homes in Ferguson, Missouri. They reminded me of Mrs. Rothman's house Mama cleaned, intimidating structures like plantations.

People say money talks. Not all the time. It didn't open doors in neighborhoods that didn't want us. Jefferson Bank and Trust refused us a home loan in Ferguson, although we'd never missed a payment.

We knew all about redlining banks practices. We were not deterred.

Because of their secret covenants not to sell their homes to Black families, I contacted Marian Oldham. She and her White husband were part of the protestors at Jefferson Banks. She referred us to Gateway Bank on Union Boulevard. Two men had raised five hundred thousand dollars to become the first Black-owned bank in St. Louis city and the state of Missouri. They gave loans to Blacks when others wouldn't.

Henry and I made an appointment.

If redlining didn't hold back unwanted neighbors, home builders had attached deeds to properties that forbid the seller from selling their homes to anyone who wasn't White. Again, Marian came to the rescue, and she suggested using the same White couple who had been the "front person" for her and her husband to buy a home. Not only were Blacks unwelcomed but so were mixed couples.

We contacted her friends and worked through the legal process.

All the scheming didn't seem to matter. On April 4, 1968, I was teaching my six graders history when we received the news Dr. Martin Luther King, Jr., had been assassinated.

Five days later, Papa died suddenly of cardiac arrest. That hurt worse than losing my babies. Henry and I called off the deal. I didn't care about that stupid house.

Chapter 31
The Truth Hurts

Victoria
PRESENT, Ferguson, Missouri, 2023

Through her own blurred vision, Victoria stopped reading. There wasn't a dry eye throughout Grandma BB's master bedroom. The children were wiping away their parents' tears.

Wow. No question Grandma BB had been denied so much in life—jobs, housing, babies, and loved ones. But she had overcome those obstacles.

Grandma BB's life came alive in the obituary. She shushed everyone. "That was more than fifty years ago. Some things have changed. Other things appear to change on the surface, but if you dig deep enough, the hate is there. For Henry and me and other Blacks, 1968 was a bad year. Papa and Dr. King died in April. Bobby Kennedy, who tried to help Blacks, was killed in June. Henry's father passed by the end of that year from cancer." Grandma BB paused. "That's in the obituary."

The raw emotions were too much like a funeral. Victoria had to turn this around. What other sad facts would be revealed in this final draft that she didn't know about?

Victoria didn't want to do this anymore. Who does a dry run of their own funeral to hear what others will say about them? *What would someone say about me?*

"You okay?" Kami appeared at Victoria's side.

"Nope." Victoria shook her head and shove the papers in her sister's hand. "You take over. I'm feeling queasy in my stomach."

Kami hugged her, then took center stage. "Okay. Let's bring it back, family," she said, then she glanced at the sheet.

Cameron's twin son, Gabriel, raised his hand. "Cousin Kami, this is getting boring. Can you tell us another story?" He twisted his lips and rested his chin on his hand.

"Come here." Grandma BB held out her arms, and Gabriel came for her hug. "Paden, why don't you take the little ones to the playroom? They don't need to hear the next part anyway."

"Yes, ma'am," Paden said and gathered his younger cousins while MJ, Malcolm's son, helped, until only the adults remained.

Standing out in the hall, Victoria swallowed. Maybe she should have gone to the playroom with the children. She'd read ahead and knew what was coming.

Chapter 32
Living The Best Life

Henry
PAST, Ferguson, Missouri, 1970s

I steered my riding mower over my acre-and-a-half lawn in the upper class section of Ferguson. Beatrice and I were happy despite life's disappointments.

Neighbors who didn't flee to westward suburbs had a taste of living on the same block with Blacks. I waved at a neighbor, Mr. Jefferson, who honked his horn as he turned the corner onto North Elizabeth Road.

"Hi, Papa Beacon," Bryan yelled as he sped on his bicycle down the sidewalk. His mother, Kathie, shook her head and waved.

I grinned and yelled back. "Slow it down, partner."

Papa Beacon. The name was sweet, even though I wasn't anyone's grandpa. My hair color matched my wife's—gray and white in my late thirties. Beatrice, my BB, said I was more handsome and distinguished, even though I had packed on the pounds. She was just as beautiful as that day forty-something years ago I saw her in that barbershop in Little Rock.

No good thing have I withheld from you, the Lord whispered. *Read Psalm 84:11.*

Children aren't a good thing? I frowned, wondering what God meant.

My will is perfect, Henry! the Lord thundered. *Continue reading My Word in Psalm 84.*

Our Darst Road property had been our second attempt to integrate the Whites-only suburbs in the St. Louis County neighborhood. Residents had put up physical barricades after the domestic workers went home to their nearby all-Black Kinloch and Berkeley communities.

This big house was BB's gift, even if the Lord never allowed my wife to have a baby. It wasn't the biggest house on the block, but it was among the biggest—a story-and-a-half bungalow with three dormers to show the neighbors we had money. The dormers reminded us of our humble beginnings in St. Louis in Mr. Chestnut's place.

We had the money to afford it. I owned and operated two barbershops while Beatrice taught school—middle at first and now elementary school.

Being around the children kept her happy as she would come home and tell what some students had tried to get over on her in class. After facing the racism while serving in Vietnam, my mindset had changed. I wanted to be *the* boss. A businessman.

Money from boarders yielded a profit, and we learned how to invest the inheritance MaDear CC left us from Pops Chambers.

My grandmother had been on my mind lately. I missed her warm hugs, gentle smiles, and soft voice. Maybe because I didn't have closure decades ago when she passed while I was away. She would be proud of what BB and I had accomplished. She wanted the best for me.

Beatrice never got pregnant again. Secretly, I had come to terms with not having children because I couldn't bear her suffering through another loss. Education was a good fit for Beatrice, my BB. She thrived on teaching young minds while thwarting bullies.

As the years raced by, we had become successful business owners. Success made our dreams come true. I tried to follow the guidelines for the anniversary gifts the first ten years of our marriage, but the tenth- and eleventh-anniversary lists didn't make any sense: tin, aluminum, or steel. We ditched the list that continued to sixty years. BB and I were going for seventy-five years since we married so young.

I didn't hold back from buying her lace and jewelry—pearls, rubies, diamonds, crystals. She will always be my young bride. That thought made me grin.

In turn, BB liked to shop—for me. My suits and shoes were her expertise. And I was always stylish—always.

We traveled the world and still penned love letters to each other, leaving them on pillows, in the bathrooms, or on the kitchen table with our bacon and eggs. We were living our best life.

Chapter 33
World Travelers

Henry
PAST, Ferguson, Missouri, mid-1990s

I was a proud homeowner as I admired the landscaping that BB and I did ourselves. After parking my riding mower in the garage, I walked to see my wife cruising down our street in her new Cadillac DeVille. She turned and glided into the driveway. BB parked and stepped out beaming, with shopping bags dangling in both hands.

I walked to her car and kissed her. "Good afternoon, wife."

"Same to you, husband." Her eyes sparkled.

Chuckling, I towered over my beauty and grinned. "What you got for me now?"

She lifted a brow and twisted her teasing lips. "What makes you think this is for you?"

I pointed to the men's garment bag from Rozell's Suits. "And I'm sure that shoe box is for me."

"You're too smart for not being a teacher," she teased, then glanced around. "The yard looks amazing. The grass is luscious and green. It makes my spring perennials sing."

Taking the bags, I trailed her into the house, entering through the breezeway.

"I've got a surprise for you." I walked ahead and cut through the kitchen into the study. Opening the desk drawer, I pulled out the envelope, then went to the heath room where Beatrice was slipping the suit out of the bag. Rust with gold pinstripes. My wife had good taste.

BB was methodical as she opened the shoebox and displayed the shoes against the suit. Two-toned brown leather and alligator skin. I wouldn't buy two-tone shoes for myself, but when my wife purchased them, I sported them proudly.

"Ready for the first dance?" I asked.

"Always."

I kicked off my work boots and slid my feet into my new shoes. Comfortable. I waited for BB to remove her heels, and I spied the red polish I'd watched her brush on her toes a few days earlier. Once she steadied her feet on top of my shoes, BB rested her head on my chest and closed her eyes.

Seconds later, we danced around the room to our own rhythm. This was our thing; our private moment to cherish all the memories we had made over the years. "Guess where I'm taking you this summer when school is out to celebrate our fortieth wedding anniversary?"

"*Hmmm.* Let's see, we've gone to Alaska, Greece, Spain, Turkey, Brazil…"

I laughed. She could remember in detail each location we had vacationed. "Let me stop you."

"Just don't stop dancing." She snuggled deeper into my chest. "This is so relaxing. I've always loved doing this since our first dance at the prom, but I wouldn't trade this for dance lessons."

"Me either." Holding her firmly, I dipped Beatrice backward. "Still guessing? I think we've gone to twelve countries—"

"Fourteen," she corrected me.

I laughed, loving her more than anything. "Yes, teacher. Well, Amsterdam, Netherlands, will make fifteen."

Her head popped up, and her eyes were wide with excitement. "Ever since we'd returned from Ghana and viewed the slave castle, my interest had been piqued about other places that played a part in the transatlantic slave trade. Amsterdam is another one of those places."

"You're sounding like the magnificent teacher you are. I'm glad you approve, Mrs. Beacon. As soon as we get back, I'll start planning our fiftieth."

The following Friday, I checked on the property on Washington Boulevard. We no longer had boarders but had converted the space into a bed-and-breakfast and hired a couple to live on site and manage it.

Next, I checked on the goings-on at the two barbershops before meeting my army buddies at White Castle. Not for the gas burgers as the locals called the bite-sized hamburgers, but for its rich blend of coffee and the camaraderie with my army buddies.

I pulled into the parking lot of our meeting spot at the Natural Bridge location. Tim and Fred were already there, standing outside their vehicles talking.

I parked my truck and walked toward them with a grin. We all sported our black Vietnam Veteran ball caps with the American flag and banded eagle emblem on top.

"How's it going, old man?" I teased and shook Tim's hand.

He pumped it back. "You got more white hair than me, buddy." He patted me on my back.

Fred, the other veteran's usual gripping handshake was weak and unsteady. He was thinner too. "Looking good, boss," he said.

"Glad you could join us this time, buddy." I frowned at his weight loss, but he hadn't lost his proud stride.

We walked into White Castle, found our normal hangout in the back corner, then ordered our large coffees and apple pies.

Beatrice would have a fit about me having rich snacks before dinner in a few hours, but she was still at the elementary school, so I could indulge all I wanted despite her protests.

"How's that wife of yours?" Fred asked as we took our seats at the table.

"Beautiful as ever." I grinned, happy to be married as long as we were. "Coming up on forty years." Some war veterans didn't have a good track record with marriages, but BB and I meant "until death do we part." She gave me space to process my thoughts whenever I withdrew from her.

Fred's first wife died about fifteen years ago, and he'd divorced his second wife last year. Tim married late after returning from Vietnam. He and Callie had been married for twenty-five years and had five children.

As we sipped from our coffee cups, Tim showed us photos of his three grandchildren.

Sadness ceased from pricking my heart at the mention of my business partners, church members, and friends having children and grandchildren. Ironically, they seemed to envy Beatrice and me.

"I'm taking BB to Amsterdam for our fortieth this summer," I said with a proud grin.

"Man, you and the Mrs. always going somewhere. I'm glad for y'all." Fred nodded.

The three of us chatted until I glanced at my watch. School was out, but BB had a meeting afterwards. "I'd better head home, but let's get together next month. Maybe Sherwin and Ed will be able to make it."

It used to be seven of us. Two died at various times. I tried to stay connected as we discussed more what happened to us after the war, not during. That was taboo.

That summer, we boarded our flight to New York. Seven hours later, while we waited at Heathrow Airport for our connecting flight to Amsterdam, we watched passengers interact with their children and grandchildren.

I put my arm around BB and squeezed. "I hope I've made you happy without babies. It would have been nice though."

She turned her lips toward me. "Henry Beacon, you have been the best husband for forty years. We have traveled, lived in nice houses, and have money. I have no regrets for what we've experienced together."

"Thanks for saying that." I choked with emotion from her sincerity.

After one more kiss, we turned back to the art of people-watching. We guessed their ages, professions, or where they lived from their mannerisms and dialects. It was a game for us whenever we traveled.

"Do you think we're too old to be foster parents?" she softly asked.

"I think we'll be perfect as foster grandparents." I chuckled. "Your students haven't discouraged you, have they?"

BB's face glowed with excitement. "They inspire me to do more. I'll check into it when we get back."

Sighing, I was up for the challenge.

Soon, it was time to board our connecting flight. Comfortable in first class, I linked fingers with my wife, said a prayer for continued traveling mercies, and closed my eyes for a nap while she flipped through the pages of a magazine.

We arrived a couple of hours later tired but excited. We ate and rested at our hotel to adjust to the time change. Our luxury suite exceeded our expectations. A half hour later, we were snuggled under the covers and drifted off to sleep.

For seven days, our itinerary was packed with Black Heritage Amsterdam Tours.

We learned that the country's capital had more than one hundred and sixty elaborate canals that ran through the city and boats were the best way to get around.

Cobbled streets didn't look pedestrian, car, or bicycle friendly, but it worked in harmony. Parked as if the water below was a curb, small, covered boats were lined up like water taxis ready to go.

The history behind the canal construction dated back to the sixteenth century.

"Charming," BB had said more than once as we admired the architecture of the tall, narrow houses with impressive facades.

We boarded the cruise boat with other tourists to see Black historical landmarks.

"I always forget about the Dutch as enslavers too," she whispered, leaning into me.

"I wonder if any of my ancestors were Dutch since our bloodline carries many ethnicities." He shrugged.

The landscape the slave traders built was breathtaking. Memorials and evidence of the Black bondage were decoratively woven into building fronts. One park sculpture looked like discarded tree branches until we looked closely. They appeared to be enslaved Blacks reaching out for help. It was heart-wrenching.

I choked along with BB and others who toured the Maritime Museum, which housed a replica of the eighteenth-century cargo ship that transported Africans for trade. I don't know which was more emotional for me—the slave castles or the ships that took them away.

As I swallowed the lump in my throat, I reflected on the Vietnam War where there seemed to be no winners. What if the Africans had come together to fight off the colonizers instead of handing over their enemies for weapons? *What if?* Thoughts filled my head.

"Hey, sweetie..." BB placed her hand on my shoulder. "You okay?"

Her voice was soft, and I looked into her eyes, which were tender.

"Yes," I managed to get out.

She rubbed my shoulder. No words were exchanged, but I knew her touch was meant to remind me I wasn't alone. "You want to head back?"

I took a deep breath and shook my head. "You wanted to see the Dutch tulips." We visited the West India House and the Hortus Bontanicus Amsterdam, then headed back to our hotel.

The next day, we took the museum tour, not that either one of us was an art connoisseur, but we booked the tour package anyway.

"I remember reading about Anne Frank's diary when I worked at the library in Little Rock, and to think my papa fought in World War II to save Jewish people like her but still so many died," BB said more to herself than the tour guide.

I had fought in another war to save lives, too, but upon return to the States, Vietnam Vets were called baby killers.

We entered a synagogue where The Anne Frank House Museum was located.

After the tours for a couple of days, we dined at Water & Brood restaurant, which was owned by a Black native Amsterdam young man and sampled native dishes like Poffertjes.

"This is some good stuff," BB said after she bit into small pancakes that were rolled like meatballs.

I nodded as I tasted the melted butter and icing sugar.

We shopped—or rather my wife shopped. We shared romantic dinners and loved on each other. The day before we left, BB wanted to see the Royal Palace of Amsterdam.

"There is so much more to explore." BB grinned with excitement.

"We can come back for a part two." I slipped my hand into my pants pocket and stared at her. Her smile made me smile.

"Next year!"

I blinked. "Next year? You don't want to go someplace different?"

"Nope." She was adamant. Mrs. Beacon aka Grandma BB was getting her way—again.

Squeezing my wife's hand, I tugged her along to go back to the hotel to pack for home and plan for our return to Amsterdam next year.

Chapter 34
Hard to Say Goodbye

Henry
PAST, Ferguson, Missouri, May 1998

My war buddy, Tim, called me before we were set to meet others at White Castle.

"Henry, can you speak in private, man?" Tim said in a low voice.

"Yeah." I stepped outside on the patio, stretching the coil cord of the receiver and shut the door. "What's up?"

"Fred won't be joining us. He's sick, man. I mean really sick." Tim paused.

My heart dropped. Not Fred. The signs were there that something was ravaging his body, but I ignored them.

"I don't know if you remember David Kissack," Tim said.

"Vaguely." I strained my brain. "A White guy, but always treated Blacks with respect."

"I found out this week that David died of Hodgkin's disease last year. It's messing with my head."

The news had been reporting certain cancers, especially brain cancer, connected to exposure to Agent Orange, the chemicals we sprayed in the jungles of Vietnam. I tried not to think about it.

Tim sighed heavily. "A time bomb is ticking inside of us to see who's next. When I went to my doctor's appointment, he mentioned traces of that herbicide found in my blood work and asked me if I was experiencing any symptoms."

What did Tim know? Rubbing the back of my neck, I stopped and faced the back of the house. It was postcard perfect with a meticulous flower garden I helped Beatrice plant. The trees provided evening shade for BB and me to recline. Okay, I needed to focus and hear what Tim was about to say. "Symptoms like what?"

"Avoiding things that remind you of what we saw in Vietnam," Tim said.

"Who doesn't?" I shrugged. "If that's the way the Lord wants me to go, I hope it's quick so I won't put my wife through it. I've made my peace with the Lord and support my church."

Why am I talking about dying? Stop it. Live.

To everything there is a season, the Lord whispered.

That reminded me of a recent sermon from Ecclesiastes, the third chapter: *To everything there is a season, and a time to every purpose under heaven: A time to be born, and a time to die; a time to plant, and a time to pluck up that which is planted. A time to kill, and a time to heal; a time to break down, and a time to build up…*

"Good for you. Well, anyway, you might want to visit our friend sooner rather than later."

BB was at school when I decided to go visit Fred the next day in the VA Hospital in Mid-Town, which wasn't far from the bed-and-breakfast we owned.

I hated hospitals.

This one even more because I knew the majority of its patients were fellow servicemen. Fred was in the hospital. Since the last time we were together, he'd revealed to Tim that he had been diagnosed with leukemia.

But what he was telling me now was something I couldn't ignore. My movements were slow, and my muscles got stiff, but hey, I was over sixty. That was to be expected.

After receiving Fred's room number, I walked down the hall. I knocked and peeped my head in the doorway. He appeared thinner and asleep. I didn't need to be a doctor to diagnose he was dying.

Taking a deep breath, I gathered my courage and stepped to his bedside. "Hey, buddy."

Fred slowly opened his eyes. It took a moment for him to recognize me. "Henry? That you?"

"Yeah." I lifted his hand in a shake. "I came to get you out of here," I joked to lighten the mood.

"Too late, my friend. I'll be on a gurney." He strained his voice. "Doctor doesn't give me a week."

I held my breath to keep from yelling out, "No!"

Fred closed his eyes as if he were already dead. I took a seat in a chair by his bed. A part of me was dying with him as memories surfaced of us having each other's back in the war, then staying in contact over the years.

Numbed from Fred's truth, I couldn't move. Finally, I stood, then I kissed his forehead, something I had never done to another man, and walked out of the room, holding back my grief until I stepped into the elevator. There were too many people inside to break down, so I held my composure.

The doors opened, and I released my pain. With each step toward the exit, a tear fell. When I climbed inside my truck, I reached for the box of tissues and used most of them.

"Lord, please don't let BB be alone when my time comes." As I stared through the windshield, I realized I needed to get home. Tonight was Chinese takeout, and my wife would be expecting it.

I needed to have a conversation with BB about headaches I've recently been experiencing. I had to prepare her for my demise. "I need to prepare myself!" I turned into the grocery store's parking lot, not sure how I got to my destination. Did I drive the speed limit? Did I yield or stop at red lights? I remembered nothing.

I walked into the Schnucks and found the payphone. "Hey, babe, I'm at the grocery store. What dessert are you in the mood for? Then I'll get the Chinese food, so it will be hot."

"I was getting worried. I didn't know where you were." She sounded relieved. "I've got a taste for red velvet."

"It's yours, baby. Sorry. I stopped by the VA to visit Fred."

"Oh no," she said, gasping. "How's he doing?"

"Not so good." I choked.

"*Awww*, honey. I'm sorry. Come home. I'll heat something up and bake some cookies."

I laughed and felt better already. "I'm coming, but I'm getting my wife her cake and our Chinese food first. Love you, BB. See you soon." I disconnected.

In addition to the cake, I grabbed a colorful bouquet of flowers, sniffed, and smiled. "For my baby." I paid for the purchases, then headed the five blocks home.

Chapter 35
Worse Nightmare

Beatrice
PAST, Ferguson, Missouri, May 1998

"Where is that husband of mine?" I shook my head, wondering if he had run into someone he knew. I was hungry and would warm up something if Henry didn't get home soon.

A knock on my door startled me, and I glanced at the clock on the wall. It was almost eight. I opened the door. Two Ferguson police officers were standing on my porch.

"Mrs. Beacon?" a tall White officer asked. He removed his cap and rested it over his chest.

The other officer was shorter, younger, and Black. He said nothing, but his eyes prepared me for something bad.

Where is my husband? Before I could ask, I had my answer.

"I'm sorry to inform you Henry Beacon was killed in a car crash on North Florissant Road. He was transported to the hospital, but he didn't make it."

Henry was dead? No. Not on our Friday Chinese food night. Not when we had just celebrated forty years. Not now.

I crumbled to the floor. I didn't recognize the scream that escaped from my mouth. "Not my Henry, not my Henry, not my Henry." The words rewound as the officers stepped inside and helped me to a chair in the living room.

My world was gone without Henry. I rubbed my forehead. He'd just told me he loved me. I needed to get details, but my mind was already in rotation, and I couldn't stop it.

Henry and I had been high school teenage sweethearts.

We married young.

We survived the war.

We built a good life together.

Why couldn't we die together?

"We're sorry for your loss. Is there a neighbor or family we can call?" the Black officer asked as he patted my hand.

I wanted my mama. She was a widow. She could help me. I needed to tell Henry's mother too. Mr. Chestnut had died years earlier.

"Friends?" he asked when I didn't answer.

Blurred faces flashed in my head, but I couldn't recall their names until Nancy's face flashed before me. We hadn't spoken in a while.

"Mrs. Beacon? Someone needs to be here with you," the same officer said.

"Nancy… Nancy Miller." My throat was scratchy., "JE-1-8382. She's not far in Kinloch," I said as my mind pushed itself to function.

Half an hour later, Nancy and Milton showed up at my doorstep, tears glossed over their eyes. The police stayed until they got there.

Taking a seat on both sides of me, they linked their fingers through mine and squeezed. "Tell us what happened." Milton, always a quiet man, took charge.

By this time, I'd registered the name of the White officer as Allen.

"Mr. Beacon was exiting Schnucks' parking lot, attempting to make a left onto New North Florissant Road when a man ran a red light and T-boned into Mr. Beacon's vehicle. Witnesses say the driver of the other car swerved but fled the scene. This is an ongoing investigation."

The other officer, Kevin Wicks, continued, "No alcohol found on the front seat of the car or on the floor."

"Henry's not a whino! Of course, there wasn't. My husband doesn't drink and drive," I snapped, feeling the blood pump into my heart.

"Yes, ma'am," the Black officer said, "but we did find flowers and a cake. He was unconscious from the impact. He was taken to Christian Hospital Northeast but didn't make it."

My world shifted.

I was alone and lost. I should have died with my husband.

"I want to see him," I said.

"I'll drive," Milton offered, and I nodded.

"And you don't know who killed my husband?" I frowned. I was buying a gun, and I would kill the driver myself.

Chapter 36
In the Blink of an Eye

Beatrice
PAST, Ferguson, Missouri, May 1998

"P rominent St. Louis businessman and Vietnam veteran Henry Beacon was killed Friday night when another driver ran a red light…" local KMOV-TV anchorman Julius Hunter broadcasted.

I turned off the television. I couldn't take the reminders of what I had lost. "I wasn't this bad off when Henry was fighting in Vietnam."

"That's because you kept yourself busy," Nancy said as she made afternoon tea for us.

"Thanks to you." Nancy made me grin. She was my first true and longest friend in St. Louis.

Nancy stayed two days with me until Mama and Mrs. Beacon arrived. Neighbors and fellow teachers came by to offer their condolences and bring food, money, plants, and prayer.

I thanked them, but I refused to accept my loss. Henry and I had a life ahead of us. Mama reminded me to pray more than once. I couldn't. I was too broken inside.

My world seemed to have more losses than victories—my babies, my husband, Papa, MaDear CC, Mr. Beacon…

Sitting on the patio where Henry enjoyed the solitude to think and decompress, I got comfortable, then began to add up my injustices as my doorbell rang. I sighed. Nancy was running errands for me while Mama and Mrs. Beacon rested upstairs. I stood and walked back inside and opened the front door, expecting another neighbor.

Lily Rae Swann Cartwright stood on my porch with a suitcase, and my cousin wasn't alone. Her husband, Mack Cartwright, had abandoned her after she'd had two daughters. Every Christmas, Lily Rae would include photos of the girls in her holiday cards as if to rub in the fact that she gave Auntie Stella grandchildren. I may not have had children, but until Henry's last breath, he'd never abandoned me.

With Lily Rae were three grandchildren. They pushed and shoved their way to come inside like they didn't have any home training. With Lily Rae as their grandmother, they didn't.

I tolerated them because I didn't have the energy to fight back against their rudeness.

Visitors were constant. By the end of the week, Henry's friend Tim showed up. It had taken him long enough to come. Anger at my injustice overtook my sorrow.

My judgment stopped as I observed the misery plastered on his face, which had to mirror mine. Somehow, I'd aged overnight. Puffy eyes greeted me in the morning. Suddenly, my timeless beauty faded, and the wrinkles of a much older woman surfaced. My gray hair was no longer an accent to my features. Instead, it held the reality that I was old—older than I had ever looked.

"Sorry, Beatrice, I wasn't here sooner. It's been hard coping—"

"I know." I nodded.

"Losing two buddies in one week." Tim bowed his head and shook it left and right.

"Wait. Two?" I wasn't expecting this news.

Tim slowly met my eyes. "Fred. You didn't know? He died the day after Henry. *Whew.*" He choked.

I wrapped my arms around him, and we cried together. Henry's friends were my friends, and the same with my friends to Henry. We liked what the other liked and disliked what the other disliked. Henry said it was because we were one.

Sniffing, Tim stepped back. "Whatever you need, let me and the wife know. We are here for you."

"I will, and I know." I closed the door behind him and sat in the living room to process the double dose of sadness.

Too distraught to make funeral arrangements, I left that to Henry's mom and Mama. The two in-laws worked side-by-side to write his obituary, but I couldn't read it. That would be too final, and I couldn't bear it.

Our master bedroom suite, which was larger than our two rooms at Mr. Chestnut's house, was my sanctuary.

I grieved behind closed doors and curtains.

I inhaled Henry's scent on the pillowcase. I read his letters.

Looked at the photos.

Dreamed about our future being snatched away.

On the day of the funeral, Mama forced me to eat breakfast to give me strength. The bacon, eggs, and coffee gave me none.

It was sunny and bright outside. Why did I choose to wear black? There should be another color for mourning clothes. Tim and Nancy's husband, Milton, had to physically put me in the limousine. I fought them. In the church, I was escorted down the aisle to Henry's silver casket, which seemed a mile away, by Lily Rae who wanted to be by my side. I didn't resist. I was too exhausted from fighting Tim and Milton.

Mama and Mrs. Beacon picked upbeat music. Good choices because I was tired of crying. Calmness engulfed me as people spoke, then my pastor insulted me when he cut short the rest of the acknowledgments, proclamations, and reflections from the program because the service ran over, and the funeral home had to get the family to Jefferson Barracks cemetery within a certain timeframe.

If I weren't in church, I would have cursed, something I never did. But I wasn't the same person. I didn't care if Henry's celebration of life lasted a day or a week. I wasn't ready to say goodbye. The undertakers could rebook the burial as far as I was concerned.

The hundreds of mourners who turned out didn't get to hear all the wonderful things my husband did. The jobs he created. The charities he poured money and energy into. The support he gave to the veterans. The way he never missed my birthday or our anniversary. Henry gave me my heart's desire. I wanted people to know that.

I stitched together pieces of that dreadful day from the funeral procession to the burial, receiving the United States flag and the bugler blowing the last note of "Taps." The respite was a blur.

A week later, I accepted a piece of me was gone. Despite my family being with me in my house, I felt alone mentally. Caged physically. Spiritually void of existence.

Lily Rae walked into the dining room with a plate of food. She took a seat in front of me, and I ignored her and glanced out the window at the neighborhood Henry and I had enjoyed for thirty-plus years.

"So, I've been thinking, with this big house," she said, glancing around, "I'd pack up his things and move." Lily Rae thought nothing of her unsolicited advice.

Something within me snapped and I squinted. I didn't care if she was related or not. "My husband bought me this house, and if I want to be entombed here as if it's a mausoleum, that's my business. I ain't moving." I used improper English, which I forbid my students to use, to get my point across. "If you don't pack *your* bags and get out, I'll throw them out on the curb for trash day." I fumed and was ready to get in a catfight. My cousin must have sensed it. I felt empowered speaking my mind and nobody was here to censor me. It was a new day.

"I was just trying to help." She jutted her chin. "That's what I did when Mama died."

Auntie Stella had died while Henry and I were on one of our trips. When we returned, we traveled to Little Rock to console Lily Rae with our presence and a monetary gift. We didn't over-extend our stay like Lily Rae had.

I got to my feet. "You can help by getting your grandchillin's and leaving early in the morning, and don't take nothing out of my house with you."

Overhearing the conversation, Mama peeped her head out of the kitchen. "Do as Beatrice says, Lily Rae."

"Yes, Auntie." Lily Rae stood and bowed her head. My cousin hurried out of my sight.

Mama and Mrs. Beacon were welcomed company. They were up in age, and I offered for them to come live with me.

"Little Rock is home," they both said.

"You always can move back to Little Rock." Mama said to think about it.

"I can't come without Henry." I teared up and grabbed a tissue from one of many boxes Mama had placed in every room. "I can't believe how much I love him. It hurts." I began to cry, and they hugged me and let me.

They left after a couple of weeks.

The first year after Henry's death was horrible. I struggled with cooking his favorite food he would never eat, buying cologne he would never wear, and sleeping on my side of the bed. I even watched some programs like Westerns because Henry liked them.

Although I was an educator, the children couldn't fill my void, and we never got to become foster grandparents either. No matter how many functions Nancy dragged me to, I had too much emptiness in my life. At fifty-seven years, I had been married longer than I was single.

Without children or siblings, Henry and I had created our own world.

I became obsessed with the investigation of the driver. I harassed the police chief about updates on Henry's case with no results.

That angered me. Bitterness became my bedfellow. How do you get rid of forty-climbing to fifty years of marriage? I didn't want to. We could have had another twenty years left. If Queen Victoria could have Prince Albert's clothes laid out every day after his death, then why couldn't I do the same?

Hollywood glam had nothing on me with my satin gowns and robes. How many times had Henry and I waltzed around the bedroom? We had danced our last dance together the night before.

Little by little, I reluctantly gave away his clothes, then his tools and other items, but I couldn't part with his shoes. And his letters, which I will read every night for the rest of my life.

I'd slip them on in the morning as if they were my house slippers. Soon, I wore them out in the yard or to the store.

I became the grumpy old neighbor, mad at the world, God, and the driver who ended my Henry's life, so I bought a gun because one day I planned to even the score. I didn't care how long it took. I would avenge my husband's death.

Chapter 37
Truth is Stranger Than Fiction
OR Payback is Real

Victoria
PRESENT, Ferguson, Missouri, 2023

Cheney's eyes were red. "I didn't know about the love letters." She sniffed and her shoulders shook.

"Yes, they were Henry's idea," Grandma BB said softly.

"Mom." Victoria ran to her mother and hugged her. "It's okay. Grandma BB knows you weren't responsible." She tried to comfort the woman who had comforted her many times.

"I can't say enough how sorry I am that my father was that drunk driver who killed Henry. I'm further ashamed he's a doctor and didn't stop to see about the victim." Cheney reached over and took Parke's hand. "Of course, we haven't been married as long as you were, but I can't imagine my life without Parke."

"Me either." Parke kissed her lips.

What's Grandma BB thinking as she eyed them? Victoria wondered. *After reading this story, I can understand Grandma BB holding a grudge, but she seems to have worked through it and accepted her lot in life.*

"I got even." She folded her arms. "My bullet had his name on it and hit its target. Too bad Mama and my mother-in-law wasn't alive to see it."

"What a twist of fate that your new neighbor would be connected with your husband's murderer," Cheney said. "I had no idea that my father would do such a thing. I've never known him to drink, and as a doctor, he broke some version of the Hippocratic Oath about preventing diseases or death when he caused injury and fled the scene of an accident."

Deli gasped and faced Pace. "Your grandfather did that?"

Pace didn't answer. Victoria didn't blame him. Who wanted to admit to that?

It was embarrassing that an upstanding doctor would commit such a crime.

"Dr. Reynolds did serve time in jail," Parke said of his father-in-law. "When he wrote me the letter confessing to the hit-and-run, I was dumbfounded and heartbroken."

Victoria's father rubbed his goatee, which had a gray patch, but he was still handsome to her.

"I'll never forget his words, *'Parke, I love my daughter, but I hate myself. I was the hit-and-run driver who killed Henry Beacon. When I found out that Cheney moved next door, I went crazy and used whatever method necessary not to visit, even if I hurt my baby girl in the process. I couldn't face Mrs. Beacon knowing what I did.*

"'I'd been drinking. The following day when I read in the newspaper about the accident and learned there were no witnesses, I kept quiet to keep my reputation intact and my secret buried. When Cheney moved back to Missouri, I couldn't believe how fate would lead her next door to my past.'"

Victoria couldn't believe her father had memorized the contents of the letter from thirteen or fourteen years ago. Grandma BB grunted. "I evened the score when I shot that sucker."

Deli gasped and jumped up. "I am so out of here, Pace. How you turned out sane is unimaginable."

She headed toward the door where Chip and Dale were stationed.

Heads turned toward Pace, waiting to see if he was going after her. He didn't budge, so Victoria asked the obvious that the others hadn't voiced. "You're going to let her leave?"

Pace looked down at his folded hands and sighed. "It's not the first time she's become angry with me."

"What did you do?" Grandma BB squinted.

"It's private."

Victoria was curious too but said nothing. She understood privacy.

"If Deli wants to be with me like Henry was with Grandma BB, she needs to know what she's getting."

"That's my boy!" Parke cheered and grinned until Pace gave him the side-eye. He sobered. "Sorry."

On the other hand, Victoria could relate to Deli's reaction. She couldn't believe half the stuff that happened in the Jamieson family before she arrived, but they provided Victoria with the security she needed after running away from her last foster home.

"Grandma BB, your shenanigans are legendary," Kidd spoke up, taking the focus off Cheney. "When I moved here from Boston, Parke coerced me to run surveillance when you had a stroke and had to enter a nursing facility for rehab. But your stunt of escaping almost cost me a death wish from my cousins. And for the record, you don't need a gun—"

"I'm a widow. Of course I need a weapon. They just don't make walking canes as sturdy anymore to break bones." She *tsk*ed.

"You have bodyguards and every adult-age male Jamieson to protect you."

"Nah." She shifted positions in her chair and crossed a leg over her knee, swinging her Stacy Adams. "A woman should always be strapped. Henry would want me to protect myself or hire bodyguards. You have to admit Chip and Dale look menacing when they're not stuffing their mouths."

With their arms folded and their legs spread, Chip and Dale flexed their biceps. Their hard expressions made Victoria giggle. They were harmless until they sensed danger.

"My short stature and my custom-made cane have tricked many fools." She grabbed and lifted her pearl-encrusted cane and twirled it as if it were a baton.

"Bodyguards, weapons, and then she added a dog." Cheney shook her head.

Grandma BB patted her chest. "I miss Silent Killer." She had adopted the retired police dog who had been injured in the line of duty.

Boy, had they gotten sidetracked.

"I have a question. Didn't you serve time in jail for shooting Mom's dad?" Victoria asked.

"I wasn't convicted but served thirty days shock time, which doesn't go on my record that has other stuff on it."

"Okay. We have come to the part of the program where the following people are supposed to give their own Grandma BB reflections, but you all have interrupted so many times, I think we can skip that part."

"Oh, no. Don't shortchange my funeral. Follow it to the letter." Grandma BB crossed her arms.

"Excuse me." Pace stood. "I'll be back."

He didn't have to tell everyone where he was going. They knew. Pace would come back. Would Deli be with him?

Chapter 38
Time Out

Victoria
PRESENT, Ferguson, Missouri, 2023

Intermission number two. People called for potty breaks, which Grandma BB protested but then decided she should relieve herself too.

While everyone was out the room, Victoria and Kami compared notes about Deli.

"You think Pace is in love with her?" Victoria asked.

"Who knows? She left, and he didn't run after her. If a man said he was in love with me, he'd better not let me leave mad." Kami shrugged. "Then again, what do I know about love?"

Grandma BB was the last one to return. She took her seat and rang her bell on the table next to her chair. "My funeral is dragging, so let's keep it upbeat."

"Yes, ma'am." Victoria shifted her papers and cleared her throat to get back into character. "Dad, you're first to give your reflections, followed by Uncles Malcolm and Cameron. Mom, you'll come behind him, then Uncles Kidd and Ace. Kami and I will be last."

"Here." Grandma BB whipped out a cordless mic and passed it to Parke.

"Seriously?" Parke gave Grandma BB a dumbfounded expression. "You know everyone can hear me just fine."

"But the person in the back of the church might not hear you, so make sure you stand in front of the mic," Grandma BB explained.

"I can write a book on Mrs. Beatrice Tilley Beacon aka Grandma BB," Parke began.

Kidd mumbled, "I'll write the sequel."

Grandma BB squinted at Kidd. She pointed from her eyes to Kidd with an "I'm watching you" gesture.

"I learned to take her seriously when I was interested in Cheney and Grandma BB had a background check on me. She wouldn't have done that if she didn't care about Cheney." He recalled more instances before passing the mic to his brother.

"All I can say is the night Parke sent me to pay Grandma BB's bond to release her from jail was one of the best nights of my life," Malcolm said.

"Excuse me?" Grandma BB squinted.

Malcolm grinned. "Hali and I had broken up, and that night we were together to get you out of trouble. I loved it—not you being in jail but making up with Hali."

Cameron stood and took the mic to appease Grandma BB. "My wife probably has more to say than me, so I forfeit my turn." He handed the mic to his sister-in-law.

Cheney sighed. "There are so many memories, I could be here a while—"

"Take your time," Grandma BB said as she shifted in her chair and folded her arms.

"For me, one fond memory was Grandma BB in the front seat of a police cruiser waving at me. I didn't know if she was pleading for help since she was grinning, but I followed her to the station and learned she'd stolen a getaway van."

"Whose getaway van was it?" Victoria asked.

"The thief who was about to rob my neighbor's house. I'm sure when he came out with the flat screen, he was shocked to see he didn't have transportation." Grandma BB was smug.

When Kidd took the mic, he choked up. "I was a broken man when I came to St. Louis. Grandma BB's roommate, Mrs. Ollie Valentine, let me know my worth when she sensed that I struggled with anger and rejection from my absent father."

"Daddy, you're nice to Mommy and me," his ten-year-old daughter, Kennedy, said, taking his hand and standing on her toes to give her father a kiss.

Kidd leaned down to receive it on his cheek and thanked her. "I remember telling her my last name meant nothing to me and neither did Samuel Jamieson who donated samples of his DNA. Mrs. Valentine was patient with me and let me know that my feelings were legit before she took me to task. She told me that it wasn't the name that made the man, but it was up to me to make my own name."

"You do know that this is my funeral, and it's supposed to be about me, not my nursing home roommate?" Grandma BB reminded him.

"Yes. Because of you in that facility, I met my future wife and a woman whose kindness helped heal me."

"Again, this is about me, people." She huffed.

Ace patted Kidd on his back before taking the mic from his brother. "I didn't meet Grandma BB under the best circumstances. I was due in court for my foolishness, but there was pandemonium in the hall. When I asked what was going on, this petite woman blocked my path, asked me if I was a friend or foe, and told me this group was supporters of the YouTube sensation Ace Jamieson."

Victoria, Kami, and all their cousins, even Lauren who was eleven, fell out of their chairs laughing.

"Daddy, you were a YouTube sensation?" His daughter was beside herself in giggles.

Talise, Ace's wife, looked as if she would add to his misery in laughter any minute as their toddler, Diamond Queen, bounced on her lap.

"I'm glad this is funny to my nieces and nephews, but I was banned from flying because of my own stupidity. I didn't want more attention, but no, some strange little woman put her fingers between her lips and whistled. That action seemed to make her dizzy."

"Ethel knew with her bronchitis she was short-winded," Grandma BB fussed. "She couldn't whistle anyway."

"Anyway, I asked Grandma BB why she and her friends were there." Ace shrugged. "I thought they were supporting me."

"Hate to bust your bubble, handsome, but courtrooms are second nature to me," Grandma BB interrupted, "but I didn't know the judge."

"Grandma BB," Victoria softly said, "this is their moment of reflection at your funeral, and you're supposed to be dead. Stop interrupting."

"Yeah, so we can bury this day," Parke mumbled.

Cheney elbowed him. "Not funny!"

"Uncle Ace, go on. I'm enjoying these family secrets, and yours is getting good." Victoria snickered.

Ace groaned. "Your Uncle Kidd was there and said Grandma BB insisted on coming, and she brought ladies from her Red Hat Society, the St. Louis chapter, because she said the other chapters had previous commitments. I thought," he said, patting his chest, "that was a good thing because I could use all the support I could get, then Grandma BB wanted the judge to give me the maximum sentence."

Engrossed in the story, the nieces' and nephews' eyes were wide as they held on to every word.

Victoria could tell her uncle was uncomfortable reliving the most embarrassing moment in his life.

"When I pleaded not guilty," Ace continued, "Grandma BB and her cohorts started chanting, 'Guilty, guilty, guilty.'"

"Did you go to jail, Daddy?" Tears filled Lauren's eyes.

"No, sweetheart. I couldn't fly on an airplane for three months. What endeared her to me was her support of my bride on our wedding day." He reached out for Talise to join him. "But that's another story."

"I think we've heard enough. Thank you, Uncle Ace," Kami said.

"I'm not on the program," Talise said, "but I want it to be known that Grandma BB will always hold a special place in my heart after she defended me to my stepmother."

Hmmmph. Grandma BB leaned forward. "I was not about to let that chick ruin a Jamieson wedding. That Donna woman knew me and my Stacy Adams didn't play. I shoved her out of the dressing room with a warning. If she tried to walk down the aisle as the mother of the bride, she would go home with a limp—not one of her big toes had better set foot in the center aisle."

Whew. Victoria's duties were almost done. Only she and Kami remained on the program for Reflections.

Kami blew a kiss. "You've been the only grandma I've ever known. I love you, Grandma BB. You taught me to tell it like it is. Before Tango, you set me up with a boyfriend in a virtual world. What was his name?" She snapped her fingers trying to remember.

"*Shhh.* Chile, that was just between you and me. Nothing wrong with pretend love since I could never replace Henry's love."

"Do not play video games when the children are around unless they're rated pre-G," Cheney scolded, and her sisters-in-law nodded in agreement.

"Good grief. It's hard enough to monitor their social media activity at home," Malcolm said.

"Well…" Victoria exhaled and smiled. "It's my turn. Although Mom and Dad adopted me, Grandma BB, you understood my hurt and you opened up your home for me to live at a safe place. You even put Chip and Dale on leave."

"Yeah." Dale frowned.

"It was all good." Chip folded his arms and grinned.

"You have been more than my grandma. You have been my confidant and counselor and taught me how to shoot a gun."

"*Ahh.*" Grandma BB shifted in her chair. "She was of legal age; I'll have you all know."

"Can you teach me?" Paden asked.

"No!" Parke and Cheney said at the same time.

"Okay, let's move on. You all have told a lot of my business. I'm glad I'm alive to hear this."

Chapter 39
The Altar Call

Victoria
PRESENT, Ferguson, Missouri, 2023

Pastor Philip Dupree, Queen's husband, stood with an unreadable expression before he smiled. "This has been an interesting exercise. Life is a dress rehearsal for death."

He glanced across the room as if he was standing in the pulpit before looking at Grandma BB. "The best thing about a rehearsal is if something is wrong, it can be fixed before the big day. In Ecclesiastes 12:14, which is in the Old Testament, the Bible says, *For God will bring every deed into judgment, including every hidden thing, whether it is good or evil.*'"

Pace reappeared. Alone.

"Where's Deli?" Kami asked.

"She's not coming back." He didn't look happy about it.

Kami exchanged glances with Victoria.

Maybe that's a good thing. Victoria wondered if Kami thought the same, but she didn't voice her opinions in front of their brother who seemed hurt.

Philip nodded and gave Pace time to take his seat by their younger brothers, then he continued, "Grandma BB, you have been a trailblazer in some areas of your life and a survivor. You've left warm memories with everyone present today, including me, but," he paused, "in First Timothy, sixth chapter and verses six and seven, Paul says, *But godliness with contentment is great gain. For we brought nothing into this world, and it is certain we can carry nothing out.*'"

"I've got a will," Grandma BB mumbled, but it was loud enough for Victoria to hear across the room.

Queen reached into her bag and pulled out an iPad, turned it on, and crossed her legs. She seemed to anticipate her husband's next move.

As if on cue, Philip turned around. "Honey, can you—" He grinned, then looked over his shoulder, and said, "Excuse me, family." Philip turned back to his wife with a smile and brushed a kiss on her lips. Queen blushed and gave Philip the tablet. "Thank you, my helpmate."

When he turned back, instead of picking up his sermon/eulogy, he looked at Pace. "Guard your heart. The woman who loves you will always have your back. Always."

"Yes, sir." Pace nodded.

"Now," Philip said as he scanned his tablet, "I know most of us have repented and surrendered to the Lord's salvation and not accepted the world's tweaked version of salvation so that God will give us a pass on the Day of Judgment. Heaven is real; so is Hell. God expanded it because of the wicked. If you want to see Jesus, playtime is over, Grandma BB. From what Parke has shared with me, I believe you and Malcolm were baptized on the same day. Malcolm stayed with Jesus, but what happened that you walked away? The Good News is the first shall be last and the last shall be first. There's still time."

He frowned while Grandma BB dusted imaginary dirt off her Stacy Adams shoes.

"Don't let the devil rob you of your reward with God. Repent and come back to Jesus while the Lord has given you this space. You've done so much for others, but only what you do for Christ in the harvest will last. It's a shame for us to live a short or long life and stand before God with no accomplishments for Him."

Philip referred to his tablet and began to read, "In Matthew, the twentieth chapter, the Scripture compares the Kingdom of Heaven with an employer who needed workers. The Bible says in the morning, he found people idle—basically, doing nothing important, so he hired them. That was at nine in the morning. He needed more workers, he gathered more at three, six, three in the morning and lastly at five a.m. All day. That shows us the man diligently looked for workers for the vineyard. How does this relate to Heaven? God is diligently seeking workers for His kingdom. What I like about this chapter is they all got paid the same, even the person who came in last. To God, His reward is fair." He handed his tablet back to Queen. "Grandma BB, there is still time for you to repent and surrender to the Lord."

The message seemed to make Grandma BB uncomfortable. "If I surrender this time, can I still keep my gun?"

"No," Cheney and Parke said in unison.

"If your weapon is legally registered, it's yours. Using it without discretion is another matter," Philip told her. "Those are my words of encouragement. Finally, I can't leave the memories of Grandma BB without asking if anyone here doesn't know who Jesus is and what He can do for you. If so, you need to repent, be water baptized in the name of Jesus Christ, and He's got something for you, and that's His Holy Spirit, which will give you more fire power than Grandma BB's gun."

Chip, one of Grandma BB's bodyguard, stepped forward. His six-foot-plus height, massive muscles, and fierce game face didn't look like a man who needed Christ. But Victoria knew that what people saw on the outside often hid what they are battling inside.

Philip waved him over and prayed for him. Chip lifted both hands in surrender.

Then a sound like a tornado approaching seemed to hit the house. The Spirit of God began to move from person to person until everyone in the room, including Victoria, was worshiping Jesus in a heavenly language.

"I'm ready to be baptized in Jesus' name," Chip said.

"We got you. After we leave here, I'll baptize you myself at the church," Philip said and nodded to Queen.

Chip grinned like a schoolboy waiting for the bell to ring.

Almost thirty minutes later, the room was still. Then the twins, Gabriel and Camille, rushed to Grandma BB and rested their hands on her shoulders. They prayed as if they were pre-evangelists in training.

Grandma BB began to repent. "Lord, I'm sorry for being angry with You a long time for taking away my babies, Papa, Henry, MaDear CC, then Mama and my in-laws. I'm sorry," she sobbed, "for thinking you left me alone in this world, but today I'm surrounded by a family You gave me. Forgive me."

"And instantly, God forgives, but with repentance comes change," Philip said. "Will you follow Christ for real this time?"

When Grandma BB lifted her hands in surrender, God's heavenly language exploded from within her mouth.

"Amen," Philip said.

The twins raced back to their mom for tissues. Gabrielle dug in her purse and gave them one apiece, and they hurried back to Grandma BB and wiped her cheeks.

Grandma BB smiled and wrapped both of them in a hug then kissed them. There was a calmness in the room, and Victoria hated to shatter the peace, but she had to bring the mock funeral to a close as instructed. "This had truly been a celebration. "Now it's time for our matriarch Grandma BB to have her final remarks."

"Final remarks? This is a funeral—of sorts—not a program for the guest of honor to give final remarks." Parke chuckled and shook his head.

"Go with the flow, sweetie. We're almost done here." Cheney patted her husband's hand.

Using her cane, Grandma BB shooed away Chip and Dale from assisting her. "First of all, thank you, my beautiful family. Despite my life's losses, I've gained so much, it's hard to describe what I feel inside." She patted her chest.

Grandma BB swallowed, then reached into a gift bag on her table and pulled out a long dark blue box. "I have something for Cheney who somehow found a special place in my heart. This is for you. MaDear CC gave me this necklace when I went to the senior prom with Henry."

"Thank you," Cheney choked and accept the gift with the utmost care. She hugged Grandma BB tight. "I love you."

"I love you, too, my first-ever daughter. Kami, you're next." Grandma BB waved her over.

Kami started boo-hooing and fell into Grandma BB's arms. Once she was composed, she stepped back. Grandma BB placed her hands on both sides of her cheeks and wiped at her tears. "You were the baby I never gave birth to." She reached into the same bag and pulled out another box. "My mother bought me this set of pearls. Wear them with love."

Kami hugged her again.

"Victoria," Grandma BB said.

Me? Victoria was speechless that Grandma BB considered her that special. Like Kami, tears clouded her eyes as she stood. Her legs were shaky.

"Minister Philip preached to me, the last shall be first, you were the last daughter of Parke and Cheney Jamieson. I was so glad when you stayed with me so we could get to know each other. You are precious to me, and I want you to have a full and happy life."

Victoria nodded. "Yes, ma'am," she whispered.

"I asked you to read my obituary because of my life's hardships and injustices. I hoped you saw your disappointments reflected in my life and the hope for blessings to come."

"I did." Victoria hiccupped.

"I want you to be happy no matter what. You have this whole family to protect and love you. Let them." She lifted the bag and handed it to Victoria. "You know how much Henry loved me and how hard losing him was for me. I survived, so here is the set of pearls my dear Henry gave me. And I have something extra in there for you. All these pearls are special and represent a wonderful moment in my life.

"This really is feeling like my funeral." Grandma BB let Victoria help her sit again, then she turned to Pace. "I wasn't sure who I would give my beloved Henry's Timex watch to that my parents gave for his graduation. I thought about your dad." She looked at Parke and scrunched her nose. "Nah."

Parke responded to her snide comments with a chuckle.

Grandma BB opened the box and stared at the jewelry. One could see she'd debated parting with it. "Great-grandson, I think if my Henry was here today, he would be proud of you." She presented Pace with the last gift. "Stay away from husseys—" She paused when surprise guests arrived. Grandma BB hinted at starting the mock funeral from the beginning.

Chapter 40
Benediction

Victoria
PRESENT, Ferguson, Missouri, 2023

"What did we miss?" Queen Robnett, her sister Rejoice, and their cousin Duchess pushed their way through Chip and Dale's security detail.

Despite their heels and sleek attire, they heaved as if they had run relay races. They were fair and golden-brown beauties while Queen Jamieson Dupree was tall and a chocolate-brown beauty.

The Robnetts' frazzled expressions gave way to relief when they saw Grandma BB in her high-back chair, swinging her leg with her two-tone Stacy Adams taking center stage.

The Jamiesons nicknamed Queen Robnett "Bee" since she was older than Queen Jamieson Dupree.

"We're not too late. *Whew.*" Queen Bee patted her chest.

Cameron was considered the hard-core genealogist guru, but the Robnetts stumped them when they showed up to a family game night and introduced themselves as the other side of the family tree.

There were so many twists to the family tree that a spreadsheet wouldn't have helped Victoria. One fact for sure was the Robnetts had four generations of Queens—two were in one family. But it was neat to hear the breakdown.

Victoria was late joining the family, so she had to play catchup. Her young cousins were taught their genealogy along with their alphabet. They quizzed her constantly to bring her up to speed.

"When I got your text," Queen Bee said, nodding at Philip's wife, Queen, "Rejoice was with me, and she insisted on coming. Then Duchess called to borrow a pair of shoes, and when we told her, she wanted to come and support Kami and Victoria. We were delayed, but we're here."

The teenagers screamed their excitement, and Duchess hugged Kami, then Victoria. Since the funeral was technically over, Victoria was ready to hang out with her cousins.

Grandma BB shooed Queen Bee away when she hurried to her side. "I'm not dead yet. You all missed rehearsal."

Queen Bee stood. "Can someone tell me what's going on?" She put her hand on her hip in a stance that reminded Victoria of Queen, Philip's wife.

"I will." Victoria spoke up. "We're here because Grandma BB is preparing to die, and she wants to make sure the program runs smoothly."

"Huh?" Frowning, Queen Bee rolled her neck.

"I'm eighty-something, and I'm not going to live forever," she said in a nonchalant manner as if she knew something that none of them did.

"You've lived two lifetimes just today," Cheney told Grandma BB.

"Eighty-three," Deli mumbled, reappearing in the doorway. "I did the math."

Queen Bee faced her. "Who are you? I thought I'd met all the family."

"I think she's Pace's girlfriend," Kami said.

She's back? The plot thickens. Victoria didn't know how she felt about Pace's friend/girlfriend. Deli acted like the Jamiesons didn't meet her standards. Too bad because the girl didn't know what she was missing. Maybe it was time for her and Kami to set their brother up with someone whom they approved of.

"*Hmmm*. A lady friend. I'm his cousin. They call me Auntie." Queen Bee carved a space next to Deli. "So how much do you know about our family history?"

"Too much," she said as Pace came to her other side and linked his fingers through hers.

They both mouthed, "Sorry" in unison.

"Well, well, well. Isn't that breaking news?" Queen Bee studied them.

"And there's more." Queen Jamieson stood. "Philip and I are expecting!" She rubbed her stomach. She seemed to ooze with excitement.

"What?" Queen Bee grinned, made her way to her namesake, and gave her a hug.

"And me too." Talise stood.

"That's it. I'm moving to St. Louis. There's a baby contest going on, and I need a husband to enter the competition," Queen Bee said.

Cheney lifted a finger. "Some of us are done."

"Speak for yourself." Cameron snickered. "Some of us are just getting started."

His wife, Gabrielle, pointed from herself to Cameron. "When we got started, you got two for one—twins. They run on my mother's side of the family."

"Oh." Queen looked shocked, then looked at her husband. "Philip, did you know about that? Twins? We could have twins too? I think I'm feeling sick." She sat down as Philip gave her sister a side-eye. "What Gabrielle meant was my mother's grandmother had twins. No one has had twins since until Gabrielle and Cameron."

Queen exhaled. "Whew. Okay."

"Like I said," Cameron said, laughing, "we're just getting started."

"I should move to St. Louis so I can help plan baby showers." Queen Bee looked at Philip. "If you have any prospects at your church, I'll move."

"I like Kansas City better," Rejoice said, "but if you move here, sis, I'm coming with you."

"Great. More Jamiesons," Grandma BB mumbled, feigning annoyance when she loved Queen Bee's spirit.

"Not Jamiesons," Queen Bee corrected. "It would be the Robnetts are coming to town."

The doorbell rang. "More food is here," Dale said and disappeared downstairs.

"I didn't order more food." Grandma BB frowned.

Since the Holy Ghost exploded in the "upper" room at Grandma BB's house, Dale seemed uncomfortable and looked for any excuse to escape.

"Did someone die?" asked a short woman with silver or goldish hair—it was a toss-up which color was dominant after a bad hair dye. She tried to squeeze her way between Chip and Dale, but they weren't budging.

"Who are you?" Victoria asked. And who else could be coming?

"Lily Rae Swann Cartwright, Beatrice's first cousin. I was coming to visit, and imagine my surprise to see all the cars outside." She dropped her suitcase and tried to elbow her way in. "Ouch. You guys are like bricks."

"Ah, naw. The devil done shown up already. Ain't no way I'm dying now…because she's come to take me to hell with her shenanigans." Grandma BB eyed her cousin as Chip and Dale came to her side with their arms folded. "What kind of bodyguards are you two if you let anybody into my house?" Grandma BB rubbed her head. "Okay, ain't nobody dying today. This has been exhausting. Maybe another day. Right now, I have an uninvited guest in my house who I need to keep an eye on. Lily Rae, why are you here?"

"I needed to get away from my daughters and grandchildren. With mama gone and Aunt Nellie, too, you're my next of kin."

"Don't remind me." Grandma BB rolled her eyes. There had to be more to Lily Rae's story, and Victoria knew Grandma BB would get to the bottom of it.

Epilogue

Victoria
PRESENT, Ferguson, Missouri 2023

"My funeral has concluded, so it's time for my repast." Grandma BB slapped her lap as she waited for Chip to bring her the serving dishes for her to help herself. "You know, I feel better that we've gotten that out of the way. We have food. We have family. Let's have a game night," she insisted.

"We haven't prepped," Parke said.

Grandma BB tilted her head and twisted her lips, giving it some thought. "You know enough about your family history. Let's see how you do on your hometown knowledge."

Parke brushed the dust off his shoulders. "I mean, I don't want to brag and cause the game to be a blowout, but I'm pretty good."

Cheney crossed her legs. "Okay, Grandma BB. Bring it. Call my husband's bluff."

"Hey, whose side are you on?" Parke acted wounded.

"The winning team, of course." She smirked.

"Excellent." Grandma BB stood. "Let me take off my burial clothes first and change into something more comfortable." She walked into her master closet.

While she was away, Parke waved his family into a huddle. "You all are honor students." He looked at Pace, Kami, and Victoria. "I need you to bring your A-game."

"What about me, Dad? I got an A in math," Chance said, and Parke rubbed his son's tight curls.

"Good. If we need any calculations, you are my man." Parke nodded at his youngest son. "Paden, I'm depending on you, too, son." He fist-bumped his children, then shouted, "Let's go, team!"

Glancing over his shoulder, Parke gave his brothers and cousins a grin as Grandma BB reappeared in leather biker pants and a jacket trimmed in rhinestones as if she was going somewhere. She had changed out of her two-tone Stacy Adams to a solid gray pair.

Taking her seat, she tapped her cane on the floor twice. "Let the games begin. Roll call," she said as if she didn't know the teams represented.

"Team Parke!" Parke clapped.

"Team Cameron!" Cameron high-fived his twins.

"Team Malcolm!" Malcolm folded his arms and rested his ankle on his knee.

"Team Ace in the house!" Ace grinned.

"Team Kidd is ready," he clapped back at Parke.

"Team Queen and hubby." Queen beamed.

"Team Robnett," Queen Bee said. "If it's local history, y'all have got the edge."

"No excuses. Get in where you fit in. Now," Grandma BB said, looking from left to right, "name the first Black-owned bank in St. Louis that became Missouri's first Black-owned bank."

Everyone looked to Parke who after a few seconds shrugged. "I got nothing."

"Buzz." Chip copied the sound of a buzzer.

"You all should know the accomplishments of Black pioneers in your city," Grandma BB scolded. "The answer is Gateway National Bank on Union Boulevard. That was mentioned in my obit."

"Which is now a credit union," Parke added. "St. Louis Community Credit Union, Gateway Branch, in honor of the old bank."

"Oh, so now you want to show up to the party and act intelligent. *Ummm-hmmm.*" Grandma BB *tsk*ed then took a sip of her lemonade. "What were the freedom rides in St. Louis?"

"Ha!" Lily Rae said. "Easy. Everybody should know about the freedom riders. If they don't, they might not be too bright."

Some shot daggers at Grandma BB's cousin.

It was as if a pack of dogs was ready for the command to attack. Chance, Parke and Cheney's youngest, stood. "Ma'am, it's rude to insult others. The average IQ of the adults in this room is between 115 and 129. My siblings' and cousins' IQs range from 145 to 179. Brightness runs in our family. My Grandma BB said, 'freedom rides' not 'freedom riders.' You must listen carefully to the question. Black men who owned their service cars from Consolidated ran into problems when St. Louis politicians wanted to remove them from service because they took riders away from the White-owned transportation businesses and cabs. To get around the violations, they didn't charge fares but accepted donations. Black leaders called them 'freedom rides' as a way to back the civil rights protests in the South…"

Victoria was proud of her little brother. She grinned and clapped. Others whistled.

"Everyone knows the freedom riders who were a group of Blacks and Whites who rode the bus through the South to protest separate bus terminals," Chance said and took his seat.

"I didn't know that, cousin," Gabriel said.

"Me either." His twin Camille shook her head.

Lily Rae looked contrite and didn't say another word.

"Ha-ha! My great-grandson shut your mouth." Grandma BB scrunched her nose at Lily Rae. "Team Parke gets the first point," Grandma BB said.

Parke high-fived his family.

Grandma BB munched on grapes as she watched them celebrate. "Okay. Another question. Name the part of the city where prominent Blacks lived. Hint: there was a high school and hospital."

The room was quiet, and most of the wives mumbled they weren't born in St. Louis.

"*Hmmm*. The only place where there was a hospital and high school with Blacks was in North St. Louis in the Ville," Kidd's wife Ava said, thinking out loud. "Sumner High School and Homer G. Phillips hospital."

"Correct!" Grandma BB tapped her finger to her tongue and did an imaginary point on a scoreboard.

Kidd leaped to his feet and pulled his wife into his arms and gave her a hard kiss. "Beauty and brains. Way to go, Team Kidd."

Grandma BB had yet to stump any of them after nine questions. "Here's the final one so you all can go home. What bank protest opened the door for Blacks to be hired as tellers and clerks?"

Pace stood. "Just a minute." He walked over to Queen Bee and whispered in her ear. She smiled and kissed him on his cheek. "Jefferson Bank and Trust."

"That is correct." Grandma BB nodded. "Pace? You gave her the answer. Why didn't you take the win for Team Parke?"

"Queen Bee needed to be on the scoreboard."

"You, grandson," Grandma BB said, pointing her cane at him, "are the reason this family has given me long life. With that said, good night. Y'all go home, and someone drop off Lily Rae at a hotel because she ain't going to stay here tonight and get on my nerves with all her yacking. I just had my coming-to-Jesus moment and I don't want to mess it up just yet."

AUTHOR'S NOTE

As I researched Grandma BB's background, I had unknowingly placed her in the Civil Rights era when I introduced her in *Guilty of Love*, 2007. The big surprise for me is I lived through the end of it. I learned many things about the accomplishments and determination of generations before us.

I was in third grade when Dr. Martin Luther King, Jr., was killed and didn't understand the magnitude of my parents' or teachers' tears.

Each generation takes for granted the liberties they enjoy. Can we name our local pioneers who made a difference? Do we know the American Black history that was never written between the pages of a book? I hope this story challenges you to not only uncover the past but to pass it on to the next generation.

Get ready for *Days Are Coming*. God has spoken, and the next installment of the Intercessors isn't for the faint-hearted. Pre-order today.

Book Club Discussion

1. What was the best part of the story?

2. Discuss how Henry's death affected Grandma BB to handle, a sickness or sudden death.

3. How did being a part of protests change Grandma BB? Have you been part of any marches or protests? If so, how did that change you?

4. How much Black local history do you know about your city?

5. Who was your favorite and least favorite characters? Why?

Research Notes

Alvin A. Reid, "Charles Oldham 'pillar of integrity' passes," *St. Louis American*, September 21, 2006.

Vida "Sister" Goldman Prince, *That's The Way It Was.*

Corinne Ruff, "80% of St. Louis County homes built by 1950 have racial covenants, researcher finds," St. Louis Public Radio, January 31, 2022.

Roy Malone, "Historic Jefferson Bank protests paved way for civil rights progress in St. Louis," *Post-Dispatch*, September 12, 2013.

John Wright, Sr., *African Americans in Downtown St. Louis.*

Leroy Donald, "Cohn's Era Ending, Once Main Street Icon, Native Retailer Fading," June 24, 2007.
https://www.arkansasonline.com/news/2007/jun/24/cohns-era-ending-20070624/

Johnnie Cole, mother, oral history.

Euralean Simmons, mother-in-law, oral history.

Linda Tate, "The 1950s," *The Wellston Loop*

https://news.stlpublicradio.org/government-politics-issues/2018-01-13/longtime-civil-rights-stalwart-frankie-freeman-dies-at-age-101

About the Author

Pat Simmons is a multi-published Christian romance author of forty-plus titles. She is a self-proclaimed genealogy sleuth who is passionate about researching her ancestors, then casting them in starring roles in her novels. She is a five-time recipient of the RSJ Emma Rodgers Award for Best Inspirational Romance: *Still Guilty, Crowning Glory, The Confession, Christmas Dinner*, and *Queen's Surrender (To A Higher Calling)*. Pat's first inspirational women's fiction, *Lean On Me*, with Sourcebooks, was the national library system's February/March Together We Read Digital Book Club pick. *Here for You* and *Stand by Me* are also part of the Family is Forever series. Her holiday indie release, *Christmas Dinner*, and traditionally published, *Here for You* were featured in *Woman's World*, a national magazine. *Here for You* was also listed in the "7 Great Reads That Help to Keep the Faith" by Sisters From AARP. She contributed an article, "I'm Listening," in the *Chicken Soup for the Soul: I'm Speaking Now* (2021). Pat is the recipient of the 2022 Leslie Esdaile "Trailblazer" Award given by Building Relationships Around Books Readers' Choice for her work in the Christian fiction genre.

As a Christian, Pat describes the evidence of the gift of the Holy Ghost as a life-altering experience. She has been a featured speaker and workshop presenter at various venues across the country. Pat has converted her sofa-strapped sports fanatical husband into an amateur travel agent, untrained bodyguard, GPS-guided chauffeur, and administrative assistant who is constantly on probation. They have a son and a daughter. Pat holds a B.S. in mass communications from Emerson College in Boston, Massachusetts and has worked in radio, television, and print media for more than twenty years. She oversaw the media publicity for the annual RT Booklovers Conventions for fourteen years. Visit her at www.patsimmons.net.

Other Christian Titles

The Jamieson Legacy

Book 1: Guilty of Love

Book 2: Not Guilty of Love

Book 3: Still Guilty

Book 4: The Acquittal

Book 5: Guilty by Association

Book 6: The Guilt Trip

Book 7: Free from Guilt

Book 8: Sandra Nicholson's Backstory

Book 9: The Confession

Book 10: The Guilty Generation

Book 11: Queen's Surrender (To a Higher Calling)

Book 12: Contempt (Grandma BB's story)

The Intercessors

Book 1: Day Not Promised

Book 2: Day She Prayed

Book 3: Days Are Coming

The Carmen Sisters

Book 1: No Easy Catch

Book 2: In Defense of Love

Book 3: Driven to Be Loved

Book 4: Redeeming Heart

Love at the Crossroads

Book 1: Stopping Traffic

Book 2: A Baby for Christmas

Book 3: The Keepsake

Book 4: What God Has for Me

Book 5: Every Woman Needs a Praying Man

Restore My Soul

Book 1: Crowning Glory
Book 2: Jet: The Back Story
Book 3: Love Led by the Spirit

Family is Forever

Book 1: Lean on Me
Book 2: Here For You
Book 3: Stand by Me

Making Love Work Anthology

Book 1: Love at Work
Book 2: Words of Love
Book 3: A Mother's Love

God's Gifts

Book 1: Couple by Christmas
Book 2: Prayers Answered by Christmas

Perfect Chance at Love series

Book 1: Love by Delivery
Book 2: Late Summer Love

Single titles

Talk to Me
Her Dress
House Calls for the Holidays (short story)
Christmas Dinner
Christmas Greetings
Taye's Gift
Waiting for Christmas
House Calls for the Holidays

Anderson Brothers

Book 1: Love for the Holidays (Three novellas):
A Christian Christmas, A Christian Easter, A Christian Father's Day
Book 2: A Woman After David's Heart (A Valentine's Day Story)
Book 3: A Noelle for Nathan

In *Crowning Glory*, Cinderella had a prince; Karyn Wallace has a King. While Karyn served four years in prison for an unthinkable crime, she embraced salvation through Crowns for Christ outreach ministry. After her release, Karyn stays strong and confident, despite society's stigma on ex-offenders. Since Christ strengthens the underdog, Karyn refuses to sway away from the scripture, "He whom the Son has set free is free indeed." Levi Tolliver, for the most part, is a practicing Christian. One contradiction is that he doesn't believe in turning the other cheek. He's steadfast that there is a price to pay for every sin committed, especially after the untimely death of his wife during a robbery. Then Karyn enters Levi's life. He is enthralled with her beauty and sweet spirit until he learns about her incarceration. If Levi can accept that Christ paid Karyn's debt in full, then a treasure awaits him. This is a powerful tale and reminds readers of the permanency of redemption.

Jet: The Back Story to Love Led By the Spirit, to say Jesetta "Jet" Hutchens issues is an understatement. In Crowning Glory, Book 1 of the Restoring My Soul series, she releases a firestorm of anger with an unforgiving heart. But every hurting soul has a history. In Jet: The Back Story to Love Led by the Spirit, Jet doesn't know how to cope with losing her younger sister, Diane. But God sets her on the road to a spiritual recovery. To ensure she doesn't get lost, Jesus sends the handsome and single Minister Rossi Tolliver to guide her. Psalm 147:3 says Jesus can heal the brokenhearted and bind up their wounds. That sets the stage for Love Led by the Spirit.

In *Love Led By the Spirit*, Minister Rossi Tolliver is ready to settle down. Besides the outward attraction, he desires a sweet, humble woman who loves church folks. It sounds simple enough on paper, but when he gets off his knees, praying for that special someone to come into his life, God opens his eyes to the woman who has been there all along. There is only a slight problem. Love is the farthest thing from Jesetta "Jet" Hutchens' mind. But Rossi, the man, and the minister, is hard to resist. Is Jet ready to allow the Holy Spirit to lead her to love?

In *Stopping Traffic*, Book 1, Candace Clark has a phobia about crossing the street, and for a good reason. As fate would have it, her daughter's principal assigns her to crossing guard duties as part of the school's Parent Participation program. With no choice in the matter, Candace begrudgingly accepts her stop sign and safety vest, then reports to her designated crosswalk. Once Candace is determined to overcome her fears, God opens the door for a blessing, and Royce Kavanaugh enters her life, a firefighter built to rescue any damsel in distress. When a spark of attraction ignites, Candace and Royce soon discover more than one way to stop traffic.

In *A Baby For Christmas*, Book 2, yes, diamonds are a girl's best friend, but in Solae Wyatt-Palmer's case, she desires something more valuable. Captain Hershel Kavanaugh is a divorcee and the father of two adorable little boys. Solae has never been married and longs to be a mother. Although Hershel showers her with expensive gifts, his hesitation about proposing causes Solae to walk and never look back. As the holidays approach, Hershel must convince Solae she has everything he could ever want for Christmas.

In *The Keepsake*, Book 3, Until death us do part…or until Desiree walks away. Desiree "Desi" Bishop is devastated when she finds evidence of her husband's affair. God knew she didn't get married only to one day have to stand before a judge and file for a divorce. But Desi wants out no matter how much her heart says to forgive Michael. That isn't easier said than done. She sees God's one acceptable reason for a divorce as the only opt-out clause in her marriage. Michael Bishop is a repenting man who loves his wife of three years. If only…he had paid attention to the red flags God sent to keep him from falling into the devil's snares. But Michael didn't and fell. Although God forgives him instantly when he repents, Desi's forgiveness is moving as a snail's pace. In the end, after all the tears have been shed and forgiveness granted and received, the couple learns that some marriages are worth keeping.

In *What God Has For Me*, Book 4, pregnant or not, Halcyon Holland is leaving her boyfriend. When her ex makes no attempts to reconcile their relationship, Halcyon begins to second-guess whether or not she compromised her chance for a happily ever after. But Zachary Bishop has had his eye on Halcyon since he first saw her. What one man doesn't cherish, Zach is ready to treasure. He's on a mission to offer her a second chance at love that she can't refuse: unconditional love for a ready-made family. Halcyon will soon learn that her past circumstances won't hinder the Lord's blessings for them.

In *Every Woman Needs A Praying Man*, Book 5, first impressions can make or break a business deal, and they definitely could be a relationship buster, but an ill-timed panic attack draws two strangers together. Unlike firefighters who run into danger, instincts tell businessman Tyson Graham to be weary of a certain damsel in distress and run. Days later, the same woman struts through his door for a job interview. Monica Wyatt might possess the outward beauty and the brains on paper, but Tyson doesn't trust her to work for his firm, or maybe he doesn't trust his heart around her.

In *Guilty of Love*, when do you know the most important decision of your life is the right one? Reaping the seeds from what she's sown; Cheney Reynolds moves into a historic neighborhood in Ferguson, Missouri, and becomes a reclusive. Her first neighbor, the incomparable Mrs. Beatrice Tilley Beacon aka Grandma BB, is an opinionated childless widow. Grandma BB is a self-proclaimed expert on topics Cheney isn't seeking advice—everything from landscaping to hip-hop dancing to romance. Then there is Parke Kokumuo Jamison VI, a direct descendant of a royal African tribe. He learned his family ancestry, African history, and lineage preservation before he could count. Unwittingly, they are drawn to each other, but it takes Christ to weave their lives into a spiritual bliss while He exonerates their past indiscretions.

In *Not Guilty*, one man, one woman, one God, and one big problem. Malcolm Jamieson wasn't the man who got away, but the man God instructed Hallison Dinkins to set free. Instead of their explosive love affair leading them to the wedding altar, God diverted Hallison to the prayer altar during her first visit back to church in years. Malcolm was convinced that his woman had loss her mind to break off their engagement. Didn't Hallison know that Malcolm, a tenth-generation descendant of a royal African tribe, couldn't be replaced? Once Malcolm concedes that their relationship can't be savaged, he issues Hallison his own edict, "If we're meant to be with each other, we'll find our way back. If not, that means there's a love stronger than we had." His words begin to haunt Hallison until she begins to regret their break up, and that's where their story begins. Someone has to retreat, and God never loses a battle.

In *Still Guilty*, Cheney Reynolds Jamieson made a choice years ago that is now shaping her future and the future of the men she loves. A botched abortion prevented her from carrying a baby to term, and her husband, Parke K. Jamison VI, is expected to produce heirs. With a wife who cannot give him a child, Parke vows to find and get custody of his illegitimate son by any means necessary. Meanwhile, Cheney's twin brother, Rainey, struggles with his anger over his ex-girlfriend's actions that haunt him, and their father, Dr. Roland Reynolds, fights to keep an old secret in the past.

In *The Acquittal*, two worlds apart, but their hearts dance to the same African drum beat. On a professional level, Dr. Rainey Reynolds is a competent, highly sought-after orthodontist. Inwardly, he needs to be set free from the chaos of revelations that make him question if happiness is obtainable. To get away from the drama, Rainey is willing to leave the country under the guise of a mission trip with Dentist Without Borders. Will changing his surroundings really change him? If one woman can heal his wounds, then he will believe that there is really peace after the storm.

Ghanaian beauty Josephine Abena Yaa Amoah returns to Africa after completing her studies as an exchange student in St. Louis, Missouri. Although her heart bleeds for his peace, she knows she must step back and pray for Rainey's surrender to Christ so God can acquit him of his self-inflicted mental torture. In the Motherland of Ghana, Africa, Rainey not only visits the places of his ancestors, will he embrace the liberty that Christ's Blood does set every man free.

In *Guilty By Association*, how important is a name? To the St. Louis Jamiesons, tenth-generation descendants of a royal African tribe—everything. To the Boston Jamiesons whose father never married their mother—there is no loyalty or legacy. Kidd Jamieson suffers from the "angry" male syndrome because his father was absent in the home, but insisted his two sons carry his last name. It takes an old woman who mingles genealogy truths and Bible verses together for Kidd to realize his worth as a strong black man. He learns it's not his association with the name that identifies him, but the man he becomes that defines him.

In *The Guilt Trip*, Aaron "Ace" Jamieson lives carefree. He's good-looking, and respectable when he's in the mood, but his weakness is women. If a woman tries to ambush him with a pregnancy, he takes off in the other direction. It's a lesson learned from his absentee father that responsibility is optional. Talise Rogers has a bright future ahead of her. She's pretty and has no problem catching a man's eye, which is exactly what she does with Ace. Trapping Ace Jamieson is the furthest thing from Talise's mind when she learns she is pregnant and Ace rejects her. "I want nothing from you Ace, not even your name." And Talise meant it.

In *Free From Guilt*, it's salvation round-up time and Cameron Jamieson's name is on God's hit list. Although his brothers and cousins embraced God—thanks to the women in their lives—the two-degreed MIT graduate isn't going to let any woman take him down that path without a fight. He's satisfied with his career, social calendar, and good genes. But God uses a beautiful messenger, Gabrielle Dupree, to show him that he's in a spiritual deficit. Cameron learns the hard way that man's wisdom is like foolishness to God. For every philosophical argument he throws her way, Gabrielle exposes him to scriptures that makes him question his worldly knowledge.

In *Sandra Nicholson's Backstory*, Sandra has made good and bad choices throughout the years, but the best one was to give her life to Christ when her sons were small and to rear them up in the best Christian way she knew how. That was thirty-something years ago and Sandra has evolved from a young single mother of two rambunctious boys: Kidd and Ace Jamieson, to a godly woman seasoned with wisdom. Despite the challenges and trials of rearing two strong-willed personalities, Sandra maintained her sanity through the grace of God, which kept gray strands at bay. But there is something to be said about a woman's first love. Kidd and Ace Jamieson's father, Samuel Jamieson broke their mother's heart. Can Sandra recover? Her sons don't believe any man is good enough for her, especially their absent father. Kidd doesn't deny his mother should find love again since she never married Samuel. But will she fall for a carbon copy of his father? God's love gives second chances.

In *The Confession*, Sandra Nicholson had made good and bad choices throughout the years, but the best one was to give her life to Christ when her sons were small and to rear them up in the best Christian way she knew how. That was thirty-something years ago and Sandra has evolved from a young single mother of two rambunctious boys, Kidd and Ace Jamieson to a godly woman seasoned with wisdom. Despite the challenges and trials of rearing two strong-willed personalities, Sandra maintained her sanity through the grace of God, which kept gray strands at bay.

Now, Sandra Nicholson is on the threshold of happiness, but Kidd believes no man is good enough for his mother, especially if her love interest could be a man just like his absentee father.

In *The Guilty Generation*, seventeen-year-old Kami Jamieson is so over being daddy's little girl. Now that she has captured the attention of Tango, the bad boy from her school, Kami's love for her family and God have taken a backseat to her teen crush. Although the Jamiesons have instilled godly principles in Kami since she was young, they will stop at nothing, including prayer and fasting, to protect her from falling prey to society's peer pressure. Can Kami survive her teen rebellion, or will she be guilty of dividing the next generation?

In *Queen's Surrender (To a Higher Calling)*, Opposites attract...or clash. The Jamieson saga continues with the Queen of the family in this inspirational romance. She's the mistress of flirtation but Philip is unaffected by her charm. The two enjoy a harmless banter about God's will versus Queen's, who prefers her own free-will lifestyle. Philip doesn't judge her choices—most of the time—and Queen respects his opinions—most of the time. It's perfect harmony sometimes. Queen, the youngest sister of the Jamieson clan, wears her name as if it's a crown. She's single, sassy, and most of the time, loving her status, but she's about to strut down an unexpected spiritual path. Evangelist Philip Dupree is on the hot seat as the trial pastor at Total Surrender Church. The stalemate: They want a family man to lead their flock. The board's ultimatum is enough to make him quit the ministry. But can a man of God walk away from his calling? Can two people with different lifestyles and priorities cross paths and continue the journey as one? Who is going to be the first to surrender?

In *Contempt (Grandma BB's Shenanigans)*, Grandma BB, the unofficial matriarch of the Jamieson clan, is getting her house in order for the perfect homegoing celebration. After all, she's eighty-something. She summons Parke Jamieson VI, his brothers, cousins, and their families to play a part in the practice funeral program—only if they follow her instructions to the letter. Since the Jamiesons are at her house with bodyguards Chip and Dale, they might have an impromptu family game night. The evening is full of surprises, especially when an unexpected visitor shows up to steal the show. With more work that needs to be done, Grandma BB plans to put her funeral on hold and stick around for a couple more generations.

In *Fun and Games with the Jamieson Men*, The Jamieson Legacy series inspired this game book of fun activities:• Brain Teasers• Crossword Puzzles• Word Searches •Sudoku •Mazes •Coloring Pages. The Jamiesons are fictional characters that put emphasis on Black Heritage, which includes Black American History tidbits, African American genealogy, and strong Black families. Relax, grab a pencil and play along.

THE CARMEN SISTERS SERIES

In *No Easy Catch*, Book 1, Shae Carmen hasn't lost her faith in God, only the men she's come across. Shae's recent heartbreak was discovering that her boyfriend was not only married, but on the verge of reconciling with his estranged wife. Humiliated, Shae begins to second guess herself as why she didn't see the signs that he was nothing more than a devil's decoy masquerading as a devout Christian man. St. Louis Outfielder Rahn Maxwell finds himself a victim of an attempted carjacking. The Lord guides him out of harms' way by opening the gunmen's eyes to Rahn's identity. The crook instead becomes an infatuated fan and asks for Rahn's autograph, and as a goodwill gesture, directs Rahn out of the ambush! When the news media gets wind of what happened with the baseball player, Shae's television station lands an exclusive interview. Shae and Rahn's chance meeting sets in motion a relationship where Rahn not only surrenders to Christ, but pursues Shae with a purpose to prove that good men are still out there. After letting her guard down, Shae is faced with another scandal that rocks her world. This time the stakes are higher. Not only is her heart on the line, so is her professional credibility. She and Rahn are at odds as how to handle it and friction erupts between them. Will she strike out at love again? The Lord shows Rahn that nothing happens by chance, and everything is done for Him to get the glory.

In *Defense of Love*, Book 2, nothing in Garrett Nash's life has made sense lately. When two people close to the U.S. Marshal wrong him deeply, Garrett expects God to remove them from his life. Instead, the Lord relocates Garrett to another city to start over, as if he were the offender instead of the victim. Criminal attorney Shari Carmen is comfortable in her own skin—most of the time. Being a "dark and lovely" African-American sister has its challenges, especially when it comes to relationships. Although she's a fireball in the courtroom, she knows how to fade into the background and keep the proverbial spotlight off her personal life. But literal spotlights are a different matter altogether. While playing tenor saxophone at an anniversary party, she grabs the attention of Garrett Nash. And as God draws them closer together, He makes another request of Garrett, one to which it will prove far more difficult to say "Yes, Lord."

In *Redeeming Heart*, Book 3, Landon Thomas (In Defense of Love) brings a new definition to the word "prodigal," as in prodigal son, brother or anything else imaginable. It's good that God's love covers a multitude of sins, but He isn't letting Landon off easy. His journey from riches to rags proves to be humbling and a lesson well learned. Real Estate Agent Octavia Winston is a woman on a mission, whether it's God's or hers professionally. One thing is for certain, she's not about to compromise when it comes to a Christian mate, so why did God send a homeless man to steal her heart? Minister Rossi Tolliver (Crowning Glory) knows how to minister to God's lost sheep and through God's redemption, the game changes for Landon and Octavia.

In *Driven to Be Loved*, Book 4, on the surface, Brecee Carmen has nothing in common with Adrian Cole. She is a pediatrician certified in trauma care; he is a transportation problem solver for a luxury car dealership (a.k.a., a car salesman). Despite their slow but steady attraction to each other, neither one of them are sure that they're compatible. To complicate matters, Brecee is the sole unattached Carmen when it seems as though everyone else around her—family and friends—are finding love, except her. Through a series of discoveries, Adrian and Brecee learn that things don't happen by coincidence. Generational forces are at work, keeping promises, protecting family members, and perhaps even drawing Adrian back to the church. For Brecee and Adrian, God has been hard at work, playing matchmaker all along the way for their paths cross at the right time and the right place.

Lean on Me, Book 1. No one should have to go it alone... Caregivers sometimes need a little TLC too.

Tabitha Knicely believes in family before everything. She may be overwhelmed caring for her beloved great-aunt, but she would never turn her back on the woman who raised her, even if Aunt Tweet's dementia is getting worse. Tabitha is sure she can do this on her own. But when Aunt Tweet ends up on her neighbor's front porch, and the man has the audacity to accuse Tabitha of elder abuse, things go from bad to awful. Marcus Whittington feels a mountain of regret at causing problems for Tabitha and her great-aunt. How was he to know the frail older woman's niece was doing the best she could? As Marcus gets to know Aunt Tweet and sees how hard Tabitha is fighting to keep everything together, he can't walk away from the pair. Particularly when helping Tabitha care for her great-aunt leads the two of them on a spiritual journey of faith and surrender.

Here For You, Book 2. Rachel Knicely's life has been on hold for six months while she takes care of her great aunt, who has Alzheimer's. Putting her aunt first was an easy decision—accepting that Aunt Tweet is nearing the end of her battle is far more difficult. Nicholas Adams's ministry is bringing comfort to those who are sick and homebound. He responds to a request for help for an ailing woman but when he meets the Knicelys, he realizes Rachel is the one who needs support the most. Nicholas is charmed by and attracted to Rachel, but then devastating news brings both a crisis of faith and roadblocks to their budding relationship that neither could have anticipated. This beautifully emotional and clean story contains a hero and heroine who are better at taking care of other people than themselves, a dark moment that shakes their faith, and a well-earned happily ever after.

Stand by Me, Book 3. An uplifting story about embracing love and giving others—and yourself—one more chance. When it comes to being a caregiver, Kym Knicely has been there and done that. Then she meets Charles "Chaz" Banks and soon learns that every caregiving situation is different. Chaz takes care of his seven-year-old autistic granddaughter, Chauncy. Although Kym's attraction to Chaz is strong, she has to decide whether a romantic relationship can survive and thrive between two people at different stages in life. It's a journey with a different set of rules that Kym has to play by if she and Chaz are to have their happily ever after and the faith and family they envision.

About *Waiting for Christmas,*

A chance meeting. An undeniable attraction.

And a first date that starts with a stakeout that leads to a winner takes all shopping spree. It's the making of a holiday romance. While philanthropist Sterling Price believes in charitable causes, he and licensed social worker Ciara Summers have a difference of opinion on how to bless others. Ciara is a rebel with a cause and a hundred reasons why helping those less fortunate is important. Sterling is a man of means who believes there is a financial responsibility that comes with giving.

The Lord will make sure everyone's needs are met, and He has something extra for Sterling and Ciara that can't wait until Christmas.

About *Christmas Dinner,*

How do you celebrate the holidays after losing a loved one? Take the journey, beginning with Christmas Dinner. For months, Darcelle Price has suffered depression in silence. But things are about to change as she plans to celebrate Christmas Eve with family and share her journey. Darcelle invites them via group text, not knowing she had included her ex. Evanston Giles is surprised to hear from the woman he loved after months following their breakup. Seeking closure, he shows up on her doorstep for answers. A lot can happen on Christmas Eve. Restoring family ties, building her faith in God, and falling in love again is just the beginning of the night of miracles.

About *Taye's Gift,*

Welcome to Snowflake, Colorado—a small town where wishes come true! When six old high school friends receive a letter that their fellow friend, Charity Hart, wrote before she passed away, their lives take an unexpected turn. She leaves them each a check for $1,500 and asks them to grant a wish—a secret wish—for someone else by Christmas. Who lays off someone before the holidays? Taye Thomas' employer did, so instead of Christmas shopping, she's job hunting. More devastating news comes when an old high school friend passed away. Could God be answering her prayers for help when she learns that Charity Hart left a $1500 check? No, the caveat is it's more blessed to give than receive. Taye has 30 days to find someone else in need to bless. To complicate matters, she's lives in Kansas City, which is more than eight hours away from Snowflake and she can't do it alone. Keeping a secret has never been so much work.

About *Couple by Christmas,*

Holidays haven't been the same for Derek Washington since his divorce. He and his ex-wife, Robyn, go out of their way to avoid each other. This Christmas may be different when he decides to give his son, Tyler, the family he once had before they split. Derek's going to need the Lord's intervention to soften her heart to agree to some outings. God's help doesn't come in the way he expected, but it's all good because everything falls in place for them to be a couple by Christmas.

About *Prayers Answered By Christmas,*

Christmas is coming. While other children are compiling their lists for a fictional Santa, eight-year-old Mikaela Washington is on her knees, making her requests known to the Lord: One mommy for Christmas please. Portia Hunter refuses to let her ex-husband cheat her out of the family she wants. Her prayer is for God to send the right man into her life. Marlon Washington will do anything for his two little girls, but can he find a mommy for them and a love for himself? Since Christmas is the time of year to remember the many gifts God has given men, maybe these three souls will get their heart s desire.

About *A Noelle for Nathan*,

A Noelle for Nathan is a story of kindness, selflessness, and falling in love during the Christmas season. Andersen Investors & Consultants, LLC, CFO Nathan Andersen (A Christian Christmas) isn't looking for attention when he buys a homeless man a meal, but grade school teacher Noelle Foster is watching his every move with admiration. His generosity makes him a man after her own heart. While donors give more to children and families in need around the holiday season, Noelle Foster believes in giving year-round after seeing many of her students struggle with hunger and finding a warm bed at night. At a second-chance meeting, sparks fly when Noelle and Nathan share a kindred spirit with their passion to help those less fortunate. Whether they're doing charity work or attending Christmas parties, the couple becomes inseparable. Although Noelle and Nathan exchange gifts, the biggest present is the one from Christ.

One reader says, "A Noelle for Nathan makes you fall in love with love…the love of mankind and the love of God. You cannot read this without having a desire to give and do more, all while being appreciative of what you have."

About *Christmas Greetings*,

Saige Carter loves everything about Christmas: the shopping, the food, the lights, and of course, Christmas wouldn't be complete without family and friends to share in the traditions they've created together. Plus, Saige is extra excited about her line of Christmas greeting cards hitting store shelves, but when she gets devastating news around the holidays, she wonders if she'll ever look at Christmas the same again. Daniel Washington is no Scrooge, but he'd rather skip the holidays altogether than spend them with his estranged family. After one too many arguments around the dinner table one year, Daniel had enough and walked away from the drama. As one year has turned into many, no one seems willing to take the first step toward reconciliation. When Daniel reads one of Saige's greeting cards, he's unsure if the words inside are enough to erase the pain and bring about forgiveness. Once God reveals His purpose for their lives to them, they will have a reason to rejoice. *Come unto me, all ye that labor and are heavily laden, and I will give you rest. Take my yoke upon you, and learn of me; for I am meek and lowly in heart: and ye shall find rest unto your souls.* Matthew 11:28-29

About *A Baby for Christmas*,

Yes, diamonds are a girl's best friend, but unless the jewel is going on Solae Wyatt-Palmer's ring finger, they hold little value to her. When she meets Fire Captain Hershel Kavanaugh, their magnetism is undeniable and there's no doubt that it's love at first sight. Since Solae adores Hershel's two boys from his failed marriage, she wouldn't blink at the chance to become a mother to them. But when it seems as if Hershel doesn't have a proposal on his agenda, she has no choice but to cut her losses and move on. But Christmas is coming. And in order to win Solae back, Hershel must resolve some past issues before convincing her that she possesses everything he wants.

About *A Christian Christmas*,

Christmas will never be the same for Joy Knight if Christian Andersen has his way. Not to be confused with a secret Santa, Christian and his family are busier than Santa's elves making sure the Lord's blessings are distributed to those less fortunate by Christmas day. Joy is playing the hand that life dealt her, rearing four children in a home that is on the brink of foreclosure. She's not looking for a handout, but when Christian rescues her in the checkout line; her niece thinks Christian is an angel. Joy thinks he's just another man who will eventually leave, disappointing her and the children. Although Christian is a servant of the Lord, he is a flesh and blood man and all he wants for Christmas is Joy Knight. Can time spent with Christian turn Joy's attention from her financial woes to the real meaning of Christmas—and true love? A Christian Christmas is a holiday novella to be enjoyed any time of the year.

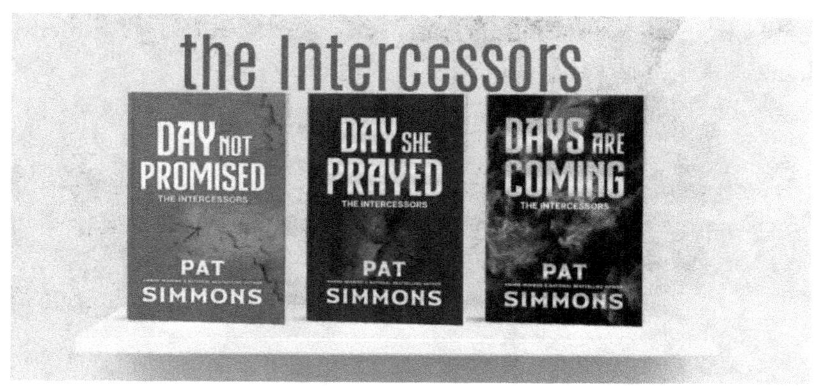

Pat Simmons introduces a new Christian fiction series that reminds readers that the bad guys don't always win, especially when the Lord fights our battles.

In *Day Not Promised*, Omega Addams thought it was a typical workday until a detour on the way home changes everything. She's almost killed, but an innocent bystander, Mitchell Franklin, takes a bullet for Omega during a gas station robbery. In the aftermath, Omega has no idea that God expects her to "pray it forward" until a spiritual battle unfolds before her eyes. Another innocent bystander is in trouble; unless Omega gets her prayer life together, others will die without Christ. It's a chain reaction that highlights the responsibility of a Christian--hot, cold, or lukewarm. It's time to get our acts together. We are our brother's keeper.

In *Day She Prayed*, New Christian convert Tally Gilbert knows the power of prayer and the pain of walking away. She's witnessed family and friends' healing, salvation, and deliverance. There's one holdout, and he's at the top of her prayer list. The love of her life, Randall Addams, won't surrender to the Lord, so Tally ends the relationship. What will it take for Randall to turn to God? Will Tally's prayers be answered, or will Randall—and their love—be lost forever?

Don't underestimate a woman who knows how to pray, has backup, and believes "The Word of God is quick, and powerful, and sharper than any two-edged sword, piercing even to the dividing the soul from the spirit, and of the joints and marrow, and is a discerner of the thoughts and intents of the heart." Hebrews 4:12.

If the devil wants a battle, he picks the wrong woman to fight.

In *Days Are Coming,* the spiritual battle is heating up in the lives of Omega and her friends. God is about to proclaim a punishment on the world because of their sins. Can prayer change things?